MEET ME AT

Castle Beach

R.S. LEDWITH

LCCN: 2025905685
Published in Norwalk, CT USA
by Seabright Press

Print ISBN: 979-8-9927119-2-9
Ebook ISBN: 979-8-9927119-1-2

First Edition

MEET ME AT

Castle Beach

One

After bringing a half dozen suitcases from her car and into the beach house, Olivia grew tired of unpacking and took a break. She wasn't carrying any more luggage. "That's what brothers are for," she told herself. Now that she was fifteen, she expected at least courteous behavior from her older brother. Ricky was three years older and much stronger. As usual, he could not be relied upon to help. He treats home like a convenience store, where he drops by only to pick up food and cash. She abandoned her suitcases, walked through the living room, and out to the front deck of her new house. The views would be impressive, overlooking the northern edge of Monterey Bay and the Santa Cruz Boardwalk, once the morning fog burned off. Ocean views would have to wait until mid-afternoon.

Olivia was alone to unpack, unsure where her parents or Ricky were. This was supposed to be a simple transfer of her summer clothes and a few personal items from her home in Portola Valley, two hours north, to this new beach house in Santa Cruz. Instead, this would be her new summer residence, beginning Father's Day and ending Labor Day weekend. She left her house and all her school friends back in Portola Valley. This felt more like an exile, even though the beach house was just a stone's throw away from the beach, or so she heard. Right now, the fog encircled the house, as if it were dropped into a bowl of clam chowder.

The beach house sat on a cliff that rose fifty feet above the river which flowed from the Santa Cruz Mountains into Monterey Bay. It was a safe place, even though the occasional big storm flooded the nearby river and beaches causing rockslides. "But that only happens in winter, and 'very infrequently,'" her mother claimed. The steady erosion of the sandstone bluffs on which the house sat was of more significant concern. Fortunately, the house was set back from the cliff's edge, so she guessed it might take decades for erosion to threaten her house and safety.

Nevertheless, just looking at it gave Olivia the undeniable fear that one morning she would wake as their home tumbled into the sea. She figured it was best not to think about it. At that moment, Olivia was more concerned by the cold brought to shore by the fog. This was supposed to be a beach house. When she first heard her dad bought a house right on the beach, she felt a familiar sting that she was not included in such a major family decision. After all, this affected her life too. Then she thought she was being ridiculous; it was her dad's gift to the family. This was a beach house. She envisioned laying out in her swimsuit on a towel with her friends, feet in the warm sand, drinks in the cooler, and the group taking an occasional dunk in the cool, refreshing ocean lapping near their feet.

When Olivia saw the house, she dialed back her snide attitude. It was a genuinely beautiful house with breathtaking views of the boardwalk and the northern part of Monterey Bay. She rubbed her arms and thought that the soreness from hauling luggage made her short tempered.

The house was of modern design with a rectangular footprint and a series of floors with tinted glass that looked like boxes stacked unevenly on a spit of land stretching upriver to her right, and down into the ocean to her left. This design allowed for a large deck on every other floor. The main floor showcased an open floor plan with a huge living room and the largest of the three decks. Downstairs was Ricky's room and a guest apartment with its own bathroom and small kitchenette. Upstairs was Olivia's bedroom and her parents' spacious en suite bedroom.

A two-car garage was attached to the main floor, a luxury for beach front property. Not that Olivia drove, she sarcastically thought. Thinking like that made her sound spoiled, even to her own ears. She then realized one of the spaces was for her to use when she turned sixteen years old, next year. She may need to change her attitude.

The roof of the house was broad and flat with a black iron railing running along the perimeter. Olivia's mom told her it would be perfect for sharing the view of the Boardwalk's Fourth of July fireworks with her friends. Olivia shook her head slightly as it reinforced in her mind that she would be watching them alone. She went to Santa Cruz several times before with her family, but it was a long time ago. She remembered cold, foggy skies, which melted away by late morning. Maybe today was colder than most. Whatever the reason, it was not what she envisioned when she thought of summer. She dug her hands deep into her hoodie pouch and pulled over the hood; she was not taking off her sweatshirt.

She passed her father walking up to the house. "You and your mom made good time," he told her, shifting a full grocery bag to his free arm. "I'm so excited we closed title and are in by Father's

Day, just as promised." It had something to do with closing a big business deal, but Olivia had not paid much attention.

The ever-present fog would wreck most of June for sunbathing. Olivia was upset about the fog in the mornings until a friend said that no native "Santa Cruzan" ever appeared on the beach before 1 P.M. Still, she had nothing to do and no one to do it with. She sighed.

On their way over from her home in Portola Valley, when they crested the Santa Cruz Mountain Summit, they could see the whole coastline was socked in with thick billowing gray fog, blanketing everything as far as the eye could see. "June Gloom" is what the newspapers called it; her mother informed them as their car raced up the hairpin turns of the highway to Santa Cruz. Now that her father bought the house, she was certain to spend all her summers here. Olivia told herself she would just sleep in longer until the fog burned off, or, she thought dryly, until summer burned off and she could go home. When their car sank into the fog bank, a light-gray mist covered the windshield, and they had to turn up the heater a notch.

She had mixed feelings about spending the entire summer at the beach. She had hoped to get a horse this summer and keep it at the stables back home. All her friends spent their summers with their horses or at the Portola Valley stables. Although her home was only two hours away from Santa Cruz, it was warm, sunny, and dry all summer long on the inland side of the coastal range. Portola Valley also had low humidity, making it ideal during the summer.

Olivia's father had called a family meeting after she brought up the idea of occasionally returning home this summer. Strangely, her brother was not required to attend. Her parents explained that she was not allowed to have any visitors at the beach house unless they were pre-approved by her parents. It was unlikely her father would allow any of her friends to visit—he always suspected that when kids got together there would be drinking beer and smoking weed, a far cry from the way her friends behaved. She anticipated a long, lonely summer.

As Olivia sat by herself on the steps to a quiet house, the car door opened, and her mom came out followed by her dad carrying a sack of groceries. "There are two more bags in the car," her mom informed her. "Could you bring them in?" Olivia stood and walked out to get the groceries. There was no one else to do it, she grumbled to herself.

"I met a friend in the produce section of the Quality Mart and told her you were looking for people to play with. She said her niece lives here all summer and is about your age. I gave her your phone number." Olivia's mom looked pleased to have been able to help her daughter. Olivia looked like she was sleepwalking, taking no notice of her surroundings and mechanically going through the motions ever since she was told they were spending the whole summer here.

"Mom, we don't 'play' anymore. People my age 'hang out' with their friends or with other people their age." When Olivia saw her mom's expression change, from one of happiness to a frown and downcast eyes, Olivia felt bad for her. Her mom tried so hard to help Olivia enjoy the summers, the way she had as a girl, and make her own fun memories of living on the beach.

"Mom," Olivia said in a nicer tone, "Thank you for sharing my number. That's a good way to meet someone." She closed the gap between herself and her mother and gave her a quick side hug before running down the steps to bring in the food. Her mom usually bought cookies and chips, which Olivia always welcomed. Snacks were "first come, first served."

On the way back to the house Olivia could hear the phone ringing, so she answered it in the living room. "Olivia? This is Beverly, Annie's mom. Your mother said you are looking to meet kids your age here at the Point in Santa Cruz."

Olivia would have to thank her mom again.

• • •

Every year on Memorial Day, Derek's family left their home in Livermore and moved into their old Victorian beach house in Santa Cruz. Each Labor Day weekend, they packed up and closed the beach house to return home to Livermore. Derek spent summers in Santa Cruz every year of his life. When he woke up on his first day of each summer in the beach house, he knew to expect an exhaustive project list his father compiled during the rest of the year. It was a lengthy list of repairs required on all weather-damaged areas of the house. If he worked hard, he could expect to take about a month to complete it, or longer if he took the afternoons off. Once he finished all the required repairs, he could finally spend the rest of the summer sunbathing, swimming in the ocean, and exploring Santa Cruz on his bike.

Derek and his dad shared responsibility for the house repairs. This year, he hoped to enlist one of his younger brothers to carry out some of his tasks when his dad was on another project. Now that his younger brother Kyle was ten years old, Derek was training him to help ferry tools up to him, using a bucket and a pulley so Derek could avoid going up and down the tall ladder multiple times a day.

His family had inherited this house by swapping it with his grandparents for their small bungalow closer to town. Derek's neighborhood was built on a bluff overlooking Monterey Bay, on the south side of the point, with the Boardwalk amusement park on the north side. The weather was temperate, with a few weeks of hot summer in August and socked-in by morning fog from May through June. Eucalyptus trees and scrub bushes of manzanita and laurel lined the creeks around his house. Derek spent the foggy months outside on a ladder and ended work when the sun finally won its battle with the fog, giving him warm afternoons to enjoy the rest of his summer.

The house effectively had two kitchens that were operating at full capacity for four months a year. Upgrading and repairing the appliances was beyond Derek's skill level, so he would focus on the other items on the chores list. Something was always breaking down, requiring Derek to bring in his toolbox and complete the repairs to keep the kitchen functioning. His father's grandparents or great grandparents built the house, Derek was never quite sure. It gave Derek a sense of ownership that his family had owned the house for so many years.

He helped his father for the past five years, and in that time, Derek gained confidence as a craftsman and painter. He and his father removed any rotted sections of wood and cut new pieces to match the original siding and trim. When assembled, those areas all required cleaning, priming, and repainting.

The small garage at the back of their yard served as their workshop until the Fourth of July when his dad declared the working portion of their summer complete. At that point, the tools were quickly stored away in the garage, and their cars parked inside to protect them from the salt air that corroded everything it touched.

Their house was known for its detailed "gingerbread trim" work. To remain true to the Victorian era, Derek's family painted it using a wide color palette. There was no formal color scheme they needed to follow, but they enjoyed the recognition granted by other owners and tourists around the area. There were many other Painted Ladies (colorfully painted Victorian homes) in nearby Monterey and San Francisco, as well as on the East Coast on Fire Island, Martha's Vineyard, and the Jersey Shore.

Derek's family chose four colors for the siding and trim about two years ago. Since then, Derek painted touch-ups where the weather took its heaviest toll. He ordered at least one new gallon of paint in each color every summer. The main siding of the house was painted tan, window frames dark blue, and exterior trim white, with a very dark blue trim accent color.

As tedious as the painting was, Derek felt a keen sense of pride each time he completed a section of the house. At fifteen, Derek was the only child in his family to work on the exterior of the house. He and his sister, Annie were 15 year old twins, and two of the five children in the family which included the three younger children, Kevin, Kyle, and Christopher, 10, 8, and 7 years old, respectively. They were just beginning to be helpful around the house. For now, they were exempt from work on the house's exterior. Annie and their mom kept the kids busy with laundry, cooking, and cleaning. To Annie, it seemed she spent most of her time trying to track the younger siblings down when they escaped from her watchful eye. Keeping track of them was often as futile as herding cats.

Unless it was raining, Derek had work to do, so on this chilled and foggy morning, Derek un-rolled his sleeves and promptly started work outside. Annie helped Derek when she could. This year she took his work list to the office supplies store to be laminated. He thought it was overkill but had to admit it made his life easier. Last year his list became a wrinkled pile of notes, smudged by rain, sweat, and damp. This year, he kept one list inside the garage, tacked to the side of the wall, and kept the other detailed list in the tool bucket hung from the ladder.

Derek employed his younger brothers, or as he liked to call them, "the Little Ones," by having them hand him coffee and sandwiches through the upstairs windows when he was high up on the ladder so he wouldn't need to waste time climbing the ladder more than necessary.

Two

One June morning, when it was still cold and the sun waged battle with the fog to allow summer to emerge, Annie came to the rear porch where Derek was working on the house, two stories up. She motioned for him to climb down the ladder to hear her better. "I'm going down to the beach at noon today to meet the daughter of mom's friend. Mom thought I might like her. The girl is new to Santa Cruz and will be staying here all summer," Annie continued. "She might also have friends or siblings you would like. Do you want to join us?"

"That sounds great," said Derek. "Give me a few minutes to put away my tools and clean up."

Annie suggested he meet her outside the kitchen, behind the house. She was packing up a picnic lunch they could take to Whale Park, across from the cove.

Derek always appreciated Annie's cooking. A few years back, she began experimenting with main courses, introducing the family to a variety of foods: tacos, enchiladas, lasagna, and many other types of dishes. She was careful not to make any of the entrees too spicy for the Little Ones. Often, she and her mom would cook something different for their parents and the older kids and serve a more child-friendly course for the younger children, like a casserole or mac and cheese. Then there were the cakes, pies, and other desserts she served as a surprise to the family. She enjoyed creating these treats, and the family both praised and devoured her delicious efforts.

Derek placed his tools into the tool bucket and lowered them down. "I really need a break. I'm going crazy chipping away paint. I feel like I am just a paint monkey, hanging from a ladder."

Annie smiled at the image of a paint monkey. Whenever Derek got new spills on his white painter's clothes and paint spattered hat, he looked, from the ground, like a colorful mechanical monkey, climbing up and down the ladder.

"Can I invite my friend Frank to join us?" asked Derek. "You met him last summer. He's a surfer and you seemed to like him."

Annie agreed it would be fun to invite him. "I know some surfers my friends introduced me to. Maybe he knows them. You might try surfing again this year," she suggested. "Just stay away from the older guys with their drinking and drugs."

"I think I am pretty good at that already."

"Are you sure? Frank could help you become accepted into the right surf group. It isn't an easy gang to break into. They will pound you if you cut them off or steal their wave."

"Thanks," said Derek as he scowled. "Now I really look forward to meeting them." They both laughed.

Derek knocked off work at lunchtime to change his clothes and wash his hands. It was still long pants and sweatshirt weather, so he picked out clothes that were warm but clean. On the way to the park, Annie asked him to carry the lunch basket she prepared. Despite the cold, there were a few people walking their dogs or strolling along the sidewalk enjoying the brisk ocean air.

The sidewalk ran along the cliff and offered a clear ocean view. Annie always walked on the house side of the road since the houses were set back from the street and offered a little more protection from the annual erosion. It felt safer to walk that way. She saw sections of the road in other stretches of cliffs that were undercut by a single storm, causing the road to crack and tumble down the cliffs. As a precaution, Derek liked to walk on the upper edge of the sidewalk as well. He and Annie walked in silence, enjoying the view.

Few visitors were at the Cove at Castle Beach this morning; the foggy chill chased off anyone interested in spending the day outdoors. The back of the cove was surrounded by a narrow road lined with beach houses, and on the sides were sandy cliffs covered with patches of ivy.

When Annie and Derek reached Castle Beach, they saw a lone visitor sitting on a blanket with their shoes on the sand. As they got closer, Annie recognized Olivia from her mom's description. She appeared slender, although it was hard to tell in her oversized sweatshirt. She had long dark hair and an olive complexion.

Derek and Annie found Olivia sitting on her blanket, frowning in general disappointment at the prospect of a cold Santa Cruz summer. Not having a good relationship with her brother was the other problem. Olivia hoped her discontent would change as she picked up a few friends during the summer. She poked a stick into the sand and it promptly broke. It was an ominous sign, she decided. Her mood matched the gloomy weather.

She realized how much she disliked having to wear sweatshirts on a June afternoon, which certainly would not be the case in Portola Valley. Most summers in California were hot and sunny. It would take Olivia some time to get used to a cold summer.

Derek noticed her frown, but it didn't have a chance against the girl's very pretty face.

Without having much to say, Olivia looked at Derek and Annie, and commented, "I can see you are brother and sister, but are you twins?"

"I guess it's true that we look alike; that's what my friends tell me." Annie swept her hair around showing off her streaked blonde hair. "We both have blonde hair with more than a touch of red. The other kids often call us gingers, and those who meet us for the first time often guess we're twins." Derek thought the whole twin thing was wearisome. He was of slight build, but Annie had begun to mature earlier than Derek and stood taller.

"Last year, I was taller than Annie, but she had a big growth spurt. I haven't had mine yet but based on how much she grew, I'm expected to clear six feet by August, as told to us by a lady in a fortune-telling booth at the Boardwalk. It cost a dollar, so it must be true." Derek worked hard to keep from grinning.

The girls failed at their attempt to play along and burst into laughter, not knowing if Derek really believed her prediction.

"I'm actually older than Annie," declared Derek.

"Derek likes this joke, even if it has become old over the years." Annie scrunched her face at him.

He looked to Olivia to see if she liked that kind of humor, and saw she was smiling and enjoying the show put on by the siblings.

"You're half an hour older than me. We're still twins," said Annie with an exasperated tone. "Even with a slight difference in height, we are fraternal twins but not identical twins." At this point, Annie usually took over the conversation. "We are both fifteen and just graduated ninth grade," reported Annie, trying to wrap up this line of questioning and avoid further confusion.

Changing the subject, Annie suggested, "I packed up a bunch of food. Let's take it across the street to the park and grab a picnic table. That way, we'll be in the shade when the sun comes out."

"I'm just saying, I am older. That makes me the first in line for the crown. That is, if we had a crown." The girls groaned.

"Is this Castle Beach?" asked Olivia, as she turned to face the cliffs. "It doesn't have a sign, but I asked my mom, and she said that is what they called it when she was a girl."

"There used to be a building that looked like a castle right there at the end of the cliff," said Derek, pointing to a flat spot at the edge of the cliff where the building once stood. "We only saw the castle when Annie and I were very young. It was torn down in the 1960s."

"As for the other beaches," Derek pointed out, "you'll find that every slight bend in the coastline gives the beach a new name." He pointed out at the beaches and swept his arm across the beach. "Castle Beach, Seabright, Twin Lakes, Black's Beach, and Fourth Avenue. The local kids like to use other little sub-names for beaches to confuse their parents."

Derek carried the basket to the park, Olivia carried her towel and beach bag, and Annie carried the blankets.

When Derek put the basket on the table, he and Olivia slid open the lid to get a peek inside. Olivia saw how much food it contained and confessed that she didn't know they would be sharing lunch. "I didn't bring any food to share. I hope you don't think I am a freeloader. I should have brought something." She was clearly embarrassed by the miscommunication.

Annie waved her hand, dismissing Olivia's concern. "Don't worry about it. At our home, the kitchen is set up to constantly serve the hungry. The house is full of kids and adults. At any given meal, we typically serve my parents, Derek and me, our Aunt Kate, and our three younger siblings. Plus, there are always a few extra neighborhood kids who always seem to show up at mealtimes."

Olivia was shocked at how many people they were feeding. At her house it was usually just her and her mom, as her dad usually worked through dinner.

"I have a brother, Ricky, who is eighteen," Olivia volunteered. "He's not very friendly and has a car, so he's able to jump back and forth between Portola Valley and Santa Cruz. I doubt you'll meet him. Otherwise, it is just my parents and me. There was a time when my brother spent time with the family, calling me his 'little sis.' He was happier back then. Now he only wants to escape with his friends in his new car. He avoids me whenever he sees me."

They were quiet after this personal confession. Derek felt bad for her. He was also glad to know he didn't have that problem at home.

Annie shook out a red gingham tablecloth and laid it flat on the table once Derek moved the basket. Olivia thought the tablecloth made their lunch seem more civilized. Derek was careful not to get involved with setting out the spread. He avoided stealing Annie's thunder from anything related to food.

Annie was known by the entire family to be a fabulous cook and baker who also enjoyed presenting her meals as much as she enjoyed preparing them. In comparison, Derek was just a good eater, but ironically, not much of a cook except as a fry chef making scrambled eggs and flipping pancakes for all the kids at breakfast time.

As they laid out the lunch spread, their conversation rolled along, mostly centered on their hometowns and Santa Cruz. Olivia told them about her life in Portola Valley. She explained that she had hoped to get her own horse this year but admitted getting a horse wouldn't make sense now that she was spending all summer in Santa Cruz and expected to stay along the shore, "to enjoy the beach," her mom told her. "There won't be any horses this year. I'm at the beach house for the whole summer."

Derek watched Olivia become animated about her family, her hometown, and her wish to get a horse. She was seriously disappointed but told her story in a funny way.

Derek concurred, "That's a compelling argument. I think you should have a horse." He liked to see her smile. "Unfortunately," he admitted, "I can't afford to get you one. By the end of the summer, I might be able to buy you a riding hat." Olivia smiled as the girls began passing around plates.

"Derek, weren't you going to ask Frank to join us?" Annie asked.

"I spoke to him on the phone at home. He said he would join us soon. He wasn't too far away."

Olivia noticed Derek had a stripe of blue paint on his forehead. The conversation stopped as Olivia pointed at the blue spot. "You seem to have some blue paint on you," she said, and identified where the paint was located by pointing at her own forehead. "It's not much but it does seem a bit out of place."

Annie reached over and touched it and felt that it was dry. "He needs to wait until we get home before he can scrub it off." Annie looked at Derek then back to Olivia. "We're trying to take him out in public more and more, but he doesn't seem quite ready yet. Until he gets it right, we can pretend he's not one of us, if that helps," Annie said with a straight face.

It took Olivia a moment before she realized Annie was joking. To join in, Olivia added, "No sense in sending him home, quite yet. We can just ask him to walk a few steps behind us."

They all laughed, even Derek. He said, "It is a painter's curse. There is always some spill or smudge that gets past me." The girls looked at it again. Derek touched the dried spill and added, "It looks a lot better on the house than on me," directing the conversation away from the paint.

"We also invited Derek's friend, Frank, to join us. He's really fun. How does that sound?" Annie asked Olivia.

"How long are you staying in Santa Cruz this summer?" asked Annie. "It's a challenge for us 'all-summer' kids to find people who are staying the full summer in Santa Cruz. Most people only stay a week or two and keep to themselves."

"I'm here from Father's Day through Labor Day, according to my dad," said Olivia. "My parents just bought a house up on the cliff, so my mom thinks we are going to sit on our deck and quietly watch our summers slip by."

Derek heard a decided lack of enthusiasm in her voice, strange for a girl who had the whole summer in front of her. Derek thought there must be more to it than a new house.

Frank rode up to the picnic area a few minutes later and wheeled his bike to their table. He gave Derek a fist bump, greeting his friend.

"Frank, it is good to see you again. Welcome to another year! Let me introduce you to the productive part of our team." Derek pointed toward the table. "The food for our magnificent lunch was prepared by my sister, Annie. You may remember her from last summer. And this is our new friend, Olivia, who came from Portola Valley in the Bay Area," he said. "She'll be around all summer. Olivia, this is Frank. He's a good friend and lives here year-round. If you ask, he will let you know that he is a surf rat."

"That's true," Frank confirmed. "After we're full, I can tell you all about surfing. At least, until it's time for dinner." He laughed at his own joke. Everyone else joined in.

Frank did a double take when he recognized Derek's sister, Annie. It had been a year since he saw her. Annie had grown and filled out, as was common for kids their age. What wasn't common was how pretty Annie had become. Frank had to look away to avoid getting caught staring. Derek and Olivia were standing quietly, assessing Frank's response to Annie. He was clearly speechless, opening his mouth then closing it, as if trying to reconcile last year's memory of little-girl Annie to the teenage girl standing before him.

Regaining his footing, Frank said, "It's great to see you again." He started to put his hand out and then pulled it back. It looked like he wanted to give her a hug, but he stalled. For a moment, Frank stood with his arms starting to rise into an embrace, but then he stopped and let his arms hang loosely at his side. "Thanks for asking me to join you for lunch."

Finally, he took her hand with both of his and squeezed it. "It is very good to see you again. Can I help you put out the dishes?" Frank and Annie wandered to the other side of the table to organize the food while Derek and Olivia returned their attention to one another.

Clearly seeing there was something going on between Annie and Frank, Olivia walked up next to Derek and lightly pressed her elbow to his side. When he looked, she nodded at Frank and Annie and quietly said, "Keep walking."

"What was that all about?" Derek whispered to Olivia. "I've never seen Frank actually speechless."

"You know exactly what that was. Your friend is smitten by your sister. Don't get in there and muck it up. He was kind of cute about it."

Annie also saw that Frank had changed over the past year. He was no longer a skinny boy who wouldn't stop talking about skateboards but instead was a polite young man who was quietly staring at her when he thought she wasn't looking. Annie snuck a glance over to Olivia, who nodded and raised her eyebrows in support of their unspoken statements which seemed to say "This guy is cute," and "I think he likes you."

Frank, in turn, continued to steal glances at Annie. Most notable, compared to last year, was that she now possessed a slim figure. She clearly was not a little kid anymore. She wore a floral swim coverup loosely cinched at the waist. Her hair was pulled back and clipped in place by barrettes.

Frank wore the typical brands of clothes worn by all the beach locals, including an orange Santa Cruz t-shirt, blue Hang Ten nylon swim shorts, and dark Rainbow® foam sandals. Annie noticed those were almost a uniform for the surf kids she knew.

The conversation resumed as they moved from general introductions to praise for Annie and the delicious food she prepared. Frank's eyes almost popped out of his head when he saw the meal Annie had packed.

As Annie continued to unload her picnic basket onto the table, Frank examined each food container and held each one up for display with an exaggerated flourish of his hand. "Here we have homemade lasagna," he said, then paused looking to Annie for verification until she nodded in agreement. "Which looks warm and delicious." He continued, "And over here is the potato salad, which seems to contain egg and sliced black olives, if I'm seeing it right." Walking down the table, he lifted another Tupperware container packed with lettuce and salad fixings. "We have a regular green salad for those trying to be slim and healthy. I wish you all good luck." He looked around at his audience, adding, "That's what tomorrow is for."

Frank sounded so much like a gameshow host that Derek couldn't help but laugh.

Once Frank spied the Mexican food Annie pulled out of the basket, he had to pause and try it all himself. Annie fed a sample of each dish to him with fresh spoons. Each dish elicited a groan of satisfaction, including the varied sauces and handmade tortillas. Frank was not disappointed, and he and Annie put on a hilarious show.

Frank was especially appreciative of Annie's enchiladas, announcing that her sauces were very authentic, much like the ones his grandmother made. Frank explained that his family was originally from Mexico, many generations back, and his grandmother only cooked authentic dishes from old family recipes. Annie's ears perked up when she heard the discussion about the recipes. She was expanding her repertoire of dishes and was always looking for new recipes to try.

Derek chimed in, "I met his grandmother and great-aunt last year. They live on Seabright Avenue, just up the road. They're old but they still enjoy cooking. At least, they keep the food coming for Frank. I practiced my best Spanish when we met, but they preferred to speak in English."

Annie beat Frank to the punch line. "It was a nice gesture you made trying to speak Spanish; however, even your Spanish teacher can't understand you." Everyone laughed.

Olivia watched Derek blush brightly as he looked away. Olivia laughed along with everyone else but touched her hand on his arm and smiled as she looked him in the eyes. His face turned even darker red. "I'm sure your Spanish is fine," she told him. "If you get stuck, I'll bet Frank would be willing to help you."

"I'm sure he would," Derek said with more than a hint of sarcasm in his voice. "I'm just afraid he might quote me as asking for an oven-roasted porcupine."

Their picnic ran into mid-afternoon as each of them shared stories of their homes and told Olivia about the places she should visit this summer.

The conversation and laughter bounced around easily, from friends to new friends. The boys were very funny. Derek told a story about last summer when Frank tried to teach Derek how to surf. Derek continued, "One thing Frank forgot to tell me was that I needed a wet suit. When I pointed out that everyone was wearing heavy wet suits, head to toe, he said, 'Do you want to be like everyone else, or are you your own man?'"

"After half an hour I was so hypothermic I could barely hold onto my board. Frank had to drag me to shore and threw me on a towel in the sun to try and warm up. That night, I had to soak in a hot bath for the rest of the evening before I felt warm again."

Frank said he didn't remember it quite like that. Instead, he told tales of surfers "shredding the tube" and tearing up "gnarly waves" until even he couldn't believe his own stories. Everyone was laughing, and Frank, ever the clown, jumped up on a neighboring picnic table demonstrating the proper stance of a true surfer dude.

Olivia exchanged glances with Annie and raised an eyebrow, laughing at their antics. Olivia also noticed Frank was constantly watching Annie when he thought no one noticed. Olivia, for her part, was watching Derek as he jumped up on the table and joined Frank in dual renditions of wave riding. Annie thought they were funny enough to be a stand-up comedy routine. By this point Annie and Olivia were laughing so hard they had tears running down their faces.

•   •   •

The air was warming up, and one by one they took off their sweat-shirts. A few new groups entered the park, setting up at their own picnic tables on the other side of a life-sized stone whale placed in the middle of the park near a small building containing relics in the Seabright Museum. Olivia caught Derek's furtive glances at her and hoped they were an indication of his interest. She was certainly interested in him. He seemed funny in a kind way, never at someone else's expense. He was also polite and attentive, making sure she had tried each different dish, and getting her seconds when she asked. And the longer they spent time together, the more she realized how good-looking he was.

Olivia noticed Derek was lean but not skinny. She thought his hands were a bit of a mess until Annie caught her staring and explained, "Derek helps my dad work on our house every day. He can never quite get the last bit of paint out of his hands. I tried one time to scrub it out with a coarse brush, but it only made his hands bright red. Now I only expect him to clean up as best as he can." As an aside, she added, "I never let him touch the food being served in the kitchen!"

The sun finally burned through the mist, warming the air in the park where the two couples were enjoying their picnic lunch. Olivia watched subtle peeks in all directions, some based on attraction and others just between the girls as they raised their eyebrows at each awkward joke shared by the guys, even though it was all good-natured. Olivia thought she would enjoy spending time with Annie, shopping, sharing lunches, and doing girl things.

She had gone from zero friends to hopefully three today, one of whom, if she was reading the signs correctly, had potential to be more.

Boys were great, Olivia surmised, but girls also need good girlfriends to share their thoughts and observations about the boys, who were probably doing the same thing. Or not. Olivia knew that boys didn't always run as deep as girls.

Derek loaded some dessert on Olivia's plate. Annie took the seat next to her, directing Derek to sit across from Olivia. He followed her suggestion and sat, causing his stomach to growl. Everyone was laughing as they continued with their picnic while the sun slowly fell behind the old museum which sat behind them. Derek found himself hoping that the four of them would meet again for lunch.

After everyone had their fill, Olivia asked Frank to tell them more about his grandmother, once he came up for air while eating the lasagna. Annie smiled as she saw how serious he was about the food.

"My grandmother and Great Aunt Nora treat us like royalty whenever we stop by," Frank said as he wiped his chin. "They feed us handmade tortillas, burritos, and things that taste great but don't seem to have names. We've got to bring Annie the next time we visit so she can learn to cook like them." They all laughed.

Derek noticed that Olivia was quiet. "Of course, we will bring Olivia too," he said, assuring her that she was included as part of the new group.

Frank continued the conversation with descriptions of his life in Santa Cruz, explaining that he had an extended family living nearby and in the neighboring town of Aptos. He had two older sisters and two younger sisters. "At our house, the downstairs floor is covered with Barbie dolls and miniature dresses. It's like a Barbie convention. Upstairs, dresses and various clothes are strewn about. Some are costumes and some are formal wear. I can't tell them apart." His description had them all laughing. "And they constantly want to do my hair. I'm not going to lie. It is chaos."

Annie told a similar story about her house, with Derek, Annie, and the younger siblings packed into the top floors of their old Victorian. "Instead of Barbies, we have action figures. No make-up, but lots of weapons," she explained. "Derek just escapes to his room, leaving me to divide and conquer the little comic book characters who rule the roost. Never walk in our house barefoot or you'll be crippled by Legos." She saw the others shaking their heads.

"If you have spare time, you're welcome to come by," Annie suggested to everyone, but looked at Frank.

"We may put you to work, though," Derek added. "Spend a summer at our house, and you could become an expert short-order cook, frying up pancakes, scrambled eggs, and SPAM. It is a one-skillet breakfast and the only skill I have besides working on the house."

The stories were funny, but Olivia also heard kindness from the older kids as they described their younger brothers and sisters. She wished for a relationship like that with her brother, but he was only interested in drinking beer with his friends and not spending time with his little sister.

Several times Derek snuck a glance at Olivia. "Is something going on here?" he wondered. Derek asked Frank about surf spots around Santa Cruz, Frank's favorite subject.

"Steamers Lane is the most famous surfing spot around. It is world-renowned, but it is mostly full of bigger guys. You spend as much time avoiding the other surfers as picking out waves," Frank explained. "I can only surf at the local spots until I get a car. Then I'll be able to get to less crowded spots."

Olivia remarked, "It seems that I'll need a bicycle if I'm going to get around this summer. I'm not old enough to drive. Frank, does that bike work well for you?"

Frank's bike was a large beach cruiser with mismatched, rusted fenders. However, he had crafted a unique rack on the side to hold a surfboard. "With a little practice, I learned to ride my bike to the beach with the surfboard firmly clipped to its side."

Derek inspected the surfboard rack. To Olivia he said, "You may not immediately need a surfboard-toting bike, but we can help you find one that will get you around town. There are lots of bicycle stores in town. With so many tourists and visitors to the city who buy bikes and then abandon them at the end of the summer, many end up at the Bicycle Recycler. It is a big used bike shop. There is no point in buying a new bicycle. We can go there and find you a good used one. Just get a good lock. We can even help you get one this week."

Annie had stacked up the empty food containers and put them next to the basket. She then pulled out a round, flat plastic container with a large knife, dessert forks, and another stack of plastic plates. "Mom doesn't let us use containers that can't be washed and reused. Avoiding disposable plastic is her thing. It works for me." She opened the large container and pulled out a whole cheesecake. She instructed Derek to get out a small jar of strawberry preserves to pour over each serving.

"Whoa! Isn't Mom going to miss that?" asked Derek.

"I don't think so," Annie replied. "She made three of them today. That's her style. She always makes extra food. It isn't much more work, and there's always someone around to eat it," Annie explained as she started cutting pieces for everyone. "We usually count heads at the dinner table to see how many plates we need. There are always a few strays that show up. The kids and their friends get involved in some sort of game and end up staying for lunch, dinner, or dessert. That's how it has always been."

Derek passed out the cheesecake slices and they ate in silence, relishing every bite. Annie even had a small pitcher of lemonade and reusable plastic cups to share. As they worked their way through dessert, the talk turned to activities for the rest of the day. It was two o'clock but still slightly overcast. Derek suggested they drop off the picnic basket at their house, borrow a bike for Olivia, and ride down the coast so Olivia could get an idea of where the stores were and they could all see where the other kids were starting to congregate.

"So, tell us about your new house, Olivia," Annie said.

"It's nice," she admitted, "but my dad said I can't have anyone over unless they're 'pre-approved'—whatever that means." More excitedly, she continued, "We certainly have room for a party using the living room and roof deck. Except for the three of you, I don't know anyone else to invite. But I'm sure my mom would like an opportunity to meet your families and others in the area."

"We should have a barbeque on your deck some evening and have Annie bring her famous ribs and potato salad." Derek was already inviting himself to her house.

Annie's eyes threw daggers at him. "In one sentence you invited yourself to dinner, volunteered my cooking, and assumed you were a 'pre-approved' guest. I swear, you're incorrigible."

Derek looked at her blankly and said nothing. After a moment, Olivia leaned over to Derek and whispered, "It means 'unable to be reformed.'"

"I knew that, but your deck sounds perfect for a party." Derek grinned.

Olivia smiled too. "I'll have to ask, but I hope we can have you and your family over for a BBQ at my house. It'll be fun. I know my mom will be pleased to plan a social event. She loves to entertain. The Fourth of July is in a few weeks, and we've got a perfect view for watching the fireworks. It'd be fun to have your family here; we can all get to know each other. I'll talk to my mom this evening and ask her to call your mom if it's okay. What about you, Frank, would your family want to join us too? Once I know it's fine, I'll let you all know."

Derek was thinking about how many people he just volunteered Annie to feed at the party. He knew his family was large, but he never could get Frank to define the number of local relatives in his clan. Regardless, even with just the three families, he figured it had to be a large group.

"You'll be surprised to see how much food Frank's family will bring," he told Olivia. "I've been to one of his family events before. A few of Frank's older siblings own a catering business. The whole family pitches in with the cooking." Derek added that it could easily come together with some excellent cooks in the mix and a roof-top viewing location for the fireworks. "Olivia's family only needs to provide the location, and we can provide the food."

If Olivia's family were so inclined, Annie suggested they could bring all three households together for a welcoming party, especially since they were practically neighbors, living only a block away from each other.

The conversation then steered to more mundane topics before the party eventually broke up to help Annie pack up the basket, and they all headed downtown.

●　●　●

The next day, the sun came out by midafternoon. Olivia enjoyed the warm, sunny afternoon, logged the summer's first day of sunbathing, and picked up a light-pink glow on her skin. She followed this with a shocking inaugural jump into the surf. The frigid waves knocked the wind right out of her lungs, but it was worth it. After the exhilarating dip in the ocean, she lay out in the sun to warm up and chase off the chill from the water. She enjoyed a leisurely day at the beach, then walked back up the hill to her home for a shower before dinner.

While she was preparing a salad with her mother, Olivia mentioned the idea of a Fourth of July party with the families of the people she met the first day. Her mother lit up with excitement for the opportunity to throw a dinner party and socialize with the neighbors. Her dad, Jack, was less enthusiastic about "partying with strangers." Since managing the family's social life was his wife Ellen's job—a job she genuinely enjoyed—her bright smile easily earned his support. He didn't expect to win tonight, so he put on his best smile and agreed it would be fun. "Cheers to the Fourth of July!" proclaimed Jack, raising his glass. "Cheers," they all said together.

Ellen scheduled a time to meet the other families and plan the gathering. Her first stop was at Derek and Annie's parents,

Beverly and Kurt Moore's, home, to see the double-sized kitchen Olivia told her about. When she entered, Ellen was speechless. The house was a Victorian farmhouse, but the kitchen was completely remodeled with wide, open countertops and fitted with industrial appliances. The counters were made of polished local granite, and all the appliances were gleaming, modern stainless steel. Emily could not get over a kitchen that contained two of everything: refrigerators, dishwashers, gas ovens, eight-burner stovetops, and microwave ovens.

Olivia thought her mom would be even more impressed if she were to see the kitchen in full use before dinner. Derek described the organized chaos of dinner preparation for a tidal wave of kids.

From the Moores' home, Beverly and Annie joined Ellen and Olivia back to tour Ellen and Jack Sutton's house. The house was modern, built only a few years before. There was a spectacular view of Monterey Bay from almost every room. The living room sported nearly 180 degrees of panoramic view through expansive picture windows running to the tall ceiling. When the tour reached the roof, Beverly and Annie stood in awe. The entire rooftop was designed for social gatherings. The large teak deck contained built-in bars and serving stations, tables and chairs casually arranged for conversation or dining, and protection provided by a four-foot-tall wrought iron railing. The rooftop view covered 360 degrees—the harbor, Monterey Bay, the Boardwalk, Wharf, downtown Santa Cruz—and was backed by the coastal mountain range and the UC Santa Cruz campus. It was like standing on the edge of the world.

After everyone had their fill of the view, they began shuffling back down the staircase. With promises to work together on the event, Beverly left for home and Ellen went to her kitchen to prepare her usual family dinner, in a kitchen that now felt like a small station in a ship's galley.

Olivia's brother Ricky joined them for dinner but didn't have anything to say about the party. He acted like Olivia was a stranger, not the little sister he had grown up with his entire life. He was large for his age, not like an athlete but rather like someone who grew large on beer, cheeseburgers, and French fries, observed Olivia. He liked showing off his new, rather poorly done tattoo of a skull and crossbones on his upper right arm.

The only time Olivia tried to be playful, nudging him into the dining room to join the family for dinner, Ricky turned and shoved her so hard she fell to the floor, slid, and struck the stone fireplace hearth. He left the house and didn't return for a week.

When asked where he would spend the Fourth of July, he declared that he would be returning to Portola Valley this week and would spend most of his summer there. Her parents were mute, clearly unhappy that he would not be staying with them as a family in their new beach house.

Their ability to communicate with Ricky was fading. Any time they asked him to help with a chore or join them for a meal, he would blow up and throw a huge adult-size temper tantrum. He would yell and carry on until he finally grabbed their credit card and his car keys, jumped into his car, and drove off to unknown places. He did not even provide an estimated time of return for his parents. He was spoiled, rude, and out of control, Olivia noted.

●　●　●

During her first week there, Olivia quickly figured out that Santa Cruz was made for kids on the move. There were bike riders everywhere, and while Santa Cruz might not be a city, it certainly had the feeling of a big town with a lot of visitors. Olivia liked being at the beach, but she didn't think she would be surfing. The water was shockingly cold, as she had learned earlier in the week. She would have to get a wet suit and a board if she wanted to surf. It seemed like a huge commitment. But summer was just getting started, so she remained open to the idea that maybe one day in the future she would give it a try.

For now, Olivia needed transportation.

The four friends picked a day to visit the bicycle shop. When they reached Derek's house, they picked through Derek's garage and selected a loaner bike for Olivia. After they adjusted the bike for her, they all rode off to the bike shop. When asked how she was doing on her first ride into town, Olivia replied, "It isn't far from our houses, but it's a longer ride than I expected! I need to get my bike legs back in shape."

Olivia was still getting comfortable riding a bike again. After years of walking everywhere, she was genuinely concerned about traffic. Derek joined Olivia as she walked her bike alongside the road when the car traffic increased. Annie and Frank rode ahead when the sidewalk widened and slowed when there was congestion. Olivia and Derek were quiet at first. Olivia assumed that he was afraid to say something embarrassing.

Finally, Olivia took control. She liked Derek but didn't want to spend all their time in silence. "Do you have to work this summer?" Olivia asked him.

"I get a couple of bucks an hour to help my dad with the house. I do my work in the mornings when my dad's here but I can work independently from him in the afternoons and earn a free day now and then. He's a teacher so he gets summers off.

Annie gets paid to watch the siblings for half the day." Derek was looking ahead at the road but listened carefully. "How about you? Do you need to get a job?"

"My parents don't require it, and they do give me some spending money, but if I want to buy something expensive, I need some way to earn income. I used to babysit in our neighborhood, but I don't know if I want to do that again. Kids are exhausting."

Derek laughed. "Our house is like that all day."

Olivia smiled. "Well, you aren't selling me on babysitting. I'll need a different plan. Maybe the shops nearby could use help." Olivia hadn't thought about what she would do this summer. Until today, she thought she would spend it reading or watching soap operas. Meeting Annie and the group had given her hope that this could be a fun summer after all.

When Derek and Olivia reached the bike shop, Annie had already picked out several bikes that she thought would work for Oliva. One even had a basket that could hold their lunches, or half a lunch if the boys were involved. Olivia smiled at the memory of their voracious appetites.

The bike shop had so many bicycles that the owner had lined them on walls, floor to ceiling, to display the new and used bikes for sale. The workshop was in a large room on one side of the store. The other side of the store had a similar layout. When Olivia peeked through a door behind the cash register, she saw a mountain of bikes, wheels, and parts. It was bicycle madness and a bit overwhelming for her. She just stood staring at the wall of bikes. "This is impossible," she said under her breath.

Annie came to the rescue. "Don't worry about the dogpile— that's what they call the tangle of bikes you just saw. They use those bikes to train kids to repair their own bikes. You don't need to worry about those busted-up junkers. There are plenty of bikes in good repair and they're lined up toward the front of the store. First look at the bikes here, and then you can start comparing them with other ones you may like. This is what I picked out for you," Annie said, flicking the bell on the handlebars of the bike she was holding. "It'll be like trying on dresses. You will know the one you like when you see it."

"It doesn't need to be too complicated," said Annie as she inspected one bike after another on the wall. "Look for ones that are in better shape, have no rust, and have gears to help climb hills. I'll tell you a secret, the most important thing is that the bicycle fits you. You don't want to be leaning over too far. That means the bike is too large. And you don't want a bike that you need to ride with your seat adjusted too high. Go ahead and start trying them. Just hop up on each bike. We'll hold it for you."

Olivia turned out to be a very efficient shopper, trying out a dozen bikes in half an hour.

"What about the prices?" Olivia asked, still looking up and down the rows of bikes at the front of the store.

"The bikes you have been considering aren't expensive," Derek said as he spun the wheel of the bike he was holding. "They're used but in good condition, and suitable for riding around town. A good choice will be a Beach Cruiser with gears."

Olivia narrowed it down to the one Annie selected for her and one she had found along the wall, which had only a few minor scratches and scrapes but wasn't rusted and fit comfortably. The guy at the shop said he had some stickers she could put on to cover the scratches. The bike even had a few gears to help her with the small hills around town.

Olivia went to the front counter. She asked about the price of the bike Annie chose and the other one she selected and learned their prices were the same. She picked out a new lock with extra keys, a new helmet (she did not want a used helmet), the basket (complimentary), and future repairs (free repairs included all summer). Finally, she put together a mental list of all the features she wanted in a bicycle, which matched the bike Annie had recommended.

Olivia completed the invoice, adding her name, address, and her dad's phone number. She borrowed the owner's phone and called her dad. She took the call over by the wall for privacy and explained to her father what she wanted. The others watched her. She nodded a few times, explained the need for a bike a second time, and then waited longer. Finally, she thanked her dad and handed the phone to the owner. "He'll give you his credit card number and ask you to deliver the bike to our house up the hill. Does that work for you?" The owner nodded and shook her hand before they all walked out into what had become a warm, sunny day.

"That was amazing," Derek said to Olivia once they were out of the shop. "Your dad bought you the bike without even looking at it." He stretched his shoulders and turned to face the newly emerged sun and drew in some of its warmth.

"He didn't need to see the bike," said Olivia matter-of-factly. "I looked at all the bikes in the shop that were my size and in good condition. I asked you and the shopkeeper dozens of questions until I was comfortable we were selecting the right bike. Annie found one I liked, and I asked the owner to explain why it was a good bike and priced correctly. I am confident I found the right one," said Olivia. "My dad usually takes my recommendations seriously; after all, he's the one who taught me how to shop."

Derek had never heard someone talk with their parents that way. It was how adults spoke to one another. He knew parents and kids didn't always trust one another to make good decisions. He observed that kids were not always mature enough to make big decisions alone. Their parents often decided what to buy, and sometimes it was a wrong fit for what their child wanted. He knew his parents often said no because they didn't have the money at the time or just didn't want to spend it.

Three

Now that they all had transportation, the four friends were free to extend their adventures much further from home. Olivia said she would like to visit the Boardwalk, but any serious shopping trip needed to wait until she had a job. To save money, they agreed to window shop, share lunches, and check out the local sights, which included seeing what strange fish the fishermen caught at the wharf that morning.

As the summer unfolded, the gang met regularly, sunning on the beach in their favorite spot, body surfing, and walking on the beach. The foursome rode downtown and browsed through the shops, the girls pointing out their favorite clothes and beach outfits in the surf shop, while the guys admired the skateboarding gear and surfing equipment.

As much as Derek and Oliva enjoyed the double dates, they were starting to enjoy time alone as a couple, and came up with reasons to travel together, separate from the larger group. Walks on the beach began to include holding hands, something that Derek had never done with other girls. If he were honest with himself, his experience consisted of a few games of spin the bottle, more a game of forcing kids to make awkward kisses than anything close to romantic.

Derek looked at Olivia as they walked on the beach. She smiled when he stopped and took her other hand. "I like walking with you." It was all he could think of to say, but it was exactly what he wanted to say. He hoped to hear what she was thinking.

She looked away with a half smile and a tilt of her head. Derek didn't want to embarrass her. "I think I'm pretty good at it, you know, the holding hands bit." He raised his eyebrows, trying to coax a response from her. She laughed.

"Is that what you think?" She squeezed his hands in response. "Do you know girls who will back up your claim?"

"Of course I do," he said, trying to be mysterious. "Plenty."

She let go of his hands. "So, you have 'plenty of girls' that have held your hands? Are there any that still want to hold them?"

"Well," he backpedaled, "I mean there could be."

"Is that so?" she asked.

"Oh, I'm just talking for fun. There's nobody but you that I want to walk hand in hand with. I'm very happy that you seem to enjoy it too." He gave her a quick kiss on the cheek, and then she gave him a hug in response. They continued their walk, both smiling, unable to make eye contact for a minute or two, each lost in their own thoughts.

As Olivia's riding ability improved, the teens explored all over town, riding together down the shoreline. They relished the lavish picnic lunches packed up from Annie and Derek's kitchen.

One day, a few weeks later, the four friends stretched out on their beach towels, soaking up rays from the first warm day of the season. After a month or so, they would develop a deep enough tan to protect them from the sun. Until then, they carefully put on sunscreen; Olivia helped Derek reach his back, and Annie helped Frank. Frank and Olivia started the summer with naturally darker skin, "blessed with an olive complexion," as Olivia's mom liked to say, and weren't as concerned with getting sunburned.

Frank sat up and surveyed the beach. It was midweek, and both the locals and vacationers were starting to congregate around the cove, spreading out their towels and setting up umbrellas; however, Frank had more important things on his mind.

"I got my mom to call Grandma and Aunt Nora," he announced. "We're invited over for dinner. Nora said we could come any time, but my mom said that meant Saturday evening. When those two women start cooking, they don't stop until everyone is full."

"You invited yourself to their house so they could cook for you?" Olivia was flabbergasted. "We should at least buy the ingredients. We should be buying extras too, otherwise, we'd use up a month's worth of groceries to feed your pack of wolves."

The four of them were quiet, each assessing the situation. It would be fun to visit Frank's grandmother and great aunt, but nobody wanted to eat all their food.

Finally, Frank spoke and broke the awkward silence. "Are your grandparents still living, Olivia?"

"We have one pair living back east and they're going strong, but we don't see them too often."

"I'm sorry to hear that," he said, and waited what seemed an appropriate amount of time to continue. "I can tell you about my experience visiting my grandparents. One pair live just down the road from us in Aptos. They traded homes with us so my parents had the bigger house once we started bursting at the seams and needed the space. They took the smaller house with an ocean view. On my dad's side, Grandmother and Aunt Nora moved into a bungalow on Seabright. They don't have much to do. They watch TV, my grandmother reads her romance novels, and my grandpa works in the shop making who knows what."

He sat up and looked at his friends. "But they love it when we visit them. Now, the little ones are difficult for the grandparents to take. Some like to sit on their lap, and others start playing with Grandmother's figurines. Something always gets broken."

They all laughed. Frank continued, "We all know the amount of activity occurring at Annie and Derek's home. It's constant mayhem. Kids are running in the house, crying, and spilling drinks."

"It's just another typical day in their lives," added Derek, recalling the picture of chaos he saw when visiting Frank's house.

"It's quite a scene," Frank continued. "When Grandpa has enough, he moves out to the shop in the garage with my dad. Then, when Grandmother has had her fill, she nods to my mom, and we pack up and go home. It may sound messy, but for my grandparents, it's the high point of the week. It just needs to be kept to small doses. Also, half the time we invite them to our house and make the younger siblings play quietly in their rooms."

"So," Olivia asked Frank, "you are doing them a favor to visit so they can cook for you?"

"They love to cook, and what's better than cooking for hungry teenagers? So we eat like locusts and down huge portions to show how much we love each dish."

Frank continued, "We bring a special pastry from the Mexican bakery, the same one they've shopped at for fifty years. In fact, Aunt Nora and Grandmother grew up with the original baker's children. The dessert is a Mexican flan that they prepare just right. It's exceptionally smooth textured, with a hint of spices that nobody else replicates.

"First, Grandmother and Aunt Nora will ooh and ahh over the dessert. They ask us where we got it, then when we tell them, they tell us all about the baker's family. In turn, we will say we're too stuffed to eat more than a spoonful, and they keep the left-over sweets for dessert over the rest of the week.

"My mom and sisters still cook traditional meals, but not often. Aunt Nora and Grandmother are the best at cooking old-style meals. They buy spices from the Mexican grocery store that are fantastic but maybe too spicy for the little ones. They also buy pork and beef from the butcher using old-style cuts which are different from those found in the American supermarkets. The differences are subtle, but altogether, the meal cooked this way seems so traditional, and I suppose it is."

Derek enjoyed Frank's description of visiting his grandparents. It was a long story, but once he explained that the visit was not an imposition, it kept Annie from getting upset. Derek wanted to keep visiting them and start bringing Annie and Olivia with him. Everyone was silent for a while. It was a very well-thought-out plan. Everyone wanted homemade Mexican food. Derek's family rarely ate it at home. Olivia's family only ate Mexican food from fast food restaurants or the food trucks in town.

"You've done this before, haven't you?" Annie asked Frank.

"Maybe a few times," he replied.

"How few?"

"Quite a few."

Annie wasn't giving up on her quest for the truth. "How many years?"

"Since I could ride a bicycle to their house."

"You are such a schemer!" Annie pushed him over and sat on him. "That's not an admirable trait, you know. We may have to talk about it, but for now, I'll join you on these visits every time you go, if only to keep you under control."

"Join us once for the meals and you'll want to return for the conversation. Aunt Nora and Grandmother are fun to spend time with."

"Well, I think that's a great idea," Derek said.

Frank rolled over, pushing Annie into the sand, which stuck to the suntan lotion on her skin. Once she realized the sand was sticking, she said, "It's time to go back into the waves." She covered their stuff to protect it from the sun, stretched out their towels, grabbed Frank's hand, and ran toward the waves. Olivia and Derek were right behind them.

As usual, the water was shockingly cold, so afterward, they stretched out on beach towels, letting the sun warm their skin and dry their suits.

They laid out in the sun and discussed various topics, from making plans for new adventures to seeing what they wanted to eat for dinner. Eventually, the sun worked its magic, warming their skin and leaving behind only the memory of the ocean's chill. Soon they were sweating enough to want another dip in the water, forgetting the shocking cold. They ran into the ocean, threw themselves into the base of a large wave, and let the bulk of its power wash over them. Each couple held hands, partly because it was fun and partly to ensure nobody chickened out.

After they hit the waves, it was mere seconds before they leapt up and screamed about the cold. In short order, they raced back to their spot and stretched out on their towels. They repeated this pattern for the rest of the afternoon. By the time they rolled up their towels and headed home, their skin glowed.

Their suntans continued to darken over the many weeks spent at the beach. Derek found Olivia's tanned skin added to her beauty. But then, everything she did touched his heart. Although he had little experience with girls, and none with girlfriends, he found himself focused on her day and night and thought that if this was how it felt to be in love, he was perfectly fine with it.

● ● ●

On a warm morning later that summer, Derek met Olivia at the beach. Annie and Frank had separate plans and said they would catch up with their friends later in the afternoon. The sun melted the fog off early, giving Derek and Olivia unlimited possibilities to enjoy the sunny day. Both were quiet, thinking about how they wanted to spend their time together. Olivia suggested it was a good day to go for a long walk on the beach together since they did not have plans and the sun was warm overhead.

Castle Beach ran south for about a half mile before it ended at a jetty that protected the harbor. Once the teens reached its southern end, they started back and walked the entire length of the beach, past the Cove at Castle Beach until they approached the cliffs known as the Point. Rising nearly 100 feet and extending several hundred feet into Monterey Bay, the Point was the remains of the shoreline still standing after ravishing winter storms. Each year, the Point gave up some land that fell, broke up, and, with time, eroded into beach sand.

Oliva showed Derek the section of the Point where her house stood, several hundred yards back from the end of the Point.

"My house is right about there," she said, pointing to the top of the point. "You can see it better from the other side. The row of houses on the river side of the point looks out at the Boardwalk and the wharf."

Derek looked up from the base of the cliff to the rock out-cropping. "It makes my heart race just looking up," observed Derek. "Your cliff house is on a solid rock foundation. It should be there long after we are grown up, and our kids are grown up." He paused, thinking about what he said. "I mean, generations: It will last generations, so you shouldn't worry," he quickly corrected.

Olivia was absorbed with her worries and did not notice his slip. "What about these piles of huge rocks that fell in previous storms?" Olivia could see evidence of the stone cliffs weathering everywhere except where ivy and other coastal plants protected it.

Derek didn't have a good answer, so he said, "Those are for people who own houses right on the cliffs. You should be fine. Your place is built on rock, not the crumbling sandstone cliffs."

She gave an involuntary shiver as she looked up at the cliff walls that would someday fall into the sea, taking her house with it. For now, and hopefully far beyond her lifetime, she told herself, the rock would stand and hold strong against the storms.

Derek showed Olivia a shortcut that was the only way to get past the Point. It was through a water-worn hole in its base, only big enough to allow two people to pass through it, shoulder to shoulder. Even then, they had to lean together to clear the low ceiling.

Holding hands for balance, they walked quickly through the hole, timing their crossing so the surging water didn't knock them over. Once through, they didn't need each other for balance, but neither let go, so they continued to walk hand in hand along the river's shore. The river was wide but shallow where they waded across.

"The river is named the San Lorenzo River, but everyone calls it the Santa Cruz River. On the other side is the Boardwalk.

It runs north for almost a mile along the shore and ends just past the wharf." Derek waved up river at a huge wooden bridge used to support the train tracks which allowed trains to operate, at one time, up and down the coast, but now only provided limited service. The bridge crossed the river gorge fifty feet above the water.

They were both out of breath once they crossed the river. Olivia squeezed Derek's hand. "I haven't been to the Boardwalk yet, although I can see it directly from my bedroom." She gazed off at the amusement park with its spinning rides and the flashing lights that ran the full length of the amusement park whenever the Boardwalk was open.

"The Boardwalk looks massive from down here," she said in a voice tinged with awe. "The rides are huge, but they always look like I could reach out and touch them from my room." This perspective was new to her, and she took it all in. She had yet to be this close to the Boardwalk. Although she saw the Boardwalk from her room, it was far enough away that it didn't seem real. It was the same with the Wharf, a long wooden pier supporting a row of buildings containing restaurants, t-shirt shops for tourists, and fishing supplies.

Olivia threw up her hands. "It's so much to take in. Someday I'd like to go out on the wharf and buy a fishing pole to try to catch food for dinner. Maybe when I have some money."

"Fishing isn't that expensive," said Derek, slowing down to give Olivia his full attention. "I have a couple of fishing poles, and we could buy bait on the pier. You catch one or two and that's dinner!" Derek looked at her, wondering how she was responding to his fishing description. Finally, he said, "Maybe another day. The Wharf will be there all summer," kidded Derek.

"I still have more to see here," she responded in a faraway voice.

"Another day would be fine," Derek answered, and they continued their walk.

Derek and Olivia were still holding hands as they walked along the beach, down where the waves were breaking. He raised her hand to his lips for a light kiss. Sometimes a wave would wash between them, splashing their hands with the sandy tide, the cool of the water in sharp contrast to the warmth of their hands and the rest of their bodies.

They walked from the waves to the base of the stairs leading from the beach to the rides as they both let the entire experience sink in. The lights pulsed toward the entrance to the rides, and loud music from the merry-go-round filled their ears. "How about a ride on the Ferris Wheel?" Derek suggested. "We could do one ride and return home in time to catch up with Frank and Annie."

Olivia wasn't sure. Her parents let her do whatever she wanted, within reason, but her mom had said several times that the Boardwalk attracted a rough crowd. Her mom once let it slip that she was only at the Boardwalk during the years following World War II and found the soldiers too attentive. Olivia had a hard time taking that assessment seriously. It certainly wasn't a place she would visit alone, but she was with Derek and his offer sounded fine, so she accepted.

They walked along the beach in front of the Boardwalk until they reached the Ferris Wheel. Derek led the way up the stairs from the beach to the Boardwalk. It was early in the day and the middle of the week, so the Boardwalk had few visitors. Music played from the merry-go-round and from the skee-ball arcade, but otherwise it was a quiet summer morning. The possibility of the typical cold morning fog scared off most of the early out-of-town visitors.

As they stepped onto the Boardwalk, Derek pointed to the Ferris Wheel. "Look! There are no lines," he marveled as they walked up to the window of the nearby ticket booth "Two tickets for the Ferris Wheel, please," Derek asked.

The woman in the booth was so old she looked as if she had been selling tickets since the day the Boardwalk first opened. She eyed Derek and then Olivia, and nodded a few times, apparently answering some questions that only she could hear. "We have a ten-pack for twenty dollars, with one ticket required per rider."

Olivia could almost see Derek deflate as their plans for a ride evaporated. She spoke up. "We are coming back one night in the next couple of weeks and plan to go on every ride in the park, but today we just thought it would be fun to ride once before we headed home. We both live here near the Boardwalk, and I see it every day from my window. I just moved to Santa Cruz this summer and have never been on the Ferris Wheel."

The woman nodded while she listened and then turned to Derek. "Is that right? You want to take just one ride with your gal here?"

He nodded. "We live here with our families, and my house is crowded. I thought this would be a private place to talk and get away from all the people at home."

Olivia spoke up, "It's quite a circus at his house."

The woman looked at Olivia and then at Derek. She leaned forward, put her head out of the booth, and squinted at the entrance to the Ferris Wheel. It was a quiet day at the Boardwalk, so there weren't enough people to fill all the rides. Derek and Olivia watched the ticket woman, both trying to guess what she would decide.

She put her hand on the crumpled pile of dollar bills and loose change that Derek had placed on the counter and slid it back to Derek. After one more look at Derek and Olivia, she made her decision.

Her grimace relaxed into a crinkled smile and her eyes widened. The hard edge of her stare was gone. "Hmm, here's what I'm going to do," she said to herself as she tore a double ticket out of the roll of tickets on the counter and turned it over. On the back, she wrote, "One Ride, Ticket for Two. First Kiss," and she signed it, "Gladys."

Olivia was holding her breath. She never expected a seasoned Boardwalk worker to give them a break, but clearly she was wrong. The ticket lady spoke with Derek.

"This is what you'll do, young man. You show this ticket to Buck, who runs the Ferris Wheel. You tell him Gladys says let the kids ride and have their first kiss. And you, Missy," she said while pointing at Olivia, "you tell Buck that Gladys said to let you keep the ticket after the ride. It's for your scrapbook." Gladys looked back and forth between Derek and Olivia as if verifying that they would follow her orders.

They nodded thankfully. It took Olivia a moment to understand what just happened. She looked at Derek who was also momentarily confused.

Gladys went back to her cynical stare and shooed them away. "Now go on. Catch that ride!"

Just as they were turning away, Gladys barked, "Hey!" Olivia and Derek looked back. "Just because you're young doesn't mean it isn't love." In the past, Olivia thought she would die from embarrassment if someone commented on her love life in public, but now she felt a warm glow running from her face to her toes. She was beginning to understand that the happiness she felt around Derek was something more than blushes or embarrassment.

Olivia took the ticket, and Derek scooped the money into his pocket. He took Olivia's hand, and they ran to the Ferris Wheel entrance for their first ride together. They were both excited and stole a few glances at each other to see if the other felt the same.

Holding Olivia's hand, Derek looked at her and saw she was watching him too. It was time to say something. "How did she know what we wanted to do? Do you think she could read our minds?" asked Derek.

"No, silly," Olivia scolded him in a pleasant tone. "We aren't the first couple to ride the Ferris Wheel. I imagine many others have thought the same thing." She squeezed his hand, but didn't mention the kiss, even though it was all she could think of. As they walked the last few steps to the ride, she was close enough that she could lean over and kiss Derek, but she wanted the kiss to come from him when they were at the top of the ride. This was his idea, so she wanted him to get the credit.

Olivia watched Derek. He kept wiping his free hand on his pant leg, looking around, everywhere but at Olivia. Olivia knew what he intended to do when they got to the top. In fact, she imagined Buck wouldn't let them off the ride if he didn't kiss her.

Once they approached the ride, Buck took their ticket, read the back, and looked over to Gladys, who gave him a thumbs-up. When the next car reached the bottom, Buck guided them onboard and handed the ticket back to Olivia and smiled. "Have a good time. When you've had enough of the ride, let me know by crossing your arms above your head to show that you are all finished." He held his arms up to demonstrate the finished motion. Of course, they didn't expect they would ever want to leave, but it was nice to have a choice.

The wheel started moving, and they were lifted into the sky.

They felt alone in the air as their car rose up to the top of the wheel. Stretched before them was the entire length of the beach, from the harbor to the Wharf. When Olivia looked down, the people below looked like ants, until her weight shift caused their seat to swing. Olivia feared it would dump them from their seats. Derek scooted closer to Olivia. She clutched his arm and asked, "When Gladys suggested we were going to have our first kiss, do you think she was guessing, or do we look like a couple?"

Derek looked tense. He was afraid to say the wrong thing and mess up their chance for a first kiss. "Fortune favors the bold," he said under his breath. The Ferris Wheel picked up speed and their seat began to rise. Derek's chest tightened.

"What was that?" Olivia asked, squeezing his hand. "Are you feeling old?" She seemed to misunderstand.

Olivia let Derek put his arm around her, and he pulled her even closer to him. The ride was going at full speed, rising above the Boardwalk while their faces were only inches apart. Derek spoke first. "I've wanted to kiss you for weeks. I don't want to wait any longer." He leaned in, his lips brushing across hers, and then he held himself still, an inch away from her lips as they rose higher and higher. The wheel slowed to a stop when they reached the top. Derek closed the gap and Olivia let his lips press firmly on hers. For a moment, their entire world consisted of nothing but the kiss and the warmth of their arms around each other. Eventually they opened their eyes.

"Finally!" Olivia said, and they laughed at her exclamation. They moved in closer and kissed again, a long, tentative kiss by a couple who, until now, had the desire but lacked the courage to follow through. When they pulled back to look at each other, they were both grinning, and she noticed the blush on Derek's fair skin glowing brightly. "I guess that was the fortune our bold-ness deserved," she said, her voice low and breathless. They both laughed. She had heard his whole statement about boldness but wanted him to explain it himself.

"There could only be a kiss if I had the courage to try." He hugged her, and she tucked her face against his shoulder. "And, if you wanted it too," said Derek.

"Or if I let you." She kissed him in agreement. "There were several times other guys tried to kiss me, but I had to push them away, explaining that I wasn't that kind of friend." She had her arms around his neck. One hundred feet up in the air, they had found the privacy they needed. "I was just waiting for the right guy. Since we first met, I knew it was you."

The rest of the ride was spent kissing, laughing, and point-ing out things of interest. They could barely make out the surfers at Steamer's Lane, the best surfing spot in Santa Cruz, as Frank often reminded them.

They kissed some more, and then Derek admitted to Olivia that he was getting hungry. After one more kiss, she agreed that they should head home to get some lunch. Eventually it was time to return to earth at Castle Beach. They would visit the Boardwalk in the future. They knew that following trips may not have today's excitement, but they would certainly retain the passion and the wonder of what was yet to come as a young couple. Until then, they would share the memory of their first kiss.

Reluctantly, they both gave Buck the termination sign. The ride went around again, and then the Ferris Wheel stopped to let them off. Derek thanked Buck and Olivia leaned down and stuck her head into the opening at the ticket booth. "Thank you, Gladys. It was great. I'll see you soon!"

Olivia waved goodbye and smiled as she and Derek walked away from the Boardwalk, hand in hand.

They reached the steps to the beach, and, carrying their sandals, ran to the tidal river. The tide was coming in. It was still shallow enough to walk through but deep enough to get their shorts wet if they weren't careful. Timing their river crossing to match the swell of the waves, they waded into the river between the Boardwalk and the Point. Within a few minutes, they were across and on the other side. Once on dry ground, they put their sandals back on to protect their feet against the searing hot sand. Olivia retook Derek's hand, and they walked on in silence. Occasionally, they both stole glances at each other. They each saw the other smiling, which made them smile even more. It was a quiet but contented walk home.

●   ●   ●

When they reached Castle Beach, they found Frank and Annie lying on their towels, soaking wet from a recent dip in the surf, and using the sun to warm them up. Annie looked up, first at Derek, then at Olivia. Olivia gave Annie a quick wink, secretly communicating the kiss. Emboldened with this knowledge, Annie wanted to make a scene, if just to celebrate a new step in her brother's and Olivia's relationship. She knew he had been agonizing over kissing Olivia. He wouldn't talk directly to Annie about it, but she caught snippets of his conversations with Frank. Now it was time to bring this kiss, and their growing relationship, into the open.

"Hey Frank, look at this. Do you see what I see?" Annie asked with a taunting tone.

Frank rolled over and sat up, put on his sunglasses, and looked at Annie, who nodded and then gave an embarrassing "smooch" sound, an obvious hint at what occurred. "I'm not sure what to see. I need a second pair of sunglasses to cut the glare of the first kiss on these two kids. Holy guaca-mole! These are some big smiles."

Derek was mortified. How could they mock him this way? Olivia just stood there, confidently smiling. Yesterday, she spoke with Annie about how to help the guys gain some courage to make the first move.

"Well, pull up a towel. We brought extras in case you forgot them when you were doing all that smooching." Frank was not going to let up.

Once they were all lined up on their towels, Frank asked Annie, "Don't you feel left out? All this romance in the air, but we failed to breathe it in. How did we miss it, Annie?"

"I don't know." She leaned over toward Frank, held his face in both hands, and pressed her mouth squarely on his lips.

Derek didn't think that it looked very romantic.

As if he could hear what Derek was thinking, Frank gave Annie a light kiss on the side of her mouth, then one along her jawline. He held her head, lightly stroking her hair back, and followed up with a softer kiss on her lips.

"Okay, guys, come on. We get it. We were late to this club. You win," Derek said. "If 'losing' means I can kiss Olivia in public, I'm okay with that."

Olivia spoke up to break the awkward silence. "I guess I'm going to have to make Derek an expert in kissing too." She leaned over, held Derek by the chin, and gave him a big, wet smack on the lips. They were all shocked, but not as much as Derek. It had taken him half a summer to muster the courage to kiss her in private on the Ferris Wheel, and here he was kissing his girl in front of his sister. He decided to take a risk. "What?" he asked his friends. "Can't a guy kiss his girlfriend in public?"

Frank and Annie roared. "May the shock never end!" exclaimed Annie. "He even has a girlfriend?" They all laughed.

"I guess that fits," said Olivia. "Now, if we are all done with the theatrics, I have a list of things I want to do before the summer ends." Olivia looked at the others to ensure she had their attention. "I want to get fish and chips from Aldo's at the harbor and ice cream from Marianne's. I heard their watermelon ice cream has real seeds in it." She barely paused while ticking off places to visit. "I want to know what the Mystery Spot is! They advertise everywhere, but we need a car for that." She looked around at her friends. "What? Don't you wonder what they are talking about? If it is a mystery, I'll bet we can figure it out!"

Derek was mystified. Where did all these demands come from?

Olivia continued to share her to-do list. "Also, I want to do some shopping. These guys need to up their game. They're no longer in elementary school, and every day can't be a surf day. It's time for some new clothes."

Annie got in the mix. "While we are at it, haven't you guys ever heard of a barber? It's time you got your hair cut and God forbid, styled. If you don't have the money, pool your resources. You wouldn't want my second kiss scooped up by another young man, just because he was well-dressed and well-groomed, would you? I know that I would like to walk down the street with a well-groomed, stylishly dressed, handsome man. Let's make sure it is you!"

The girls laughed at their jokes, while Derek stood, not knowing what to do. Frank began doing modeling poses, hoping he could elevate his game, but without spending any money it would be a challenge. He pulled his pockets out and showed the girls they were empty.

Olivia looked at him and laughed. "If that's the way it is, then the clothes and the haircut will be my early birthday gift to each of you."

She turned to Annie and said, "When they look good, we look good!"

Their list was written, revised, and rewritten with the addition of new clothes to buy and long overdue haircuts. The original list included restaurants to visit, caves to explore, and touristy t-shirts to buy. As they reviewed the list, one by one they became drowsy and dozed in the warm sun.

Although Derek was a late bloomer when it came to kisses, Frank later admitted the truth, that he and Annie had their first kiss just that morning. While Frank put up a good show in front of his friends, he revealed to Derek he had been too scared to risk his friendship with Annie by taking the next step. It was not the first time Frank had kissed a girl, but he shared that this time it was something special.

•   •   •

Grandmother and Aunt Nora greeted them all at the front door, and graciously accepted the dessert presented in a pink box. Olivia watched Grandmother and Aunt Nora at the door shaking hands with the guests. They ushered in their visitors and commented on how pretty the girls were and how much the boys had grown.

When the two young couples entered Grandmother and Nora's house, they walked through the living room onto an outdoor patio to receive glasses of iced tea or lemonade. Frank quickly stepped into the role of the group's talk show host. He obviously enjoyed it. Whenever he gave an opinion or told a story, he paused for someone else to correct him or add details that he had left out. "We had another plate of flan for you tonight, but it didn't make the journey," Frank explained.

Grandmother and Nora exchanged glances, waiting for Frank's typical story to begin.

Annie couldn't leave Frank's comment alone. "We had more than enough, but by the time we reached your front door, they were all gone. We had to continue down to the bakery for another box before visiting." She gave a light elbow jab to Frank's ribs.

"Well, I had to make sure they were good. I'd hate to bring something that was undercooked."

Olivia noticed Frank was in trouble with Annie again, but she didn't miss the smile Annie had for Frank when he wasn't looking.

"How were they?" Derek questioned.

"Fantastic. Like a snack before dinner." Frank rubbed his belly and smiled.

"More like six snacks, I'd say," offered Annie. She bumped shoulders with Frank. Her true feelings were demonstrated by how close she sat to him and not by the banter about the missing desserts.

Although Frank took the role of Master of Ceremonies, it was easy to see that Annie was the leader of the group. She and Frank maintained a steady dialogue as she corrected him, asked him to behave, and use proper table manners. Frank's social gaffs were minor and almost intentional, just enough to keep a dialogue going between Frank and Annie. Then the conversation included the others, with Frank asking for Grandmother's opinion on which fork was for which food. Derek issued his proclamation of the correct utensil, if that were the subject, only to be overruled by Olivia, who agreed with Aunt Nora and Grandmother's answers.

Based on all the smiles around the table, it was clear the evening at Grandmother and Aunt Nora's house was a big hit.

The older women enjoyed meeting their grandson's new girlfriend and they were equally charmed by his friends Derek and Olivia. The girls talked about recipes and cooking techniques, promising to visit the Seabright house again before leaving for school. There were many discussions about the pictures on the mantle—two related families spread out over two, three, or more generations. It was fun for everyone.

The conversation moved along smoothly as they discussed all the activities and new developments of the summer. Over the years, the two older women had attended all the family events, and there were many of those, but they didn't often have this much quality time where each person could speak up and share their views without interruption. Frank had two older sisters, Gabby and Vanessa, who were so involved with their boyfriends that they hadn't come by the house in a while. There were also two younger girls who often came along when Frank's mom wanted to visit her mother. Grandmother adored the little granddaughters, but they were young and required constant attention. It was hard to have much conversation between adults and teenagers with young children running through the house.

After dinner, Frank took a moment to give his friends a history lesson.

"My great grandparents were the first to come from the old country, Guadalajara, Mexico, and settle here. At that time, there weren't many houses suitable for year-round living. Instead, most of the development was along the shoreline and consisted of beach houses with small bedrooms, few bathrooms, and no air conditioning. There wasn't insulation, but it was cool enough that people would come from San Jose or Monterey to stay here during the summer and escape the heat of summers inland. My grandfather was a carpenter and helped buyers of these old homes convert them to all-season dwellings.

"At the same time, he quickly secured several lots where he would build homes for his family, including his wife, and for his mother, who is my great-grandmother, and one for his sister, my great aunt Nora. They chose the lots to be a mile or two inland from the shore and away from the summer fog that rolled into the bay and kept most of the neighborhoods socked in every morning until midsummer.

"The houses were built in the style of the times: some were Victorian houses, like Annie and Derek's house, with a design from the late 1890s. They had elaborate roof lines with numerous dormers and turrets added to make the houses more attractive. The house for my great-aunt was built in the craftsman style: straight lines, trim with squares, and designed with simplicity and functionality in all the features. To emphasize the natural beauty of the wood, the buildings were finished with linseed oil to show off the grain of the wood or shellac to give a clear finish to interior wood trim.

"My grandparents came to live in these houses when they were young. They married, stayed in their homes, and raised families. My mother lived in the Seabright house and moved out when she realized we needed more room. Now we are the next generation and are expected to raise our families here. The only problem is there are more of us than there are houses. My dad is working to acquire more lots and build houses for us, but the lots are more valuable now that highways allow commuters to live in Santa Cruz and work in the cities around San Jose. It keeps the price of houses up." Frank spoke as an expert on Santa Cruz. "My dad says that houses have always been expensive, so we shouldn't use that as a reason to postpone plans to buy a lot, build a house, get married, and raise families as adults have done for generations."

Everyone was silent. Finally, Olivia said to Annie, "I guess we have weddings to plan."

Derek gripped Frank's shoulder. "Don't worry, I'll be your best man." They all enjoyed a light moment in the conversation. Oliva and Derek exchanged glances, as did Frank and Annie, digesting the idea of marriage. Questions that floated in the air were: "What would marriage be like? And would it be with my girlfriend or boyfriend who is here right now?"

Even though the questions didn't require responses, the discussion of marriage had been raised, although in jest, and there it stood. Each of the four of the visitors paused for a moment while they peeked into the future. It was fun to think about the next phase of their lives and pretend this was their house and they were adults and the kids around this table would grow old together.

The light conversation resumed and continued throughout the evening, making for a lively discussion as they each described their summer activities. Nora had a soft spot in her heart for the pretty new addition to the table. Olivia had been quiet, soaking up the stories, sometimes with surprise, sometimes with horror, but mostly with laughter or a kind comment. Derek had visited before and pushed past his initial shyness. He told them about the repairs and restorations he had to conduct on their house.

He explained that the work wasn't hard, so when he finished his morning chores at home each day, he planned to offer his services to neighbors around the Point.

"When I'm working at home, I'm just another kid helping with chores, but when I talk with the other property owners about making repairs, they see me as a carpenter. Because I can get on a ladder and make the necessary repairs to the water-damaged shingles, I am able to charge my labor at market rates. They can't do the work themselves, or more often, they know how to make the repairs but no longer want to get up on the ladder. By now, climbing ladders is second nature for me." Derek looked around the table but couldn't read the expressions on anyone's face.

Annie spoke up, "Derek, nobody likes going up on ladders, especially as high up as you go."

"Yeah, dude," Frank chimed in. "I'm pretty brave on a surfboard, but you wouldn't catch me climbing up to the third floor to pull shingles off the side of the house." Frank was uncharacteristically serious.

Olivia spoke up. "I've never been up a ladder, and I don't like him being up there. But I have sat and watched him do his work, and I can tell that he is incredibly careful. It is like watching an acrobat, the one who piles up a stack of chairs and then climbs up to the top, adds a chair, and then does a handstand." Everyone looked at her in horror.

"He does handstands on top of the ladder?" Grandmother asked.

Olivia knew that Grandmother was kidding, but she had to be clearer. "He moves slowly and steadily when climbing. His tools are carefully hung, each in its right tab on his belt, or in a bucket attached to the ladder, and he never reaches too far or makes any sudden movements. He is very deliberate. I can tell he has experience and doesn't take any extra chances."

They all turned as one to Derek, wanting to hear his take on this new development.

Derek held up both palms. "I don't do handstands," he said with mock seriousness.

"He would if Olivia asked him to," Frank added, smiling until Annie stared him down.

"Okay, then. If you know what you're doing, it sounds like a fine business plan," said Grandmother. "Frank's grandfather and I came from families that weren't afraid to do hard work. What you are describing is skilled labor. It is the first step in providing for your family. I know that Annie and Derek's families have been skilled workers here in Santa Cruz for many generations. Over the years, they sometimes worked with my family on the same projects."

Nora looked at Olivia. "What does your father do?" she asked in a kind tone. This was the newest visitor to their house, and from the glances Olivia exchanged with Derek, it was likely Grandmother and Nora would be seeing more of these two couples this summer.

"My father is an attorney in San Francisco. He comes down to Santa Cruz occasionally, but otherwise he works long hours and spends most of his time in the office." She wasn't well-versed in what type of law he practiced.

"That's a fine profession," said Nora. "Are you going to become an attorney too?" Nora asked.

"I don't know," Olivia replied. "I am not sure what he does except read and occasionally yell at people on the phone."

They all laughed. "That sounds like most attorneys I've known," Nora commented. "Becoming an attorney is not easy. You must go to college and then spend three more years in law school."

"She's really smart," Derek commented. "She gets straight As."

"Derek!" Olivia squeezed his hand under the table. "I'm just like everyone else."

Aunt Nora looked at Derek and then at Oliva. "I wouldn't say that." Turning to Olivia, she said, "You speak well and carry yourself like an adult. You and Annie are also good influences on these two young men and probably keep them in line, which is a difficult task. Without your input, I suspect they would become wild hooligans. I'd say you are quite exceptional."

Frank leaned closer to Derek, and, using a stage whisper, asked Derek, "Are we hooligans? It sounds like it could be a cool gig." The girls ignored the boys' silly comments.

Annie said, "I remind Derek every day that he is very lucky to have a girlfriend like Olivia. He certainly isn't going to do any better."

Olivia glared at Annie, hoping to stay out of this exchange. Now that everyone was embarrassed, Frank came to the rescue. "I like to think I'm exceptional for bringing together this great group of people. But I'd be more exceptional if I could have another enchilada." Everyone laughed.

After dinner, Derek and Olivia split up from their friends and walked the short distance to Olivia's home on the Point. Both were thoughtful about the topics broached during dinner. Wanting to be the first to bring it up, Derek asked Olivia what she thought about the marriage talk. "Have you ever thought about being married and what it would be like?"

Olivia had to think about it as she continued walking with Derek, holding his hand. "It is a long stretch to think about marriage when we are still so young."

Derek listened, interested in hearing her point of view.

He could clearly see how smart Olivia was. She was articulate and spoke carefully about one of the most important topics in their lives and still presented her ideas in a way that was neither threatening nor argumentative.

Derek said, "I can see it, with you of course." He grinned at Olivia, pleased with himself for avoiding that pitfall. "But I think that once we're older and able to be self-supporting, then the conversation will be more interesting. Where would we live? When would we start trying to have kids? Can our love continue like it is now, driving us, helping us overcome demanding situations we encounter, making us smile when we are together?"

Olivia was impressed that Derek jumped right into the topics of love and family. She had some thoughts of her own. "I'm not worried that we can earn enough to live apart from our families, once we get through college. But I'd like to know if we would be mature enough to be supportive and kind, so our disagreements don't become fights. It would be a shame to overcome all the obstacles to find a partner, 'The One,' if you will, and then blow it up by being competitive and insensitive to the most important person in our life."

She stopped in the middle of the sidewalk and faced him. Derek took her other hand. "I don't think that would be a big problem," she said. "We are already good friends, and we don't talk like that with one another now. I hope we won't change. What are your thoughts?"

Resonating in Derek's head was Olivia saying "we."

This was a real conversation about real possibilities. Derek was aware of the warmth of Olivia's hand in his. He felt they had elevated their connection tonight. He wasn't planning to get married any time soon, but he was thinking that when the time came for a wedding, he hoped it would be Olivia standing across from him as he recited his vows.

They walked in a comfortable silence the rest of the way home.

*   *   *

The next morning, Frank's grandmother and Aunt Nora were exhausted and slow to rise. They had put away all leftover food and turned in for the night much later than usual. Over the next few days, there would be enough time to put away the dishes and discuss their impressions of the young people.

Nora awoke to the smell of her favorite traditional, percolated coffee. They normally drank whatever was on sale at the local food mart, but meals like these stirred up memories of the food she cooked for her family every day. With laughter and banter supplied by the kids, it had been a delightful evening.

When Nora sat at the table, Grandmother put down the dish towel and joined her. There was so much to say, but there was no hurry. Grandmother refilled her own coffee cup, while filling Nora's.

Frank had always ensured he made time available to meet with his elders, ostensibly to eat their food. It was true the young man ate a lot, but they knew he also came because he enjoyed their company. They noticed how nicely the kids got along at the dinner, telling funny but warm-hearted stories.

Nora sipped her coffee and spoke first. "The young men seem to have done well for themselves." She looked at Grandmother and saw her nodding. "Derek's girl is quite pretty. They make a lovely couple."

After a moment of reflection, Grandmother offered up her

observations. "It was nice seeing Frank with a girlfriend. He is still a funny boy, but now he has a mature and thoughtful side that wasn't here last year." Grandmother stirred some sugar into her coffee and took another sip. Satisfied with the results, she resumed. "Annie will certainly keep him on his toes, and she's very pretty, too. The girls do mature fast, and the boys bring up the rear. It was meant to be like this, so the girls have time to guide their boys to the path of becoming men. All the jokes and games being played are the same as when the boys and girls were children. But now, the boys have stepped on the path to becoming men, caring more about the feelings of their girlfriends than they do about winning an argument."

Nora agreed, adding her observation: "The boys are developing a gentle and caring side. Their focus is no longer just on themselves or their friends; instead, it is on their girlfriends, and now, on their relationships. This is a necessary step toward maturity. If they can keep that perspective, they will have a happy life."

"I expect we will be seeing more of Annie. She was busy writing down your recipes like someone who hopes to cook like us. She seemed extremely ambitious."

"Olivia appears to be a long-term girlfriend as well."

"You're right. Let's hope the boys can keep up."

Nora and Grandmother were quiet after recalling the events of the evening. There was laughter and handholding under the table. They each shared long stories about their experiences, while the others were quiet. Then, when the topics were suitable, the storytellers would switch with the listeners, all carefully orchestrated by the older women who would listen partly to the stories and partly to the conversations among the couples.

After reflection, Nora commented, "These are not just young

crushes. Their sensitivity to one another's feelings was at a level that most adults never reach."

"Derek is quite ambitious with his woodworking business. It is a viable choice, as Santa Cruz doesn't offer many other types of jobs. Most people with legal or financial skills will leave Santa Cruz and move to the Bay Area, where they are well paid. Olivia might do that, but the other kids have deep roots here."

"How did these boys catch the attention of such wonderful girls?" Grandmother sipped her coffee and pondered the ways of young couples.

"It's one of life's great mysteries," said Nora.

Four

At the end of the summer, Derek promised to stay in touch with Olivia, hoping to call her every night, but Annie had another idea and suggested Olivia and Derek correspond the old-fashioned way—in writing. It would keep their interactions private and personal. "If this relationship is meant to last," said Annie, "it will generate an impressive stack of letters to show your children and grandchildren." Annie laughed.

Olivia agreed with Annie. Each week they would check the mail for correspondence. Derek was not happy about this suggestion and was angry with Annie for selling it to Olivia. But Olivia seemed to like the idea, so he eventually supported it; he wanted to keep her happy, so he went out and bought a box of cards and stamps for the coming year.

While Frank and Annie had a calm and cool relationship, as if they had always been together, Derek had a different type of relationship with Olivia. Over the summer, his love grew and strengthened, burning hot and bright as they entered the last week of summer. When he and Olivia headed to their respective homes on Labor Day, there was a sense of inevitability they would remain together as a couple when they returned to Santa Cruz the next year.

For now, Derek tried to avoid thinking about all the pitfalls and traps that could cause this summer romance to derail once they returned to school. Issues such as misstatements or poorly expressed sentiments were a danger for hurt feelings. They both knew that school was full of romances and flirting that could grow into full relationships. Derek and Olivia agreed that a romance at their home school could come along and grow to replace theirs. They agreed that it could happen and there wasn't much they could do except to avoid going out with two different people at the same time. Otherwise, their love would need to be strong, and fun, and remain important for it to survive the school year. They were both confident in their first love, sure that they could weather the coming year apart.

As the summer raced toward Labor Day, their day of departure, Derek was closely tuned into Olivia's moods and fears. When she became quiet and teary, he knew how to bring up good memories of the past summer and point out that their relationship was more than just a fun way to spend the summer.

All four had agreed to meet on Father's Day at the Cove of Castle Beach next summer. Unlike the other couple, Derek and Olivia limited their conversations to correspondence via mail. Olivia reminded Derek that one of the attractions of using the post office to correspond was to see their relationship come alive and grow and document their feelings toward one another.

Olivia knew Derek was not as supportive of this plan as she. She decided to spice it up and see what Derek had to say. "If we ever decide to share these letters with our children or grandchildren, they'll have firsthand documentation of the love we share." It was meant to be funny but thought provoking.

Derek took the reference to future offspring in stride, setting aside that conversation for a later date. Knowing it made Olivia happy, he was willing to go along.

Fall and school came, and the letters began. All the arguments aside, they had fun sending letters to one another and waited eagerly each week for a reply. Olivia and Derek each struggled to express feelings they never felt before. They used cards with drawings of sea birds, waves, and beaches that they signed. They pushed themselves to say what they were afraid to say in person. Olivia concluded her letters by penning, "With Love," and at the end, "Your love, Olivia." They weren't at the point where they could say they loved each other, at least not yet. For now, this was acceptable, along with the promise to see each other next Father's Day at Castle Beach.

Duing the school year, Annie and Olivia's friendship grew. They shared long phone conversations discussing boys in general and their boyfriends in particular. A consistent theme was why guys were so slow to understand girls' feelings. More than once, Annie exclaimed, "They're such knuckleheads!" Girls they knew at school tried to attract the guys they liked. If it were only that simple; instead, girls were ignored by their crushes while they tried to shake off the boys they were not interested in attracting. "It's a complicated dance," reflected Olivia, "and nobody seems to know the steps."

Most of their conversations were about their own guys. Annie reported to Olivia anything she picked up on Derek and his social life. This year, he spent all his time on various sports teams and in the gym working out. Olivia was pleased to hear that he did not have a girlfriend, not that there weren't plenty of girls who were interested in him, reported Annie. He just seemed uninterested, or maybe oblivious, Annie wasn't sure.

Annie suggested that this summer, Olivia buy the best fitting swimsuit she could find to shake Derek out of his seeming disinterest in girls and to capture his attention. "It doesn't have to be a bikini," Annie advised. "Get something that looks like it was spray-painted on." They both laughed until they cried. They each flipped through various swimsuit catalogues until they found a couple that would be sure to catch Derek's—and any other breathing male's—attention.

"Also, get an expensive pair of sunglasses and a haircut styled like one of the magazine fashion models. Guys don't notice much but they do wake up when something new comes along." Annie was pleased with her advice to Olivia. Now it was Olivia's turn to help Annie crank up the heat.

"For you, Annie," Olivia began, "you've already hooked your fish, so to speak. He's helpless. You just need to continue reeling him in." Her advice was like Annie's, shock her boyfriend out of any possible interest he might have in anyone else by showing up this summer with a hot new swimsuit. Over the past year, Annie's figure filled out while she remained slim. Olivia recommended she buy the bikini that would emphasize her new figure and get it one or two sizes smaller than designed. "Just don't get it so small that the straps snap on your first day in the ocean. If the suit doesn't get Frank's attention, you can go for plan B and let your top slip away under water and splash around, claiming it was torn off by rough waves. I'm sure Frank would enthusiastically offer to help you find it," she teased.

"He probably wouldn't let anyone else in the water until he found it." Annie laughed and blushed in embarrassment.

Derek stuck his head in Annie's room. "What's going on in here? Something you can share?" When she shook her head, Derek said, "Tell Olivia, 'Hi,' for me. Ask her to call if she has time." It was a standard routine since he knew Olivia would call when she was back in Santa Cruz. Until then, he was living for the occasional short call with Olivia and her frequent letters.

Derek and Frank talked weekly on the phone. Conversations bounced around from everything related to surfing to dreams about getting an old car running that Frank bought and planned to restore. Unfortunately, the car was mostly in pieces and sorted in boxes, and neither Frank nor Derek knew anything about putting it back together.

Both guys eagerly awaited the start of summer and hoped their relationships with the girls would pick up where they had left off. Only time would tell.

Frank and Annie's relationship fared well during the long school year spent apart. This long-distance relationship was made easier by frequent calls after they parted on Labor Day weekend. Annie enjoyed her calls with Frank all year, but she encouraged Derek to write his love notes by hand. Olivia was the architect of the plan and had a stack of letters and cards from Derek, each of which she read and re read until the next one came. Olivia reciprocated with postcards and letters.

Annie felt that this form of communication taught both Derek and Olivia to express their feelings. There were also the calls Annie made to Olivia that she occasionally shared with Derek, allowing them to share a short conversation and maintain contact. Derek stopped complaining about the limits placed on his use of the phone. He enjoyed writing and receiving a card each week.

Occasionally Annie walked away from the phone, leaving Derek and Olivia for a private conversation like they had during the summer. Derek loved hearing the tone of Olivia's voice and the slight hesitancy she would have when discussing memories from the prior summer.

Derek and Olivia would get right up to the edge of saying, "I love you," but then they would back away, each too timid to be the first. Annie would show up and the moment would be lost, filed away for the next phone conversation. For now, Derek would just wait until next summer to reset the rules.

Derek found exchanging letters was enjoyable. He spent considerable time drafting his responses. He wrote how much he cared for her but, more often than he wanted to admit, had written intimate notes only to crumple them up after writing "I love you" at the end. He still lacked the courage to send those letters to her.

When Olivia's correspondence came, he would first skim through it, hoping to find that she had shared her declaration of love first. Not finding it, he would go back to the beginning and read it slowly, repeatedly, realizing that she also found it challenging to write what was in her heart. Derek knew she was fond of him. She wrote several times that she "liked him a lot." But like his letters, hers always seemed to fall short compared with what he wanted to hear and matched the struggle that he went through when he wrote letters to her.

He was happy that they kept up the correspondence at a pace of one letter a week and otherwise kept it light. They read each letter repeatedly while they eagerly awaited the next one.

Derek and Olivia exchanged many letters over the school year, but Derek only had a few good pictures of her. His favorite was of Olivia at the beach with the cliffs behind her and a hint of the ocean along the edge of the photo. It was taken at the end of last summer when her tan was deep and her swimsuit was getting thin, leaving much less to the imagination than originally designed. She refused to give him another picture, only saying that all her pictures were terrible. The photos he had were enough to help him remember her.

Derek wondered if she had changed in appearance. For that matter, he asked himself if he had changed as well. This year, he played water polo and was on the swim team—both of which had rigorous workout regimens, so he was in great shape, but physical change was slow and hard to recognize even though he was getting stronger over time.

Derek liked spending time with Olivia and wanted to enjoy the coming summer with her as he had last year. He appreciated that she was pretty but also thought she was funny and kind. They laughed whenever they got together. She was the first girl he had ever been this comfortable around. She made him feel special.

Five

The school year finally ended, and summer arrived on a bed of fog. Annie and Derek moved from Livermore with their family into their Santa Cruz summer home. They arrived immediately after the school year ended and eagerly awaited Olivia's arrival on Father's Day weekend.

The day before Father's Day, Olivia talked her mom into taking her to downtown Santa Cruz so she and Annie could shop for new swimsuits together. It was only through Annie's great charm and tact that she was able to convince Olivia's mom to let the girls shop alone. In return, they agreed to show her their choices later that evening. It took multiple stores and hours for the girls to try on swimsuits, model them, and finalize their selections. They held hilarious dressing room fashion shows for each other before settling on their actual choices.

Derek and Frank were not invited on the shopping trip so the guys would experience the full impact of the girls' purchases when they wore them on Father's Day. Along with the swimsuits, the girls planned to flaunt their new sweat suits, sunglasses, sandals, sun hats, and tote bags, all courtesy of Olivia's new American Express card which successfully covered their purchases. "You can pay me back in food," Olivia said, still trying to think of anything they missed.

Annie was nearly in shock. They stood at the checkout counter of yet another exclusive beachwear shop, running their hands over the fine fabrics of their new clothes before their purchases were carefully tissued, folded, and placed into multiple shopping bags. Annie never made that many purchases in one day.

Olivia asked for another minute while she disappeared into the back of the shop. She returned with four light cover-ups of different styles and colors. Olivia casually placed them on the counter. "Take the two you like, and I'll take the other two," she said to Annie. Olivia was checking these new additions against the suits they had already selected. Annie would be happy with any of them. She was careful not to look at the price tags, fearing she might faint.

"Are you sure your dad is okay with this?" asked a shocked Annie.

"Of course. I'm careful not to surprise him with this many purchases, but he knows to expect this at the beginning of each summer, and maybe one or two smaller purchases in July." She separated the four cover-ups, two for Annie and two for Olivia, and stepped back. "I always tell my dad that he doesn't want me to wear the same suit so often that it wears out and I have a 'wardrobe malfunction.' When he learned what that was, he stopped complaining about buying extra outfits."

On the way out, they stopped by the Sunglasses Hut kiosk where each girl bought what Olivia described as "real sunglasses." Annie assumed that meant they were much more expensive than those at the clothing store, plus Olivia thought they looked very chic. It was entirely Olivia's show, with Annie along for the ride.

"These sunglasses are to die for," declared Olivia.

The first week Derek's family was back in Santa Cruz, he worked hard with his father to get ahead of his annual home improvement responsibilities, earning him more time with Olivia when she returned.

The fog dissipated before noon, so Derek dressed for warm weather. Sometimes heavy fog did not burn off until late afternoon. Today it was warm, like an August afternoon with only a wisp of moisture in the air.

Last fall, the four friends set Father's Day as their new summer kickoff. Derek awaited summer's official start when Olivia's family settled back into their home on the Point. Derek could barely contain his excitement at seeing Olivia again while Annie threatened to pound him if he mentioned her name one more time.

Father's Day arrived and Annie was already at the beach. Annie and Olivia agreed to start the day on their own before the guys joined them later that day. At noon, Derek walked down to the beach, and from a distance, saw people with folding chairs and blankets. He knew Annie would be in the exact location in the cove, which they agreed was their spot. As he approached, he saw Frank and Annie lying on their blankets. Nearby, Olivia was standing on a blanket next to them still bundled up in a sweatshirt and sweatpants. As she turned and looked at him her eyes widened in surprise.

The first thing Derek noted was that she was still beautiful. And yet, there were subtle changes in her face—a sharper jawline and shaped eyebrows were features of her new look as a young woman. Derek arrived when Oliva was changing out of her sweats revealing her new swimsuit. Olivia smiled at Derek and pulled her sweatshirt over her head. Then, completing the motion, she removed her sweatpants and folded them carefully before placing them on her towel.

While her sweatsuit fit her well, giving a hint of her figure, the swimsuit was a whole different story. It was pastel yellow with small, blue polka dots on a one-piece suit. It fit her perfectly and covered all the key curves without overly straining. It didn't look too small, but it certainly hugged her figure beneath. He was speechless; this suit was dangerous.

Derek was struggling not to look too hard but was failing miserably. Frank was only too willing to increase his embarrassment by teasing, "Hey, Derek, what do you think of Olivia's new swimsuit? Do you think it's a good color?" He waved toward Olivia but continued speaking to Derek. "Over here, Derek. If you keep staring that hard, you will burn off all the polka dots."

There was general laughter from the girls, so Olivia decided to take charge and hug Derek as her greeting. Derek was still speechless as he looked at her, taking in the changes over the past year. She had always had a pretty face, but now she had a new haircut that made her dark hair frame her face. Either she used a light touch with makeup, which enhanced her natural beauty, or she was wearing no makeup. In any event, she was perfect. Her designer sunglasses made her look like a celebrity, and her skin already had a rich tone, her bright-yellow outfit emphasized her tan.

Olivia's suit was a one-piece with a low, scooped neckline and cut higher on the hips, in the latest fashion. It was not excessively revealing; nevertheless, her beauty caused him to fall in love with her just a little more. He had expected her to buy a one-piece because bikinis were impractical in the waves. Every girl wearing a bikini into the surf knew the risk that her top or bottom might be torn off by the pounding wash of a big wave.

Derek noticed that the day was warm for June, with only a high overcast layer of clouds, perfect for an inaugural dunk into the waves. He could tell Olivia had taken some time to look her best for him, and she had succeeded beyond all measure.

Derek still had the dilemma of determining how to return the greeting, but he was afraid to be presumptuous and kiss her, so he took her hands and looked her in the eye. "It's great to see you, Olivia. How was your drive over?"

Olivia looked at him with an impish grin on her face. "No kiss today? Will I need to wait half of the summer again before you finally kiss me?"

Derek was frozen, then tried looking around for help. This wasn't how he wanted to start the summer with Olivia thinking he was a kid without dating experience or not knowing how to treat his girlfriend.

Derek didn't know what to say, but her laugh was kind when she pulled him closer and kissed him on the lips while standing in their space on Castle Beach. He knew how he felt about her. Her kiss removed all doubt that she still cared for him. They both made it to Castle Beach on Father's Day. It just might take a minute or so for him to unfreeze, Olivia assumed, and gave a soft chuckle.

Derek and Olivia took a private walk down the length of the beach, first to the jetty in front of the harbor, and then back to the Point, down by the Boardwalk.

They compared their experiences at school over the past year, sharing highlights and some embarrassments. Olivia learned that she wasn't physically coordinated enough to join a sports team. At least, that's what the girls on those teams told her. In his music class, Derek could not understand how to make the proper sound from the recorder, a hard, plastic, flute-like instrument that was handed out by their music instructor. Derek didn't care, as the instruments sounded like frightened geese, even when played correctly.

Olivia told Derek about several books she had to read over the summer and the equal number of book reports due in fall. Derek did not recall receiving any school assignments over the summer. He needed to confirm with Annie whether he missed the assignments or if he was just lucky and did not have any due in fall. He probably wasn't paying attention when the spring semester came to a close and teachers struggled to maintain focus in the classroom.

Olivia mentioned she bought a guitar and was learning some popular songs. She complained that she was so bad that nobody would ever listen to her sing. Derek said he would listen and promised to encourage her, no matter how she sounded. Derek told her he was taking karate classes and was considering getting a surfboard.

Conversation came easily, and it was a pleasant walk along the beach. The water was calm and fishing boats began appearing on the horizon, returning from their morning run. The cliffs along the coast and the dozens of small houses facing the water appeared to have made it through the winter without suffering any significant winter storm damage.

When Derek and Olivia returned to lay on their towels, Annie and Frank were just returning from a dunk in the waves. It seemed like such a short while ago they all said goodbye at the end of last summer. Now they were back, and the two couples picked up where they had left off. Olivia and Annie quickly returned to their roles as best friends, sharing secrets quietly and throwing furtive glances at their guys.

Derek often drove his father's truck to the hardware store for supplies and occasionally stopped for ice cream. When he had time, he spent it preparing meals with Annie and Olivia or babysitting the Little Ones, who were on their best behavior for their pretty helper.

While last summer culminated in a first-kiss crush, this year felt different. Derek and Olivia still held hands and kissed, but this year, they were together every day for every possible moment. In the evenings when they returned to their homes and retired to their rooms, they still called to talk late into the night.

Derek and Olivia agreed that when summer ended, they would return to their lives at their schools with their old friends and old activities. During the school year, they would each attend school dances in groups, but neither wanted other romances or secret relationships. They were each only interested in the love they shared over the summer with one another.

This was more than last year's first romance. It wasn't just the thrill of having someone who cared and enjoyed kissing them. The closer they got to one another, sharing the good and the bad, the more they felt a sense of wholeness, like they were meant to be together.

●　　●　　●

Preparation for the big Bicentennial Fourth of July celebration started a week ahead of time. It built on the success of the prior year's celebration, but everyone knew this would be even better. Annie took control of making the pies and cakes, while Frank's family contributed Mexican food, both popular and traditional dishes. Olivia's mom, Ellen, was only responsible for setting up the deck as a serving area, although she could not help but prepare several large racks of pork ribs using her favorite family recipe BBQ sauce. The Little Ones were responsible for cooking pack after pack of hot dogs and hamburgers for the younger crowd. The event was planned and executed with military precision and professional catering expertise since Frank's family operated a catering company.

When the food was finished, the dishes and serving trays cleaned and stacked in the catering trucks, there was just enough time to get back to the roof to view the fireworks. This year promised to be the greatest fireworks display in the history of Santa Cruz—to commemorate the United States's Bicentennial—two hundred years since the Declaration of Independence was signed. This was to be a once-in-a-lifetime fireworks display.

Over 50 people attended the party. The fireworks began and it felt like each explosion was going to land on the roof, when in fact they were executed safely offshore from a barge towed into the bay. Olivia, Derek, Annie, and Frank all stood together at the railing enjoying the show. Standing in the corner of the railing was Olivia's mother, smiling as she presided over a remarkably successful rooftop party.

Before the end of summer was near, Frank came up with the idea of setting up Christmas lights in Derek's backyard to better enjoy the summer evenings. Each Saturday night, they moved the furniture around to make a dance floor and opened the gate at the end of the driveway to let in all their friends. People brought food and dessert, and dressed in Hawaiian shirts or t-shirts with obscure logos. They danced to music by the Beach Boys and retro surf bands which gave off the summer romance vibe. The music lasted the full evening until midnight.

Frank brought his DJ equipment in the back of a truck and his surf buddies helped with the security, maintaining a no-alcohol policy and sending home anyone who had already been drinking. Annie and Olivia patiently taught Derek to dance, even if people were watching. Frank and the girls enjoyed seeing their best friend start to cut loose.

There were no complaints from neighbors as long as the music ended promptly at midnight and their guests left no mess in the street. When the lights flickered at the approach of midnight, everyone joined together in a ten-second countdown while they scrambled to find their sweethearts or potential sweethearts. This was a friendly group, and summer romances were popping up all around. At midnight, all the couples kissed and then either went home or somewhere more secluded. As the summer progressed, the number of couples kissing at midnight grew. In the center stage were the two couples that were examples that summer romances can build and strengthen on nothing more than hope and love.

With their second summer winding down, each couple had to face another inevitable goodbye. For Derek and Olivia, the end of summer led to a familiar but difficult period of long-distance romance and uncertainty over the likelihood that their relationship would last another year apart. Olivia expressed to Derek her belief that this year's goodbye was harder than last year's because they now had more invested in their relationship.

Frank had no fears at all, or at least, didn't share any. "We're meant to be together," he told Annie. "If we don't make it," he paused for effect the way Frank often did, "we had a great time trying."

Annie told Frank she didn't doubt him for a minute. They were a steady couple. "Our relationship is built on our personalities that are a perfect match. We have fun and enjoy being together as much as possible," she said. They would face another year apart, but with Frank's faith in their relationship, Annie was not afraid at all.

Annie tried to explain to Olivia that there was nothing to fear, but Derek and Olivia's relationship was different. It was constantly at the forefront of their minds and burned hotter than anything either of them ever experienced. They enjoyed being together to look after each other, whether at the beach, at dance parties, or during the day.

Derek knew it was almost impossible for him to keep his mind from wandering into the real world, where high school kids had summer romances and then broke up, and relationships didn't last a lifetime. When he explained his fears to Olivia and that there were only two more summers before they left for college, she calmly told him to let go of the future. "The future will take care of itself." She told Derek later that sometimes she was afraid too. "School years are long. Even unintended romances have a way of happening, causing break ups for even the best of long-distance relationships."

As they talked, Derek suggested that the best way to make it through the school year was to let go a little bit and allow each of them to attend dances or social functions with their group of friends and keep friendships light.

"That doesn't sound appealing," said Olivia. "All the guys at my school are immature. I'd never go out with them. But you probably have a great school with plenty of girls to date."

"I don't want to go out with anyone else," Derek assured her.

After they thought about it for a while, Olivia addressed the situation they both were avoiding. "I'd be very happy staying together with you throughout next year, but if either of us wants to go out with someone else, we've got to be honest and break up. We can't go out with two people at once. We can go out on group dates or attend school dances, but it wouldn't be with a girlfriend or boyfriend. We'll enjoy our school year. If we are still interested in each other, then we'll meet again at Castle Beach next summer." Olivia tried to keep the conversation light, but tears swam in her eyes.

● ● ●

Summer winded down, ending like a race car coasting into the pit on an empty tank of gas. Each passing day reminded them that these were their last few days in Santa Cruz. Derek and Olivia felt a tinge of melancholy mixed in with the contentment of being next to the one they loved.

One week before they each left for school, Derek took Olivia to the park bench at the end of his street, facing the ocean. They sat looking northwest into a darkening sky, watching the sunset starting its magic. Finally, Derek took Olivia's hand and turned to face her directly. "I don't want to talk about tomorrow, the end of summer, or school. I want to talk about right here, right now." Olivia listened, unsure where this speech was going but content enough to wait.

"Right now, I am happier than I ever thought possible. I am with you, and just being with you is enough. It was the best summer of my life, and it still is. I've tried to understand why, but all I can say is that I've fallen in love with you." Derek kept eye contact. "I love you, Olivia."

She was jolted to hear it aloud after only talking about it while sharing secrets with Annie. But after some reflection, she wasn't surprised he felt that way because she felt that way too. Olivia put her arms around Derek's neck. "I love you too, Derek. I'm so happy to know you feel the same way!" She hugged him tightly and rested her head on his shoulder. She pulled back to see his eyes shining on the brink of tears. Her tears flowed freely down her cheeks. They kissed, touched their foreheads together, laughed, and moved closer together, enjoying the moment as much as possible.

Summer was ending, and despite their promises, there was no certainty they would return next year. All they had was now, and for one evening, it was enough.

When summer ended, Olivia returned to her house in Portola Valley and cried for a week. Derek returned to Livermore with his family, but when he got there, he wouldn't leave his room. He missed the final days of summer before school began because he didn't want anyone to see his tears, which kept silently springing up without his permission.

It wasn't lost on Derek that Annie and Frank talked on the phone during the entire school year. Every evening since summer ended, Annie would spend time in the phone nook under the stairs talking with Frank. Derek became used to the muffled sound of her calls. She talked quietly and then ran to her room for hushed phone conversations on the personal line Derek reluctantly set up for her. After completing his homework, Derek read or played with his younger siblings.

Derek tried arguing with Annie, but Olivia agreed with her best friend, and wouldn't respond to any requests for phone calls from Derek. So, the school year went by at an agonizingly slow pace. He spent more time with his family than in the past. He admitted that at least he was getting good grades. He focused on his schoolwork and had no one to talk to since his parents limited his social life so he would avoid friends who were 'bad influences on him,' as his dad liked to say. His friend group broke apart, with two friends moving out of the area and two others getting in serious trouble with the law.

Derek was fortunate he was not with his friends the night they decided to steal a couple of cases of beer from behind the local liquor store. They were quickly caught. When Derek's father learned about his friends' arrest, he banned Derek's use of the phone and grounded him for the little remaining school year so he would avoid their influence. Without contact, his ties with his old friend group were effectively severed, keeping Derek from getting caught up in their misdeeds.

Derek wasn't surprised at his dad's reaction, and luckily, Derek was able to avoid being associated with their legal troubles. Still, it was lonely without friends to hang out with and knowing his girlfriend was unwilling to talk with him.

Six

Derek noted that this would be the group's third Father's Day. This year it came, like any other June day in Santa Cruz, with cold, damp fog that never ceased to surprise him. Derek wore his best sweats over a new swimsuit and joined Frank carrying a picnic basket to the beach. Frank came to see Annie every day since her family arrived in Santa Cruz after the school year. Today, the two took over the kitchen for a few hours, cooking, baking, and concocting a special lunch for their friends. They were excited to be back together in Santa Cruz; even the freezing weather couldn't dampen their enthusiasm.

The Cove at Castle Beach came into view as Derek, Frank, and Annie descended to the beach on the last stretch of sidewalk. It was sparsely populated, except for one person who stood alone in the section of the beach they had claimed for themselves, next to two towels and chairs.

The minute Olivia saw them she leapt off the sidewalk and took off, running toward them at full speed. When she reached Derek, she threw herself into his arms. He spun her around twice and then put her back on the ground, kissing and whispering in her ear. "I missed you, Olivia. Let's stop living in remote places and move here." They laughed at their private joke and Olivia reached out to Frank and Annie, whom she hugged individually.

They were all talking at once. Frank talked about how much surfing he had done, and Derek included himself in the surfing conversations even though he hadn't yet learned how to surf. Annie just listened in for a while, then leaned over to Olivia. "We have all summer to talk privately. Let's let these fools ramble on for a while. They're so cute." Frank pretended not to hear. He was just so glad that everyone enjoyed being together again.

Derek and Frank picked up the basket and carried it to the park. Olivia and Annie returned to the beach and gathered Olivia's towel and gear. Everyone helped set the table to prepare their meal at the park. The picnic table was quickly set with a wide assortment of casseroles and salads, cold fried chicken, barbecue ribs, and a mountain of fresh brownies, still warm from the oven. The boys ate silently, offering servings to the girls periodically, and serving themselves when food on their plates was low. The boys remembered their manners from last year and asked for help when they thought it prudent. Annie pushed good manners on the boys all last year, and they were on their best behavior.

Eventually, when everyone had eaten their fill and told their most pressing stories, Frank suggested they walk along the shore to help their food digest and to continue talking. They carried the lunch basket up the sidewalk and over to Annie's car. Once it was packed up, Derek drove to his house and unloaded the food into the kitchen. After getting caught up with Mr. and Mrs. Moore and answering the onslaught of questions they had for Olivia, they returned to the beach.

Later that week, when Derek and Olivia sat in the shade at Whale Park, Oliva explained that she needed to talk with Derek. "My brother is in town." She was wringing her hands and could barely look Derek in the eyes.

Unclear about the importance of this information, Derek asked, "Am I going to meet him?"

"If we are careful, you won't. He's unstable and has a history of violence. He didn't like hearing that I had a boyfriend. He said he was going to pound you. I take him very seriously based on what he has done to others. If you see him, you need to run."

"I don't know what he looks like, and I don't usually run." Derek was becoming nervous. "Can't your parents talk with him? This town doesn't allow violent people to roam and pick fights for no reason."

"I'll bring you a picture of him. We can still walk together, but maybe we should ride our bikes to allow for a fast getaway."

She explained that Ricky always had two big friends by his side, so they could fight with anyone they chose. People at home gave him a wide berth. The ones who fell prey to his crew knew better than to press charges with the police or report it to their parents.

Ricky's problems went a long way back but increased once he got his license. His driving history was littered with speeding tickets, wrecked cars, and legal issues. Their father had attorneys dedicated to solving Ricky's problems, from defending against the legal charges to settling the civil ones. He was hurting people, but for some reason, their father wouldn't acknowledge that Ricky needed to be stopped before someone might be killed.

Derek told her he would be careful, but he couldn't make any promises.

The rest of the summer swept along smoothly, each week warmer than the previous one. Derek and Olivia rode their bikes all over town, getting to know the shopkeepers and eating at local diners. As they headed south along the coastal roads, the names of the towns shifted from one to another, each town with a distinct personality. Derek was never much of a shopper, but he did like to browse with Olivia. She didn't need anything, but occasionally, he would buy her a pair of earrings or a bracelet. Their bikes were ideally suited for cruising along the small roads and sidewalks.

● ● ●

Finally, fate seemed to catch up with Derek and Olivia.

It was late summer, and Derek had thus far avoided a confrontation with Ricky. He and Olivia continued enjoying walking on the beach and taking long bicycle rides. One afternoon, they were getting back from the beach when Olivia stiffened. She tried to turn them around unnoticed, but Ricky's raspy voice called out to them both. "Are you the guy trying to screw my sister?" he asked Derek. They were passing by the park, but there was no way to run from Ricky and the two large guys with him.

"I don't know you, and I'm not trying to screw anyone," Derek replied.

"Leave him alone, Ricky. If you hit him, your parole officer will find out, and you'll go back to jail," Olivia pleaded.

"You stay out of this," Ricky said to her. "I'm just protecting my sister from a crazy man."

Ricky walked over to Derek, and without further conversation, Ricky hit him fast and hard in the face, breaking Derek's nose. He delivered two quick shots to the ribs before Derek could escape, pulling himself around a picnic table. Ricky stopped and pointed at him. "Don't let me see you again. Wherever you hang out, it better not be near this beach." Ricky and his friends walked off, laughing at Derek.

Derek flopped down on the bench and let his head hang. He was sure he had a concussion, and his ribs hurt with every breath. The pain was terrible. He didn't know what to do. He could barely think.

"Derek, can you hear me?" It was Olivia. She ran around and into his line of vision. "Oh my God! I've got to get help! Stay here, I'll go get someone."

"I need to go to a doctor. I'm really hurt." By this time, Derek was hunched over, holding his ribs, with blood pouring from his nose. "I don't want to get you in trouble with your brother. Can you get Annie and have her bring the car? I need to go to the emergency room. Or maybe I need to go home. I can't afford a trip to the emergency room."

Olivia ran to Derek's house and saw Annie out in front. Olivia yelled that Derek was hurt and Annie immediately brought her car around. They carefully loaded Derek into the back seat and quickly took him to the emergency room, as instructed by Olivia when she jumped into the passenger seat.

At the hospital, the doctors reset Derek's nose and packed it with cotton. Olivia took care of the paperwork. The doctors took x-rays of Derek's ribs and found he had two cracked ribs on each side. They asked if he wanted the police to get involved, but Derek refused.

The nurse wrapped a bandage around his chest and gave him a couple of pills and a prescription for mild pain killers. Olivia paid the substantial bill with her credit card and directed the paperwork to be sent to her father.

It took Derek the rest of the summer to fully recover. During his recovery, he didn't spend any time near the beach and only focused his time working on the family's house and training at the karate dojo, working with his karate instructor, Shihan, about his predicament. His karate school was not a fight club but taught a philosophy to respect others and to fight only when necessary. In this case, Shihan recognized Derek needed specific skills tailored to defending himself from these thugs. When Derek healed enough to work out, he began training, preparing to protect himself against multiple assailants, with or without weapons.

The month of August was hard on Derek and Olivia. They knew Ricky was the problem and that neither Derek nor Olivia was to blame for the fight. But knowing something and believing it is sometimes difficult. Derek was furious that Ricky's parents let him come to Santa Cruz. He was dangerous and openly expressed his hatred toward Derek. Derek simply wasn't safe. Olivia quietly blamed Derek a little bit, or maybe more than a little bit, for being unable to protect himself from Ricky. It was not fair that Olivia was angry at Derek, nor was it fair that Derek blamed Olivia for her brother's behavior. Both Derek and Olivia had feelings of resentment toward each other simmering below the surface.

In addition to her concerns, Olivia had to deal with her father, who was angry that he got stuck with Derek's medical bill, overlooking the fact that Derek did not press charges. Olivia told her father that Ricky started the fight and if Derek had pressed charges, Ricky would be in jail, but her father was not listening.

Olivia and Derek continued to see each other through the end of summer, but they both felt things were damaged between them, so they didn't discuss the next year. By the end of the summer, they didn't have anything to say and sat inside his garage in awkward silence, avoiding another confrontation with or about her brother. The summer was slowly running out, and by the end, Derek was partially relieved they both would be returning home soon.

• • •

The next week, Frank's grandmother and Aunt Nora arranged another dinner at their house for both young couples before the summer ran out. Once again, the food was tremendous, and they all enjoyed the visit.

As usual, the guys over ate and talked well into the evening. Eventually, Annie suggested it was time to go. After many hugs and promises to return, they gathered their items and walked down to Annie's car. Just before they got in the car, Aunt Nora pulled Derek and Olivia aside. Holding their hands, she said, "Something's wrong with you two. I remember how things were last summer; it isn't like that now. Please visit next Wednesday for lunch. We'd love to chat." Derek looked to Olivia, and they both nodded. "We'll be there," they agreed.

On Wednesday, Derek and Olivia rode their bikes to Seabright Avenue, where the two older women lived. As they parked their bikes in the side yard, Aunt Nora met them. "It's just me today," said Aunt Nora. "You get to hear about my story. Grandmother has already heard it a million times. She was there for most of the major events in my life." She laughed.

The food was already made, so the kids helped set the table in Aunt Nora's open courtyard. The fog never reached her house, situated a mile from the beach, making the air comfortable and warm. Olivia commented that it was enjoyable here on the patio, under the big tree.

"I eat out here most of the time, especially when Grandmother is out. She gets cold quickly."

They enjoyed quiet, easy conversation through lunch. When

they were done, Derek cleared the table, Olivia set out a tea service, and Nora brought out the pastries. Finally, she was ready for her lesson. She waved toward the living room.

"Just because you see pictures of me with my husband and we are smiling, doesn't mean we were always happy. See here." She gestured toward a photo. "He's not looking at the camera. We had a terrible fight that day. We weren't even married then; it was my sister's wedding, and he was interested in another bridesmaid. Nothing happened, of course. If it had happened, his picture wouldn't be on my mantle." She smiled as much for this memory as for the kids' sake.

"There's more to being a couple than we admit. A quiet dialogue is constantly running between the two of you. Most of the time, it is silent. No words. But still, it is a simple set of dialogues and hopefully some communication. Like, 'Who is he looking at now? Does he know her? Why didn't he hold the door for me?' or 'Was she still angry? What did I do? Did she like the little gift I bought for her? Why does her mom seem like she is angry with me?'

"These conversations need to be listened to, brought to the surface, and expressed. If you put words to them and talk them through, you have a chance to be happy together. If not, these personal stories will weigh you down until you aren't excited to see each other." She paused to allow these ideas to sink in. Aunt Nora could almost see the tension in the room begin to fade, Olivia's shoulders relaxing, and eventually, Derek taking Olivia's hand.

"I see sadness and a sense of loss with you two. I know what you had when you came by last year. And don't think it wasn't real because you are young or only together for part of the year. You are young, it's true, but in many ways, your relationship is the same as one found between adults. It is important to peel away the layers of doubt, anger, and resentment so you can get back to the light, carefree relationship you should have at your age. That relationship is still with you, otherwise you wouldn't have come today to hear an old fool woman offer you hope." That elicited a smile from Derek and Olivia.

"There are many concerns competing for your attention. For example, we could dwell on whatever issues you are facing, such as: will we make it as a couple? Does his family like me? Is it ok if I don't join him as a surfer? He doesn't think I see it, but when we watch the waves, he spends too much time watching the surfer girls."

It was amazing how well she could read the issues weighing down Derek and Olivia. In many ways they were common problems among any new couple. "I'm just guessing here with these issues." Aunt Nora added, "only you two know the real issues which are causing you so much heartache."

They both squirmed under her gaze. "Hold both hands," Nora commanded. "Look into one another's eyes. You've allowed these thoughts to take over your hearts. When you were here last year, your hearts were full of love, and your minds were calm. You were so happy just being together that you didn't allow the unfounded thoughts we all have running through our minds to weigh you down. At that time, being together was enough."

"So, how do you clear your minds?" Aunt Nora asked rhetorically. "That's easy," she replied quickly. "You talk to each other. That's why long walks on the beach are so popular. Nothing is competing for your attention. Talk about trivial things first. Solve them. Put them to rest. Kiss when each issue gets unraveled and replaced by love. Then, when you are ready, it will be time to tackle the big problem causing you so much pain."

She looked at them both and waited. Finally, she asked, "Which of you will bring it up? Don't worry. We aren't going to resolve it now." She waited.

Finally, Olivia spoke up first. "I have an older brother. He has issues."

"You could say that again," Derek interjected.

Aunt Nora looked at him and shook her head slightly.

"Yes, he has problems," replied Olivia. "He took them out on Derek earlier this summer and hurt him badly. Derek didn't press charges, which he should have, but my father still thinks it was Derek's fault. So, this year, we haven't been able to have much of a summer. We spent most of it indoors. I'm tired of hiding. I want a beach vacation where I can go with my boyfriend into the water and not be afraid."

"And you think that is Derek's fault?"

"No! It's not his fault. He didn't pick the fight."

"Did you ask your parents to make Ricky stay away from Derek and live at your other home?"

"It's not that easy."

Nora looked over at Derek and waited. Finally, she asked. "I understand why you don't want to go to the beach. Do you think it is Olivia's fault?"

Derek paused and then pulled his hands away. "Her parents should have locked him up. He doesn't belong here. I can't live like this, waiting for him to appear around every corner. I don't like hiding."

"Well, there's the problem. Or maybe there are several problems," Nora said. "You two have some work to do. But I'm telling you your love is still real and important. You can solve your issues; I'm sure there are more than we discussed. When you settle a problem, stop and celebrate. Share kisses and quiet time. But behave!" They all laughed, and some of the tension left them.

"Olivia, ask your parents to take your brother home for the rest of the year. Give Derek a break. And you, Derek, use that time to learn how to protect yourself. I know the Shihan you study with. He is an excellent instructor and a deadly fighter. I lived in Santa Cruz when he first arrived. He fought every karate master in Monterey Bay and beat them all. You can be the best as well. Work harder, work longer. Become strong and confident. You don't need to fight but you need to be confident you can defend yourself. Make your opponent wonder whether he can beat you." She leaned forward, expressing the gravity of what she would be saying. "Regardless of which course he chooses; ensure you can win decisively. He needs to know that—if there's a fight—when it's over, he can't afford to fight you again."

●   ●   ●

On Olivia's last day in Santa Cruz, she called Annie and asked where she could find Derek. Annie sent her to Castle Beach. "That's a good sign," Annie suggested. "When he's down at the Cove, he's usually thinking of you."

Olivia walked down to the cove and found Derek sitting on his towel in the same spot they claimed as their own—ever since they threw towels there every day for the past three summers—or at least before Ricky came to Santa Cruz. Today was one of the few times she saw him at the beach since the fight. Olivia asked if she could join him. Derek nodded and assumed there was nothing more to say. Out of habit, he pulled a second towel out of his backpack and invited her to sit beside him. Olivia joined him, smoothed the towel out, and tucked her legs under her.

She had a few things she wanted to say that could directly impact their future together. She spent long hours with Annie over the past few days trying to get this right. It was important.

"We didn't have a good summer for a number of reasons," Olivia started. "I guess that was to be expected once Ricky attacked you. You spent more time with your surfing crowd than with me. I can never compete with surfers. I don't surf, and half of the girls in that group are trying to keep you for themselves." She was talking as much to herself as she was to Derek.

Olivia was winding down. "This school year, I expect to be alone—well, no boyfriend. I hope you are alone too. What we have is good enough that it should survive a little competition. For me, I'm going to say no to the boys. For you, keep up the surfing, avoid drinking, and say no to the surf skanks." They smiled at her reference to the girls who hung out with the surfers. Derek had referred to them as surfer girls. Olivia did not see them quite that way. Her label stuck.

Olivia sat up on her knees and pulled Derek up, so they were eye to eye. She pulled him into a tight embrace. "I want you to know that I still love you, Derek. I hope to see you right here next Father's Day. I hope next summer is better."

"I love you, Olivia," Derek responded. "I wish we hadn't wasted this summer. I'd like to try it again next year too."

"It's almost Labor Day," she said. "I think next year is already here." Olivia leaned in as Derek gave her a long, soft kiss. She pulled him in closer with her arms around his neck and met his kiss with her own. Now, they had something to look forward to.

Seven

All summer long, Derek had campaigned to his parents, trying to get them to allow him to live in Santa Cruz for his senior year and graduate from Santa Cruz High School. Frank encouraged him too and began introducing Derek to his friends. Socially, he would have a head start with Frank's friends.

Derek's group in Livermore had fallen apart the previous year when his dad grounded him. They weren't good students, and they increasingly got into trouble; not to the degree that Ricky did, but still, Derek thought he might end up on the wrong path if he stayed in Livermore. It was time to try something new.

Derek had a few activities he wanted to continue. First, he needed to follow through with his karate training. If he wanted to protect himself and walk unafraid on the streets, he needed some defensive training.

He also wanted to continue to surf. This past winter, Derek spent time at Steamers Lane and at a few smaller breaks where he watched and learned about surfing. There seemed to be the same group of kids every day. Derek did not expect to surf every day, but there was a big crowd that met before school, many of whom became friends.

Derek had bought a surfboard and wet suit. After that, he only needed transportation to haul his board and gear to the beach. His old car had given up the ghost a few months earlier and he needed a replacement. Eventually, Derek settled for a small pickup truck with over two hundred thousand miles on it, and more rust than he cared to think about.

Finally—and this sounded unbelievable to him—he enjoyed spending time with Frank's grandmother and Aunt Nora. They both gave Olivia and him great advice throughout the summer. Their advice probably saved his relationship. He liked their food and wisdom, but he especially enjoyed how they would ask a question and sincerely listen to his answer. He could take his time explaining himself, and nobody rushed him to finish or talked over him. Growing up in a family of five kids, there was never time to talk one-on-one with his parents, and when he did find the time, it didn't last long. His parents were great, and he enjoyed talking with them, but the mayhem at home wore him down.

This coming year was an important one. Some decisions he would have to make would be pivotal. He'd need to have a home where he could think through the issues he faced, now that college was rapidly approaching. He needed a quiet year at his family's beach house without being surrounded by the chaos of his whole family.

Derek bounced his idea off Annie and found she had already talked with their parents about year-round living at the beach house. Annie finally broke it off with her on-again, off-again boyfriend in Livermore after deciding he would never amount to much, so leaving him behind was no problem. She was much happier with Frank. Her parents thought living in Santa Cruz was an excellent idea for Annie, but they thought it was unwise for her to live alone. They didn't think living alone on the Point was a good idea for anyone since it was isolated, and the houses were mostly empty during the off-season.

Now that Derek would be sharing the house with her, it placated their parents. Derek also came up with the idea of offering a room to their Aunt Kate. She agreed to stay with them at the Point for the coming year to provide adult supervision, at least enough to satisfy their parents. Derek thought it funny that Aunt Kate was "adult supervision" when she was only a few years older than him and Annie. She had recently graduated from college in northern California and returned to Santa Cruz while trying to decide what to do with the rest of her life.

●　●　●

In the end, their plans fell together better than anyone could have hoped. Both Annie and Derek convinced their parents that it would be best for them to live at the Santa Cruz house year-round so they could have a quiet place to study. College tests and applications were coming soon. Derek wanted to avoid all the usual commotion at their family home. In addition, this arrangement would allow him to continue his karate training with Shihan.

Derek, Annie, and Aunt Kate settled into their rooms and set up a chore list, deciding to divide and conquer the responsibility of maintaining the house. As Derek walked up the front steps with a box of Aunt Kate's belongings, he passed Frank coming down the stairs. "Hey! Are you helping Annie with her unpacking?" They both stood awkwardly in the entryway. Derek wasn't sure what was happening, and Frank was not certain he was welcome.

Annie came to the rescue. She pulled the box from Derek's hands and put it on the ground. "Derek, say, 'Hi,' to my guest. He'll be visiting us from time to time. It's more like September to May, but he'll also help his parents at their house. So, it's probably best we don't overcomplicate our world by giving details of our room assignments. Frank's parents support this arrangement, as long as his grades remain high." Annie stared at Derek until he looked away.

"My sisters each had similar living arrangements when in college," said Frank. "It helped pave the way for my parents to accept this more sophisticated living arrangement. My parents also see the benefits of living in a quieter house. And I promised my mom I wouldn't misbehave, and I'd focus on my studies." They laughed knowing it was a rather loose standard, if promised by Frank.

Derek was silent as he digested this new information. As far as he was concerned, it worked, so he replied, "I'm not totally sure what that means, but welcome to our home, roomie." He opened the front door wide, gave Frank a friendly punch in the arm, and made room for Frank to bring in another box from the car.

It was difficult for Derek to accept that Olivia would not visit him in Santa Cruz during the school year. The highway between Portola Valley and Santa Cruz was fast, narrow, and mountainous. It was known to be dangerous; it was decidedly not a good road for an uncertain driver, and Olivia was slow getting her driver's license. She also knew her parents were not comfortable with her driving skills, and they would not entertain discussions about driving to Santa Cruz during the school year. Her father implied that having Derek visit her in Portola Valley might be acceptable, but they would need to discuss it later. Olivia took that as a victory.

A victory for Derek was that Olivia finally agreed they could talk on the phone during the school year. Derek was thrilled. He could finally talk and express himself freely; keeping to the written word was always such a struggle, although he treasured her letters and knew she felt the same.

Even though they agreed to exchange phone calls, she left him with a stack of sealed greeting cards, each with a date written on it. The first card was dated "September, the day after Labor Day." Derek took that one with him, leaving the other cards in his bottom desk drawer. He sat on the bench at the end of the street, looking out into the bay, and held her card carefully in both hands. The sun was dipping toward the horizon, and people strolled about, all oblivious to the importance of the letter clutched in the hands of the quiet, serious young man. Derek and Olivia managed to salvage their summer, ending on a high note. Her kiss was strong enough to carry them through the difficult conversation they faced about attending colleges on opposite coasts.

They had shared a bittersweet moment, with the near certainty of a long-distance relationship for the next four years, offset only by the strength of their love, which they expected to carry them through.

Derek sat down and opened the envelope. Inside was a card with a drawing of a small girl handing a flower to an even smaller boy, silhouetted against a pastel-colored sunset. Inside the card was a sheet of paper folded in four sections, the edge ragged where it had been torn from a school notepad.

Dear Derek,

I am guessing you are sitting where you can see the beach. Maybe at Castle Beach Cove or on the bench at the end of your street. I'm only in Portola Valley but it already seems I'm in another country.

Derek looked out at the bay and was impressed that she knew where he was reading her card.

I'm trying this approach, writing a series of cards to you and asking you to open them only on the date shown on the envelope. After that, you can send me cards too, if you'd like. I was planning to send you one card a month, but when I finished one, I wanted to write you another one. The next thing I knew, the sun was rising, and I had finished 25 cards; one per week up until Christmas. I hope you enjoy reading them as much as I enjoyed writing them.

This past year was difficult, with a never-ending string of ups and downs. Looking back at it, I can see that we were caught up in a cycle of trying to protect our relationship from the fear of seeing Ricky again and concerns that it would cause our break up.

Derek stopped reading and pulled a handkerchief from his pocket. Reading the card was as close to her as he would get to Olivia for many months, but the card smelled of her perfume, and the handwriting and words were hers. There was no way he could keep from crying.

We have something great, which means we have something great to lose. But it's funny. I don't fear that we will be defeated by outsiders who want our attention, and don't kid yourself; plenty of girls would do anything to steal you away. It's also possible that some guys would find me attractive in a beach-girlish way. Ha, ha, ha!

What I mean is, if we want to stay together, we can control our destiny if we have faith in our relationship. We should have a little faith that we are smart, strong, and in love enough—can you say that: in love enough? If we care and want to be together, we will find a way.

So, I close with this thought: We can choose to be afraid and unhappy, or we can assume we will be a couple that lasts 50 years. It's our choice. As for me, I choose to believe in our love for the long run.

I love you and will cherish you forever.

Love,
Olivia

P.S. Please get used to listening to the stereo in the evenings. Frank and Annie are embarrassed to think you can hear them when they are—you know.

Derek sat on the bench and cried his eyes out. He was overcome with a sense of fear and loss. He knew Olivia was right; they could make it if they did not let fear consume them. But here he would be for nine months, sitting on a little bench barely an hour away from Olivia, thinking about the coming year when he and Olivia would be apart, and the years beyond with her at Harvard in Boston. He was overwhelmed. Yes, they could now talk, but it was not the same as being together. Why was this year so much harder than before?

When Derek finally returned home, it was well past dark. He waved goodnight to everyone and went straight to bed. It was going to be a long year, he admitted to himself.

• • •

Santa Cruz High School started at the end of August. For the seniors, it was their last chance to enjoy high school. There was a sense that time was running out as each senior frantically tried their best to prepare a future for themselves in the post-high-school world. For students stretching to get into highly selective universities or secure scholarships, grades were a significant factor, and performance in class was taken seriously.

The group enjoyed a broad assortment of meals prepared by Annie with help from Aunt Kate and sometimes Frank and Derek. "We eat like actual adults," announced Frank. Everyone laughed and agreed it was good to finally eat "real food" and not the chicken nuggets and spaghetti routinely served when their whole families were present.

Fall came quickly with shorter days, wisps of fog, and cool breezes. Derek, Annie, Aunt Kate, and Frank spent much of their spare time on the back porch over the second floor of their house, enjoying the ocean view and watching the tide shift in the bay and fishing boats pass in and out of the harbor.

One day, Frank proclaimed, "Fall in Santa Cruz is the best season of the year!" He shared his logic, "The sun is out, the skies are clear, the water is warm, and the air is cool in the shade."

It was true. Fall on the coast was refreshing, and while most people left town to start school or go back to work, the four of them enjoyed the temperate evening weather, followed by glorious sunset displays. Some days, they walked to the cliff and followed a narrow trail down to the beach, with Frank and Derek carrying the food and the women carrying the picnic blankets.

During a busy fall, Olivia tried to discuss college selections with Derek. He replied that the topic was pointless; her parents only allowed her to apply to colleges in Boston while his only allowed him to apply to colleges in California. Harvard, her mother and father's alma mater, and plenty of other high-quality private schools existed for her in Boston, each too costly for Derek and his parents. Olivia petitioned her parents to consider a west coast school, but to no avail. Even top universities like Stanford, Berkeley, and UCLA were rejected by Olivia's father for reasons she could not fathom since those universities were top ranked. Olivia realized her efforts were futile.

After Olivia's last conversation with Derek, she felt like a final stake was driven through her heart, dashing their dream to attend the same school while increasing the likelihood that their relationship might not survive.

In addition to school and sports, Derek started managing a few of the properties around their neighborhood, keeping watch while the owners were away for the winter. As he explained to Annie, Frank, and Kate over dinner one evening, it was like babysitting an empty house. The owners wanted him to keep an eye on their vacant houses, set timers for the lights, and ensure no uninvited guests crept into the house during the off season. He also checked the houses after each storm to make sure they were water-tight and there was no storm damage. Periodically, he scheduled a cleaning service for the interiors to vacuum and clean the bathrooms and kitchens and maintain the homes at a cleanliness level that would satisfy any owner who wanted to return to their house on short notice.

The work was not hard and did not take up much time, but he was building a list of clients and had to go the extra mile to ensure they were all satisfied customers. If he did a good job, a property management market survey showed he could charge considerably more than he initially expected.

The best part was that he could hire out the maintenance work. If the job required cleaning, he hired a service. If the job required heavy lifting, cutting tree branches after a storm, or stacking wood, he enlisted Frank and their friends in exchange for a quick cash payday. Derek's years of home maintenance working with his father were paying off. His property management business began.

Both Annie and Derek were seniors this year, with a final need to earn top grades, compose equally important essays, take SAT tests, and complete college applications. It was a busy and stressful year. Frank also shared many of the same classes, which led to marathon study sessions.

Once their applications were submitted, there was nothing they could do to change the selection process. They simply had to anxiously wait for spring, when college acceptances—and rejections—were sent to prospective students. They each applied to several good California universities and colleges within a couple of hours of home. Still, the schools were expensive, even if they could obtain one of the elusive scholarships reserved for the top high-school students. In addition, they realized scholarships did not always cover room and board. Without a substantial scholarship, most of their top school choices were out of reach. They all hoped for the best.

In the evenings, the three seniors tried to steer conversations away from the future and college. They found avoiding the topic was nearly impossible, and schools, majors, and living options snuck their way into most discussions. They knew they would be on edge until acceptances were received in the spring. It was a long time to wait.

Frank and Annie's acceptance letters came in April. Each letter was thin, stirring momentary panic that they had received rejection letters. This fear subsided when Frank tore his envelope open first and read the golden words, "We are pleased to inform you that you have been accepted to Cal Poly San Louis Obispo." When Annie heard Frank read his letter, she tore hers open to reveal the same acceptance letter.

Frank hugged Annie and together, they fell onto the couch. Kate and Derek jumped into the pile as they all rolled around on the moving pile of accepted students. There were tears of relief as the months of waiting came to an end. The letter announced that each of them qualified for financial aid, with details of the scholarships and admissions to follow the next day in a separate envelope.

Derek quietly went through the rest of the mail, hoping his letter had been sent in the same batch. Sure enough, at the bottom of the mail stack he found a similar letter addressed to him from UC Santa Cruz. Quietly, while the others were still poring over their letters, Derek carefully opened his letter to reveal a similar letter from the University of California, Santa Cruz granting him admission to the University and promising more details, including scholarship information, to follow in the coming days. He stood mute, holding the letter and wondering if Olivia had received letters from the schools she had applied to in Boston.

Frank took note and gently took the letter from Derek, reading the acceptance letter. He also saw Derek's tears, which were different from the ones shed by Frank and Annie. Frank placed the letter on the coffee table and drew Derek into an embrace. Annie and Kate joined them, supporting Derek. Everyone was hugging and crying. The tears were for each of them, and also for each other, too. The emotions were too complicated to separate out. In one sense, they had each stepped across the line from high school to college. Frank and Annie were moving ahead to the same college, knowing that their issues with tuition and housing had yet to be settled, but moving one day at a time with faith that they could solve any problems as they arose.

Derek was happy to have the acceptance letter in his hand, but it also was proof that he would be living in Santa Cruz and not with Olivia in the coming year. He had not heard from Olivia so he assumed her letters had not arrived. He didn't know if she applied for early admission, which would have granted her acceptance back in November or December. They had not discussed her applications. Now it was time to find out as acceptances were expected to be delivered before April.

The call was short. Olivia congratulated Derek for his acceptance into UCSD. They didn't have much to say about it. Derek's grades ensured he would be accepted to the University of California at the campus of his choosing. He had always expected to attend UC Santa Cruz. It was near Santa Cruz, which Derek now considered home, and he expected to receive a nearly full scholarship.

When asked, Olivia admitted that she received her acceptance letter to Harvard a week ago. She said there were probably other schools that granted her admission, but it didn't matter.

None of them were in California. She would attend Harvard, as was always expected. Her parents were pleased and were taking her up to Boston next week to walk the campus.

Derek noted a sense of defeat in Olivia's voice, much like the way she had sounded when they first met, and she described her new beach house in Santa Cruz. Derek felt that, once again, Olivia had received a valuable gift but was expected to march on the path set down by her parents. He felt it was a shame that she would not enjoy this major stepping stone to her future. Instead, she continued to play the dutiful daughter.

Derek and Olivia agreed to talk soon, and as they hung up, tears began to fall. For Derek, they were tears of frustration. They would not be attending school together. For Olivia, the tears came from fear that she and Derek may not survive the long-distance relationship.

●　●　●

Derek surfed nearly every day before school with the Steamer Lane gang. As a result, he had a group of surfing friends and others he met through Frank at Santa Cruz High. The surfers were in the water year-round at several select spots along the coast, so it was inevitable Derek got to know them. Almost all were decent and not too aggressive, once they knew he was a "local," or one who lived in Santa Cruz year-round. After a few weeks, they allowed him to join swells at Steamers Lane, the central surfing spot on the northern edge of town.

He was also getting to know the girls, including Wendy, a petite young surfer, with short blond hair and pale-blue eyes. Whenever she saw him, she gave him a big smile that would embed itself into his memory for the rest of the day. When she pulled the lanyard to unzip the back of her wetsuit and emerged in her tight little one-piece swimsuit, he couldn't look away.

She told him about her plan to pursue a career as a professional surfer. Based on what he had seen, Derek believed Wendy had a real shot at making the pro surfing circuit. More than that, she made it known that she was interested in Derek, lining up near him in the waves, parking her truck near his, and staying around to talk after surfing.

Yes, Derek told himself, she was very cute, and she liked him. Based on Derek's history with other girls, having two girls interested in him at the same time was a rare situation. But it was over before it began. He would not lead Wendy on any longer. It would not be easy, but he had to let her know his heart was with someone else.

On a warm early May afternoon at Steamer's Lane, Wendy and Derek were standing on a wide space above the cliff, watching a resolute group of surfers trying to coax a few final rides from a calm sea. Wendy asked Derek if she would see him over the weekend at Steamers Lane. "High tide is mid-afternoon," she told him. Derek started to be evasive but then knew it was time to be straight with Wendy.

He dropped his truck's tailgate and invited Wendy to sit next to him where they could watch the waves and talk.

He held her hand when he told her that he liked her. His feelings were probably deeper than that, he explained, but there was another girl he had been seeing during the summers. She lived in the Bay Area, a couple hours north of Santa Cruz. Recently, it wasn't always clear that they were together, but still, he felt that he had to be straight and wouldn't go out with Wendy during the school year and have another girl during the summers. He explained that he cared for her, but it couldn't get serious because he had already given his heart to Olivia.

Wendy cried and admitted she saw the signs when he wouldn't let things become more serious. She was sad, not angry, but it hurt all the same. She wanted to know why he couldn't choose her. Wendy said they were still good together, there was no need to break up over a long-distance girlfriend. She tried to convince Derek that his relationship with Olivia was only a summer fling.

Eventually, there was nothing more either of them could say. Derek held tight to his position. Wendy told him to keep in touch if things changed, but she didn't mean it. When her tears had dried, she had no more arguments. Wendy told Derek that with school ending next week, it would be best if Derek found a different stretch of beach to surf for a while. She didn't think surfing together would be the best plan.

Annie went to talk with Derek who was up on the ladder, as usual. "Got a minute for me?" she asked. Derek came down carefully and gave her his attention.

"I understand you've been seeing Wendy, the girl from the surf gang." She put her hands on her hips and glared at him. "Don't bother trying to find out how I know. Remember, 'Knowing Everything' is my super power. And Frank didn't rat you out." She was very angry, and it showed. The red blush on her face was almost pulsating. "How could you do this to Olivia? The girl who's your better half. Without her, I'm afraid to say, you just suck. If you head down this path, it won't be long before everyone knows you're a cheater and you ruin your reputation and your relationship with Olivia. And everyone knows, once a cheater, always a cheater.' And doing this to Wendy? If she were a skank it'd be easier for me to see you break up, but she's a great gal with lots of friends, and she deserves better."

She was calming down slightly. "You," she said, pointing to his chest as she paused to choose her words, "you deserve a swift kick in the ass. This is going to end badly for you."

Annie stormed off before Derek could explain he had already broken it off earlier that day. At this point, she wouldn't believe him anyway.

Eight

During the school year, Derek had hoped Olivia would drive down to visit him in Santa Cruz, but it never happened. Instead, she remained in Portola Valley and Derek focused on a disciplined schedule of working, studying, surfing, and karate training. He pulled nearly perfect grades his last semester of high school, earning him the Honor Roll Scholarship each California high school offered to its top ten percent of seniors, but the victory was hollow as nothing could stop Olivia from moving to Boston to attend Harvard College.

Father's Day was unseasonably warm. Frank, Annie, and Derek stretched out on their towels to catch the early summer rays. Frank moved back home earlier in the week before Annie's family moved in for the summer. Since all encounters with Annie's parents this school year seemed to go well, Frank was not concerned with her parents. Of course, the fact that he and Annie studied hard and produced straight As, made up for most of their parents' concerns with the living arrangements.

Derek was nervous about Olivia's return to Santa Cruz this summer. He didn't know how much their future college moves would affect their relationship. Lying on his beach towel, Derek scanned the visitors as they approached the beach. In many ways, nothing had changed. They would see each other during the summer and go back to school in the fall, as they had done during years before.

His heart leapt when he recognized Olivia in her faded gray sweats and the gentle way she carried herself across the sand. Derek stood up carefully and walked toward her before Annie and Frank even saw her. It was the moment he had been waiting for since last August, and he was lightheaded. She smiled and he reached out his arms for her. He closed the gap between them and pulled her into an embrace that was so familiar last year and now as fresh and comfortable as the sun-warmed blanket that awaited them.

There was no holding back, like last year. Derek tucked Olivia's head into his chest then pulled back to give her a soft, long kiss. "I love you," he said. "I can't believe we made it here another year." Derek ran his hands down her shoulders and looked at her. She now looked like an athlete, with firm muscles and gentle curves. She was no longer a schoolgirl; at eighteen years old, she was a young woman.

She said she loved him back. For a fleeting moment, Derek was concerned he wasn't as fit as she and almost pinched his stomach to see how much fat he was carrying. Derek knew he sported the build of a young man. He built his powerful muscles through competitive sports and not just in a gym weight room. He knew she picked him as her boyfriend, not because of his athleticism, but she said she was drawn to his kindness and his sense of humor, which was never at someone's expense.

They slowly meandered down the beach before joining the others, allowing for a private conversation.

Olivia spoke first. "I have something to confess. Back in Portola Valley, I spent time with a group. These were my friends who went to parties and socials together. Some were couples, others were just friends."

She had prepared notes and practiced them for this part of her story. She couldn't afford to ruin their relationship over this. "There was one guy who was a friend that watched over me at dances and gave me rides to and from the parties. He wanted to be my boyfriend. I didn't think of him that way. I know when I visit Portola Valley, he'll want to see me. He was starting to want more but I wasn't serious about him. I made it a point to stay in the group when he was around.

"The spring formal was coming up and my friends kept asking me to go with him, even though they knew you and I were a couple, and they also knew I wasn't planning to attend. So, when he asked me, I agreed to go with him, just as a friend-date. It was awkward because I knew he wanted this to be more serious than just a date with a friend. He tried to kiss me on the dance floor, and I lost it. I knew I wanted to be dancing with you—not him. I ended up sitting in the corner crying. It was a terrible evening." Olivia absently dug in the sand with her foot.

"I made sure he knew it was over and that I couldn't see him anymore. I never felt about him the way I feel about you. He was entertaining and very nice, but I didn't feel that he was listening to me. I'd bet I could ask him a dozen questions about me, and he wouldn't get half of them right." She laughed wryly. She looked at Derek to make sure he understood. "With you, I knew we were a couple because you liked me and wanted to hear my opinions and thoughts. With you, I felt cherished. You respected me. And still, we shared some very nice kisses."

They both smiled, knowing that they had gone well beyond "a few nice kisses" last summer, even if they had not gone "all the way." As if reading his mind, Olivia teased, "Will we need to wait much longer before we can do that?"

"Anyway, I live in a town where people have lots of money. That's where my father wanted us to live. Except for time with a few close girlfriends, I wouldn't say I have fun there. I don't like those girls and find it wearisome going out with the guys from our town. All they want is to get me out of my clothes. It never worked, but they never stopped trying. It was exhausting and demeaning. But you might have better success with me this year…" She smiled, letting him digest that thought. "They sure won't."

"I do know this: I love you, Derek. I may be young, but I know what love is. It was difficult last year to be together, afraid of Ricky attacking you again. But last year I remembered I have a box of letters that you sent. I read and re-read them all. What we had was real. It can be real this summer and in the future too. That wasn't a good summer for us, so I'm offering a do-over this year. I have no hard feelings about the arguments we had regarding Ricky and my parents, and the careless accusations we threw around.

"So, what I'm saying is, here I am at Castle Beach. I'm here for you."

Olivia paused before adding, "It's time to say goodbye to Wendy too." Derek spun his head to look at Olivia.

"Yes, I know about her, your little surfer girl. I have friends everywhere." Derek's jaw dropped and his shoulders sank in shame. He was frozen like a little boy caught stealing cookies from the kitchen.

"Did she keep her suit on?" Olivia asked in a voice that was so quiet, Derek wouldn't have understood her if he hadn't expected her to raise the question. Derek nodded. "Yes, we only met at the parking lot after surfing. I should never have let the flirting go this far."

Olivia was quiet. Derek couldn't read her expression.

After an awkward silence, Derek confessed, "I was talking with her for a couple weeks. We stayed after surfing and just talked. It was fun in the beginning, but I felt like such a lousy guy." He couldn't look at her. "I liked having someone here who was waiting to talk to me. But it was a bad idea from the beginning."

He finally sat up and looked her square in the eyes. "I broke up with her yesterday. I couldn't go further with this unresolved."

"How did she take it?" Olivia needed to know.

"She was sad, and cried, but she wasn't surprised. I wasn't responsive to her and finally when I told her, she was starting to suspect that I had someone else."

●　●　●

June rolled into July. The fog was less frequent, allowing more time for lying on the beach. Out of the two couples, Annie and Olivia had the only reliable cars. Derek had an old pickup truck, but it was always on the blink, so he used it only for local errands. Annie's car was a four-door Honda that was small, but good with gasoline. Frank and Derek took turns filling its tank.

Olivia's mom lent her a sporty Mercedes; however, Olivia was so nervous about driving that she didn't use it much. Instead, she joined Annie in her Honda when the four friends went out.

Frank's car was little more than a garage full of parts. He claimed that one day the pile would resemble a car, once he got the pieces together. Derek wanted to help but did not know the first thing about cars.

They all took Frank's word for it that there was a car somewhere in the garage. He hoped to finish the restoration before he left for school. Frank and Derek spent hours at night poring over books on how to restore a Mustang. It didn't look that hard when the guys in the book pulled the engine and rebuilt it. Frank knew this was a difficult step and was happy to skip it since the engine was already out of the car and sitting on a wheeled dolly. His problem was finding a way to attach it back into the car.

When he bought the Mustang, he got it cheap because it was disassembled and had been for the past ten years. Frank used Derek's truck to transport the fenders and small parts. Frank had a friend who worked at a tow shop who helped with a flatbed trailer to transport the engine, chassis, and heavy parts off the truck and to his garage floor. The girls frequently stopped by to watch Frank and Derek look at the car while they guessed where each piece went. They added commentary and laughed at the boys and their seemingly impossible task.

One evening, when Frank was eating over at Annie and Derek's house, they were having their usual conversations about the car and how to get it moving. Annie's mom called out from the kitchen, "Derek, you should remember Uncle Robert is a serious car guy. He's rebuilt a dozen cars and sold them just for fun. He lives nearby in Aptos. I'll bet he can help get your car running."

Frank and Derek were stunned. Why hadn't they thought of this before? Right after dinner, they called him, and Robert said he would pick them up in 20 minutes and give them a ride to Frank's garage. Annie was home and said she would pick up Olivia and be back in a flash. They could all ride over together.

Soon after the call, they heard a deep rumble in front of their house. Everyone poured out of the house to see Robert and his car. It was stunning, a muscle car that Frank told everyone was the latest hot item in collectible cars. Robert explained that it was a 1968 Chevrolet Chevelle SS.

One of the kids asked, "Why is it called an SS?"

Robert replied, "It stands for 'Super Sport.'"

The Little Ones all went, "Ooh."

The car looked like it just rolled off a showroom floor. It was deep blue with two white racing stripes running down the middle along the center of the car. The paint glistened as if it were wet. The tires were glossy black with a thin white strip on them. It was a dream muscle car.

Robert explained that he built many cars over the years as a hobby, selling ones as they were completed to raise funds to buy the next project. He said he kept this one the longest. He enjoyed participating in car shows and had won several trophies. He enjoyed driving a finished car with nothing that needed to be done. Still, he had the urge to restore another one and was interested in seeing Frank's Mustang.

The kids went inside after a promise to get a ride in his car sometime this summer. Derek, Olivia, Annie, and Frank piled into the Chevelle and Robert drove across town to Robert's place in Aptos. It was a modest house set back from the road. Behind the house was an old-fashioned wooden barn. It was big and wide enough for three garage doors.

"I wanted to show you my shop first. It makes the most sense to work on Frank's car here in my garage, where I have my tools and paint booth."

The barn was old and showing years of wear. The girls looked at the garage, and Annie leaned over to Olivia for a side comment, "Perfect match for a beat-up car."

Robert opened the door and threw a light switch, which lit up the entire shop. What they saw inside was nothing they expected. It was more like a James Bond film where the evil criminal hides his modern, high-tech shop in an old, abandoned building. The shop floor was finished with glossy gray paint and the walls were lined with tool boards with every imaginable tool, each clean and hanging on metal pegs with a black outline indicating where each tool belonged. All the tool spaces were full and carefully organized.

The garage contained a professional shop with more tools than Derek could imagine. With all these tools, Derek figured Robert could restore just about anything. Anything, but maybe not Frank's pile of parts. His stomach dropped, knowing how important this was for his friend.

One car bay was empty, presumably where Robert parked the Chevelle. Another bay contained a fully restored car that Frank called a Woody Surf Wagon. Robert offered the details, saying it was a 1951 Ford Woody. Regardless of what it was called, it was the perfect beach cruiser with side panels made of polished natural wood, and long enough to hold surfboards on its roof rack.

The last car that occupied a bay looked more like Frank's than any of the others. To the girls, it was nothing more than a pile of parts. "I'm not sure what this is," Robert said jokingly. They all stared at it and the girls wondered why he hadn't thrown it away yet.

"It is some type of 1930s Ford coupe," he said. "It's not worth much until it's restored, but when finished, it'll make a great Hot Rod."

This revelation gave the guys hope; with Robert's help, Frank's pile of parts had the potential to be assembled into a running car.

"Let's go see Frank's car," Robert called out. "As long as it hasn't been through a fire, we can restore it, and a 1965 Mustang is always worth restoring."

Everyone walked back out to the Chevelle in silence. Robert led the way. Annie took Frank's hand and gave it a squeeze. Derek was impressed, looking at Robert's beautiful cars. Sometime in the future, Derek mused, Frank might own a restored car like Robert's, or maybe Frank could learn to restore one himself. But he knew Frank had to face the fact that it might take a few years to restore a car to that level of perfection.

Robert's house was in Aptos, a small shoreline community just south of Santa Cruz. Frank's house was on the Santa Cruz side of the town line. It was only minutes before they arrived at Frank's house, a well-maintained Victorian home with a wraparound porch.

Frank lived there with his parents and four siblings, all girls, including two younger sisters who lived to torment him, and two older sisters attending college who returned home in the summers to work and hang out with friends. Frank's mother insisted they also spend time with their family. In his family, there were five kids during the summer, leading to a level of noise and commotion familiar to Annie and Derek.

Robert pulled into Frank's driveway and turned off the engine. It was a quiet night filled only by the buzz of the crickets and the croaking of frogs. The crickets momentarily ceased their calls with the arrival of the car. After Robert turned off the engine, the insects resumed their din as Frank's front porch light came on and his parents and the girls came out to see who had arrived. Frank Sr., Frank's father, was the first to respond. Looking at the Chevelle, he said, "Now that's a beautiful car. It was everybody's dream when I was in school."

Speaking to his dad, Frank explained, "Robert restored it himself," pointing at Robert's car. "He said he could offer advice on putting the Mustang together so it could look like his car. He's Annie's uncle and has a full auto shop in Aptos. It's amazing."

"That pretty much covers it," said Annie, pulling Frank over to her by his shoulder. She didn't know how it would go when Robert saw the parts that were his car. Frank walked over to the garage and rolled up the door. He flipped the main switch, and a single bare light bulb came on. The rear of the car rested on two wheels, but the front was propped up on two cinder blocks. The chassis didn't have much else attached to it.

Frank's garage walls were covered with odds and ends, all dirty and greasy. There were two doors, fenders, a hood and trunk, windshield, suspension pieces, and box after box of nuts and bolts, and miscellaneous small parts. The engine sat alone on a rolling dolly. The car was a white, two-door coupe with two broad blue stripes running down the middle of the top and along the hood and trunk, but that was years ago, when it was assembled. Now it was an underwhelming pile of parts—at best.

Frank's dad mercifully kept the conversation going. "Frank found this in the newspaper. Some hippies were selling it just north of here in Felton. They wanted their garage cleared out. I don't think Frank paid much for it, but it took a few days to get all the pieces picked up and brought over here. We had to get a flatbed truck to bring the chassis home. If you can help put it together, then God bless you. I'm good with my hands, but I build houses, not cars; I'm afraid Frank's on his own with this rebuild."

When Frank Sr. stopped talking, Robert did not respond. The group was silent as Robert focused on inspecting the parts. He was busy squatting down, looking at the engine, wiping away the dirt from a badge riveted to the engine block. Then he looked at the fenders, particularly one that looked like a front fender.

He looked at the interior, or what remained of it. The upholstery piled up at the end of the garage was not in bad shape, but the driver's seat showed deep cracks in the leather. Finally, he stood up and wiped his hands on a handkerchief he pulled from his pocket.

"I'm not an authority on Fords, but every car guy knows the story of how Ford introduced their new line in 1964 called the Mustang. They made millions of them over the years." Robert walked slowly around the car as he spoke. "However, during the first few years, they made batches of special edition Mustangs with more powerful engines and unique add-ons. You could find them for a couple of thousand dollars when I was in school. They were fast and easy to fix. As the years went by, the baby boomers grew up and wanted to own the cars they lusted for in high school or college, so they started buying them up. The SS was the holy grail of Chevys, but the Mustang GT 350 was the car Ford fans coveted."

He walked over to the fender on the wall and pointed at the name plate painted behind the driver's side front wheel. "Look here, Shelby Mustang GT-350. Under the dust, the car was painted with a white body and two wide blue stripes running from front to back. This is the original paint job. See, there are no colors under the white, no body repair. It's never been restored.

"Now I know you think it is a piece of junk, and you'd be right if all you cared about was its age. But Frank's car is not junk. It is one of the most highly sought-after Mustangs in America. The only question remains: Which GT-350 is this car? Look at the engine. See that red cobra on the valve cover?"

One of the little girls piped up, "I don't know what a valve cover is, but I don't want to be anywhere near one with a snake on it."

Olivia threw her arm around the little girl and squeezed her shoulder. "I won't let them get you."

"This was one of the Shelby Cobra lines. A guy named Carol Shelby was hired to make racing cars for the track and the street. Shelbys are the main collectable Mustangs. Some are worth hundreds of thousands of dollars. If this is one of the rare Mustangs, it should be restored by one of the top shops in the country to get the real value out of the car. Of course, when they get this valuable, you wouldn't want an amateur like me to restore it. But if it is valuable, I'm sure we can figure out a way for you to make a deal with a reputable shop. They would do the work for a share of the profit. With the right deal, they might throw in another, less valuable Mustang for you to drive while this one is being restored. Of course, once the Mustang is finished, you'll have to sell it to cover the tab for the restoration shop. Also, you don't want to park a car in your garage that's so valuable you're afraid to drive it."

"How did it happen that someone sold this to me for less than a thousand bucks when it could be worth far more than that?"

"The obvious answer is the seller didn't know what they had. It probably sat in the garage for 10 years after someone took it apart to restore it, and then gave up. Plus, until it's cleaned up and re assembled, it isn't worth much. Now, it is still just a box of parts, but it could be restored into a very valuable car. I know a couple of guys we can talk to who'll give us an estimated value. Monterey is a big car town with many shops that would vie for a chance to restore this. Then, depending on how much it is worth, we should talk to a restoration shop that would partner with you to restore it for a share in the profits when you sell the car. I don't know how much it's worth, but I'd say it could cover your college expenses with enough left over to buy you a nice car for transportation. One that isn't so rare." Robert was still staring at the car, wiping the dirt from his hands on a rag.

Everyone was stunned into silence.

●　●　●

It was getting late, so Robert left Frank at his house and took Derek, Annie, and Olivia home. Derek asked Robert to drop them all off at Derek's house. He wanted to walk Olivia home so they could talk along the way. There was a lot to digest. The discovery was shocking—Frank's disassembled car that they all previously thought was a pile of junk, was worth far more than anyone expected. It might even help pay his college costs. Because his savings for college fell short of the actual costs, even with financial assistance, Frank could not see how he would afford to attend a university.

Annie had saved for college her whole life, but it still wasn't enough. She once told Frank that her college expenses, even with scholarships, would saddle her with significant student loans.

Derek and Olivia walked up the street to Olivia's house. "That was quite an adventure," Olivia said. "Can you believe how much ridicule Frank received for buying that junker, and then it turns out it could be worth a fortune?"

"I was only hoping Frank had enough money to get it running," said Derek. He thought about the sudden turn of events. It would change things dramatically for Frank's finances, but it did not solve his immediate need for transportation.

"I wonder if Frank can get a car like the Woody in Robert's barn to use this summer," said Derek. "Frank doesn't need a collectible; he needs transportation for two surfers and their boards."

Olivia was quiet. "Is that all you need a car for?" she asked Derek. She waited for him to talk. Finally, she said, "For such a great boyfriend, sometimes you can be so thick."

She waited for Derek to spot the error in his logic. Nothing was coming, so she continued, "Since I've confused you, let me tell you what you should have said: 'Oh, Olivia, how great would it be if we had a car! We could go on dates at a restaurant without a million little kids yelling and throwing things during dinner. We could also use a car that wouldn't break down if we went for a drive together.'"

She held his hand and swung their hands back and forth as they walked. He was smiling, listening to her joke around. She continued talking, apparently having more to say on the topic of cars. So he grinned and listened.

"Wow, Olivia, would you like me to take you shopping?" she said in a strange deep voice, apparently meant to mock him. She was smiling too, enjoying herself by cutting loose and kidding Derek, which she didn't do very often. They laughed and talked all the way to Olivia's home where Derek kissed her good night and dropped her off at her front door.

●　●　●

The rest of the summer rolled along, although they were all so busy it seemed the summer could last forever. Frank and Robert spent days visiting collectible car dealers and restoration shops. In the evenings, they pored over car collector magazines. Once Frank selected a restoration shop, he could negotiate a deal that would give him an older rebuilt—but reliable—car to drive during the summer. As for the value of the car, Frank and Robert were pretty sure they knew how much it was worth, but they were tight-lipped.

Because Frank was dealing with potentially high financial value and uncertainty, Olivia suggested he hire someone to help him protect his investments. She volunteered her father's legal service to draft a contract between Frank and the restoration shop for restoring and selling his car. Her dad was glad to help a fortunate young guy start out. In the end, Frank insisted there be a provision to pay him a small amount for his services.

Nine

Olivia found Derek up on a ladder, as usual, working on a stuck window. She held the ladder and leaned back to look at him. "Can you come down for a minute?" she asked, yelling at him two stories up. Recently, he seemed to spend more time on ladders than on the ground. She worried he would reach too far out to one side or the other and crash down onto the parking area. She tried not to think about ladders.

Derek hung his hammer in his tool belt. "I'm on my way down. It sounds like this is important if I've got to climb up and down the ladder again."

Olivia waited quietly until he was firmly on the ground. "My brother, Ricky, is back in town. I spoke with my parents and tried to get them to hold the line and keep him at our house in Portola Valley, but for whatever reasons they had, they said that Ricky would be coming to stay with us for the rest of the summer." She burst into tears, clutching herself.

Derek tenderly pulled her into an embrace and spoke in her ear. "Don't worry. It'll be different this time. I'll be fine. Are you sure you're safe?" he asked her.

"He arrived today and has two big friends with him. They've never threatened me. I'm mainly concerned about you. If you want to leave town, I'll come with you. I don't know why my parents won't tell him to stay away. He's over twenty-one now."

"Where does he live?"

Olivia stayed in Derek's embrace, clinging to his shoulder. Finally, she pulled back. "He normally lives with us in Portola Valley, but he's been in and out of jail. Most recently, he was in the Redwood City Jail serving the end of a six-month sentence."

"What did he do?"

"He got into a fight." She looked Derek in the eyes. "He beat the other guy half to death." She looked away. "Ricky's dangerous. I don't want you to get hurt."

Derek led Olivia by the hand to a small bench by the fence in his family's front yard. "Olivia, listen. He needs to know he can't keep us apart. Ground rules need to be set. If he doesn't listen and he insists on a fight, I want you to stay out of it. Be safe and get to my house. No matter what happens, don't try to stop a fight; I don't want you to get hurt. Please stay here—until any fight is over. You'll be safe since there are always people around—can you promise me that?"

She looked confused.

"I'm going to be fine. It's not the same as last year. This time, I'm expecting him, and I am ready. I've trained to protect myself, should I need to," Derek spoke in a soft, calm manner.

"There are three of them," said Olivia. "What are you going to do about that?"

"I'm going to do the same thing three times," Derek told her in a calm, confident voice. "First, I will un-invite them to Santa Cruz. If they don't leave us alone on their own, I'll make them understand they should leave."

He held her hand, and together they walked into his house to call his best friend. "Frank? This is Derek. Ricky's back. It's time we cleaned up the street," Derek said with a sharpness in his voice that only his friend would be able to hear.

Frank heard the phrase indicating Ricky's return. He responded softly, repeating, "It's time to clean up the street. That's a tall order. Do you have a place where we should start?" Frank could tell this was serious and hoped to lighten the weight on Derek's shoulders.

"I don't want a fight, and I don't need you to fight. Just be a witness. Could you be here in ten minutes?"

Instantly giving his full attention, no joking around, Frank took a deep breath and exhaled slowly. "Robert is here with me. We'll be on our way now. Should I bring anything?"

"Just come as quickly as you can. I think I should be alright. I'm ready for him, but he's not ready for me." Derek hung up the phone and sat for a few minutes with Olivia in silence. Derek sat without moving except for the light tapping of his fingers on his leg.

Derek had Olivia call her house. Ricky picked up.

"I heard you were back in town," Derek said to Ricky into the phone which was now on speaker.

Derek's tone was low and steady, "It's time you got the message that Olivia and I are together, and you aren't wanted here."

He waited for Ricky to respond. The silence stretched out and then he heard Ricky speak to someone on his side of the call. "It's that kid that was seeing Olivia last year. He says I'm 'not wanted here.' What a polite little punk. Let's pay him a visit."

Derek continued, "You can leave now, or, if you decide to stay, leave Olivia and me alone."

Ricky sneered, "I have a couple friends with me who like it here in Santa Cruz. We're spending the rest of the summer here. You shouldn't mind—you'll be dead."

"That's quite a threat," Derek told him. "I don't care who your friends are or if they stay, just leave us alone."

There was another long pause while Ricky spoke with his friends. Before they were finished, Derek cut him off, "So, what are you going to do?"

Ricky said, "We're coming over to kick your ass."

Derek was more than ready to end this conflict with Ricky. He wanted to spend this summer with Olivia in peace. "Ok. Meet me at my house in twenty minutes. You know where I live." Derek hung up the phone.

Olivia was too shocked to cry. She followed Derek outside where they sat on the bench in Derek's yard as he suggested. Derek was calm and didn't speak. Now that he was ready, he waited. Ricky and his two friends would arrive shortly but so would Frank and Uncle Robert.

Derek remained silent, allowing him to clear his mind as he watched the end of the street for Ricky to arrive.

Olivia sat next to Derek when Robert and Frank came down the road, the roar of the Chevelle SS heralding their approach. Frank jumped out when the car stopped, only long enough for Robert to drop him off. Olivia watched as Robert parked his car down the block, keeping the area in front of Derek's house clear. Word of Derek's pending fight with Ricky spread fast. Derek's family and friends soon lined both sides of the road. Although it wasn't clear what would happen, Derek's clan was there to offer their support as best as they could.

Robert looked from Frank to Derek. "What's going on here? I don't want anyone to get hurt. Derek, let us know if you need any help. Should I call the police?"

"I'll be fine," said Derek without taking his eyes off the end of the street. "There might be a fight when Ricky gets here; the choice is his. Please be a witness for me."

Robert nodded in agreement.

Derek was the first to see Ricky and his friends approach. There were three guys, clearly older and bigger than Derek. The one in front had a baseball bat.

Derek gave Olivia a fast kiss. "I love you. Don't be afraid. I'll be fine." He then let her go and pulled Frank aside. "If things go south, use the hose by the front door and blast them with a full stream of water in the face. Do not jump into the fight. I didn't train with a partner—I can do three-on-one. Three-on-two is more difficult to coordinate." Derek stepped into the middle of the street and waited. Derek recognized the first guy as Ricky. He was laughing as he approached Derek.

Ricky was the first to talk. He had the bat and swung it like a slugger aiming for the fences. "Derek, you're doomed. I'll try not to kill you, but no promises."

"You hit me with that bat, it's a felony. You'll go right back to prison. We have witnesses. Is that what you want? Can't you just leave us alone this summer?"

"I brought my own witnesses," Ricky said. "I'll take care of you first, then anyone else who wants can take a shot at me," Ricky sneered to the crowd.

Derek stood tall and stared Ricky in the eyes. It was true Ricky was bigger than Derek, but Derek was also a year older than the last time they met. He was no longer a kid. Back then, Ricky took him out with a sucker punch. This time, Derek was prepared. He expected Ricky would start with another fast, one-shot attack. This time Derek was ready to hold his ground. He did not want to risk losing Olivia or another summer together.

Derek stepped to the side of the street. "Now, hold on a second. If we're using weapons, let me see what I can find." He backed up toward his house, never taking his eyes off Ricky. Reaching into a small pile of wood at the side of the driveway, he pulled out a long stick, maybe five feet long and an inch and a half in diameter. "Look what I found. It's a closet bar. For hanging up clothes, but also good for jabbing assholes like you. Is that what you want?"

Ricky laughed again, even louder. "Go ahead, see if you can find some more garbage to help you fight me. It won't matter. I'll still kill you."

Derek took the stick and shifted it from one hand to the other to find its center of gravity. He spun it up over his head, down, and around each side of his waist. Then he started spinning it in front of him, faster and faster, until it became a blur. He stopped the bar suddenly, turned it around above his head, chopped it down to his waist, stepped forward, jabbed it toward Ricky, and shouted, "YA!" It was clear he was prepared to fight.

Without taking his eyes off Ricky, Derek spoke sharply to Ricky's two friends. "This fight isn't yours. I want you both to walk back to your car and get the hell out of here. Never come back to Santa Cruz. If you get involved in this fight, you'll get hurt." He waited.

Ricky looked at Derek and then at his friends. "Hey, come on, he's just a kid. We can do this." The two guys were not so sure. They looked at Ricky and then spoke quietly to each other.

Without a sound, they turned around and walked quickly back up the street and out of sight. Now, it was just Derek and Ricky.

Derek began talking loudly to Ricky and the curious people watching from the street. "You show up at my house, three guys and a baseball bat? You just got out of jail, and you want to start a fight? I can defend myself. I can just knock you down, call the police, and let them do the rest. That's the least of what will happen if you try to fight me. It'll be self-defense for me. Don't think you can come into my neighborhood and start a fight in front of my girlfriend, family, and friends. If you try anything at all, I can assure you you'll get hurt. So, what's it going to be? Will you get in your car and leave Santa Cruz forever, or will you fight me, get hurt, and then go to prison?"

Ricky took one step back, paused, and then charged at Derek, his baseball bat held high. Derek quickly skip-stepped back and to the side as the baseball bat swung within inches of his chest. Derek was faster than Ricky, waiting only for the bat to turn past him when he charged, using his stick to pin the bat against Ricky's chest. Derek pushed Ricky and then stepped back and, showing great control, tapped Ricky on both sides of his head using a side strike with each end of his stick. He could have hit hard, ending the fight, but he wanted to show his control and capability.

Ricky became enraged and tried to swing the bat again at Derek. Derek pivoted away again, striking his stick downward on Ricky's collarbone, hearing a loud crack as it broke. Ricky was teetering, side to side, barely able to stand. Derek stepped forward and gave him a sharp front kick to the groin, launching him across the street where he landed on his back. Ricky did not get up; instead, holding his arm to his chest, he gave short, sharp screams as he struggled, and failed to get up. The crowd breathed in collective relief.

Derek walked over to Ricky to see if the fight would continue. It was clear it wouldn't. Derek tossed his stick into the wood pile by his house and went over to Olivia, who was standing with Derek's family which now flooded into the street. Once they were satisfied Ricky wouldn't be causing any trouble, they surrounded Derek, patting him on the back in awe of how fast the fight was decided. Someone called 911. When the medical team arrived, they tended to Ricky, who was making whimpering noises but not moving.

Derek turned his back on Ricky and returned to his front yard. He had no interest in Ricky or his injuries.

Olivia watched the fight from the bench at Derek's house. She felt safe surrounded by the rest of his family, but she had stood frozen when Ricky advanced toward Derek, swinging his baseball bat. Just as quickly, Ricky was on his back, howling in pain. He would not be threatening them anymore. The fight was over.

Olivia ran over and clung to Derek. He wrapped his arms around her and told her in a soft voice that it was all over. She had been terrified that Derek would get hurt or even killed. However, when it was clear Ricky was not getting up, she finally relaxed. Ricky's two accomplices were gone and would not be a problem. They left and never looked back. This was Ricky's fight and not theirs. When Ricky recovered, he would not risk being beaten again by Derek.

●　　●　　●

The paramedics transferred Ricky to a gurney and into the ambulance for his ride to the emergency room, not without a considerable amount of screaming from Ricky due to the pain from his broken collar bone.

The police arrived and assessed the situation. They talked to the crowd who watched the fight. Uncle Robert acted as spokesperson with the police officers, recounting the details of the fight.

The officer approached Derek to interview him. Derek was still talking with Olivia and comforting her about the fight. He gave his story to the police. It was short. "This is where I live. That is my home right there." He pointed at his family's house, behind him.

"This guy came down the street carrying a baseball bat with two other large men and wanted to fight me. I only met him a few times before. He had his own grievances which I didn't understand. I had to protect myself. It was fortunate there were building supplies near the house to help me protect myself from his bat." Derek gave Olivia a squeeze. "I got a break."

The police officer finished writing in his notebook and then asked the bystanders if that was an accurate account of the fight, and they all agreed that Derek's story was consistent with their observations.

"I think you should call his parole officer in Redwood City," Derek suggested. "From what I've heard, this guy has a history of starting nasty fights."

Derek watched the police officer pick up the wooden closet bar. "Was this your weapon?" he asked Derek.

Derek nodded.

"Why did he want to fight you?"

"He didn't like me going out with his sister."

"Did you know he was bringing a baseball bat?"

Derek shook his head no. "Why would I expect someone to come after me with a baseball bat?" After a beat, Derek continued, "I don't know much about him. I saw him a few times at his family's beach house, but we didn't talk. He was a weird guy. I hadn't heard from him in almost a year, and then he said he wanted to kill me. I took the threat seriously when I heard he was coming to my house."

The police officer stopped writing in his notebook and looked at Derek. "Let me get this straight. You were confronted by three guys, one of whom, Ricky Sutton, age twenty-one years, had a baseball bat. When they showed up at your house, you had no weapon except this stick." The policeman paused until Derek nodded, affirming the story.

The cop continued, "So, Ricky started the attack by swinging the baseball bat at you. He missed. You returned the attack, hitting Ricky three times with your piece of wood, plus you delivered a kick to him which knocked him across the street. He was the only one who was hurt. The other two characters walked away from the fight. There's no information on them." Derek nodded again.

The police officer concluded, "In my opinion, this incident can be closed. I'm recording Derek fought in self-defense. I'll file a report and share it with the Redwood City Police Department to follow up with Ricky's parole board. You're lucky you weren't killed."

Derek gave a final nod.

The police officer thanked Derek for his time and went to speak with the paramedics. He compared the story against the paramedics' description of Ricky's injuries before he closed his notebook. It appeared the police were done with their investigation.

The officer walked off holding the clothing bar, swinging it lightly, like one who knew it could also be used as a martial arts weapon. The police officer threw the stick back on the woodpile, went back to his police car, and drove off. It was just a piece of building material. At least, that's how it would be described in his report.

•   •   •

Derek and Olivia were still standing in the front yard when Olivia's parents approached them. Her mom stopped to check on Ricky before the ambulance took him away. Her dad came over to talk with Olivia. "He picked up right where he left off with Derek," Olivia said to her father. "It didn't turn out as he expected, though."

Olivia's father turned to Derek. "I'm glad you weren't hurt. Your Uncle Robert told me how it happened and that it was over quickly. You must have trained hard to get that good."

"I didn't have a choice," said Derek almost apologetically. "He would have killed me if I hadn't protected myself." It wasn't said with pride. It was simply a statement of a fact. "I tried to avoid the fight. I gave him several chances, but he had no intention of backing down. I'm sorry about hurting your son. I didn't know another way."

Olivia's dad shook his head slowly. His movements were those of a man ten years his senior, caused by the stress of raising a troubled child. His family would face years of sorrow yet to come from Ricky. To Derek, he said, "You were protecting yourself and possibly Olivia too. I cannot explain what happened to Ricky or how he grew up to be such a violent and angry young man."

Derek had nothing to say. He hoped this chapter of his life would now be over for good.

Olivia went over to hug her mom. There were a few times she felt her mother's lack of support, and she seemed to side with Ricky, while Olivia was a model child. Maybe her parents simply did not need to worry about her, so it appeared that they cared more for him. But right now, all those concerns were washed away. Olivia knew her mom was her biggest supporter, and nothing would change that. Olivia's fear of a confrontation between Ricky and Derek was over. She felt incredible relief.

Olivia was certain Ricky would stay away from Santa Cruz and, more specifically, steer clear of Derek. After a few days in the hospital following surgery, Ricky would spend time in prison. Olivia thought her parents' concerns would last a long time since Ricky was in a constant cycle of violence and jail. His parents had no idea how to steer him toward a peaceful life.

Olivia's father took her mother's hand and slowly walked up the road toward their house. After a couple of steps, her mom spoke to her father who paused and then continued to their home while she returned to Olivia, who was waiting for her. After Olivia's mom gathered her thoughts, she shared that they needed to return to Portola Valley to help Ricky recover and deal with the resulting legal issues. They expected to be in the Bay Area for an undetermined amount of time and wondered if Olivia was comfortable staying in Santa Cruz for the rest of the summer without them. They knew she would be safe here and away from Ricky.

Olivia's watched her mom struggle with her emotions. This was a difficult and trying day, to say the least. Her mom explained they not only liked Derek, but they trusted him—and trusted him with Olivia. Both she and Olivia's father noticed he was good with Olivia, treating her with kindness and care. Her mom said that they recognize she and Derek are no longer kids but young adults. She continued to say they were impressed with his behavior, not just today, but through the years, and that it was clear he loved her. If she and Derek were to start thinking of a long-term future together, she wanted Olivia to know that both parents approved.

Olivia squeezed her mom's hand. Both Olivia and her mom were crying now. Her mom said if Olivia chose to stay in Santa Cruz, she could trade her Mercedes with the family's sedan, so she would be more comfortable driving. Olivia smiled.

Once home, Olivia and her mom continued their conversation in a quiet corner of the yard. Her mom said they would put money in Olivia's account to pay for her food and gas. They wanted her friends to join her occasionally for meals so she would not feel alone in the big house. Her friends were welcome over anytime—just maybe not both Frank's and Derek's entire clans at once—since those were large families. Olivia and her mom laughed at that understatement.

To Olivia's shock, her mom even said she could have Derek stay with her for the rest of the summer—and Annie and Frank too, if they wanted—as long as those living arrangements were fine with the other parents. A quiet lecture on the importance of birth control followed, much to Olivia's extreme embarrassment. Her mom quickly added that they did not want to become grandparents at this time.

Thoughts swam in Olivia's mind: She and Derek were finally free from the threat of Ricky's visits! Her parents actually gave their approval to live with Derek this summer—in their house? A smaller car and living expenses for the rest of the summer? Is this really happening? Olivia almost pinched herself in disbelief.

All Olivia could do was nod and reply quietly, "I think that will work for me." She held back her bewilderment.

Her mom slipped back into her polite, social voice. "Now that that's settled, we'll be sure to give you a warning if we plan to come by, to give you time to tidy up the house, if necessary. I don't want to walk into the house unannounced and have your father think you're living like a slob."

With that, her mom turned to leave, but not before giving Olivia a sad smile and a wink before attempting to walk away. Olivia hugged her a bit longer. Their relationship had changed. Was this a glimpse of their future as she became a grown-up daughter, talking with her mother, who was, for the moment, acting more like a big sister? They shared an extended glance, acknowledging that even with Ricky's tragedy in Santa Cruz, life went on.

"Just like that, everything changed," Olivia thought, as she gave her mom a final squeeze of their hug and then watched her parents walk back into the beach house to pack.

After the police and ambulance pulled away, Derek approached his dad so they could talk together while Olivia was talking to her mom. Derek's dad expressed how impressed he was with Derek's ability to wield the stick, or bo, as it was called in karate, and his confident poise and self-control. His dad explained how terrified he was that Derek might not be able to defend himself against three big guys. He was most impressed by the way he warned off the two other guys by making it clear they were unwelcome, and that he preferred not to fight, but was prepared to fight, so they left peacefully. His dad continued to say how proud he was of Derek.

Derek wanted to explain that his performance was not a fluke but resulted from focused preparation. "I worked out for hours at the dojo, almost every night for a year. I practiced with all the weapons we had, including knives, nun chucks, and the long bo, which I used today.

"Ultimately, I had to be ready for just about anything if Ricky came back. I didn't want to end up in the hospital like the last time. My goal was to make Ricky question whether fighting was a good idea. I expected there would be more than one member of Ricky's posse, so if I could get them to fear I would win, maybe they would all walk away, knowing it wasn't their fight. Ultimately it worked—for two of the three guys. I hoped by quickly bopping him on each side of his head, he'd realize I knew what I was doing and was just showing him my skill—not intending to do any harm—as long as he backed off."

Derek stepped back and bowed to his father in the style of his dojo, in the way a karateka shows respect to his elders, with both arms crossing his chest then striking downward to his sides, both hands held in tight fists. Meanwhile, Derek saw Annie motioning to the side, signaling that others wanted to speak with him. Derek's siblings, family, and friends all came by to congratulate him. The Little Ones gave him a pat on the back, proud of their big brother.

Eventually, Derek felt his energy drained. The adrenaline wore off and all he wanted was to lay down. As soon as he could, Derek went to find Olivia.

Ten

From the front yard, Derek and Olivia watched her parents drive away. Olivia saw her mother give her a slow wave. It was hard to miss the sadness in her eyes.

Olivia led the way into her house. Previously, Olivia never had Derek in her house without her parents at home. There was also the unacknowledged anxiety that Ricky might show up unannounced when Derek visited. Today was different: Ricky would not be visiting for a long time, if ever, and a sense of peace and relief were present in the atmosphere.

Olivia led Derek by the hand up to her room on the second level. They entered her bathroom, where she started the shower and slowly removed his clothes. He stepped into the shower. Olivia also removed her clothes and stepped in as well, taking the soap bar and washing him down. He stood silently. Then she took a face towel, soaked it in the warm shower stream, and gently washed his face and neck and shampooed his hair. Derek didn't say a word. She gave him a light kiss on the lips and turned off the water, reaching out of the shower for a towel for each of them. She dried his hair and then the rest of him as he stood silently. She took one of her bathrobes, wrapped it around him, and tied the sash. Olivia pulled on her other bathrobe for herself, knotting it at the waist.

When they were both dry, Olivia led Derek into her bedroom and walked over to the bed. She reached around him and flipped back the covers. They sat on the side of the bed, and she held him in a soft embrace and waited. "You are safe now. You won. It's over," she said to him quietly but in a firm voice. And then she repeated it, again and again.

He began to breathe deeply while she continued quietly, "You are safe." And then he started to cry. Quietly but with big, deep breaths. He sobbed for a while; then he cried silent tears while she held him.

Finally, he spoke. "I've been scared for so long. I have been to so many practices where I've been hit and knocked down then forced to get up again. My primary teacher, Shihan, knew I must practice while I was truly scared, and be willing to take the pain when I was losing so I could continue fighting until I won."

Derek looked up at Olivia, not seeing her but allowing himself to remember round after round of practice fights. "All that practice was to make me ready for the one moment with Ricky. Most of the time, I knew I could do it, but not always. Sometimes I was very unsure. I've been living for this fight for the past year, and now it's over." She still held him. She waited.

Finally, she loosened her embrace and moved back. He held her face with both hands and placed his lips against hers. It was a long, deep kiss, pressing home his love for her and hers for him. They were facing a new future. "I love you, Olivia. If I didn't fight him and win, we would never be safe. I did it for us." She kissed him again and gave him a quick hug.

Olivia held him at the waist of his robe. "I am very proud of you, not just for winning the fight but for doing what it took to stand up to Ricky and for training hard for so long. I didn't know how hard it was for you. You never told me the details." She looked at him and gave him half a smile. "I'm proud of you for winning too."

When he was breathing normally, and appeared to be back in the present, she changed the subject. "My mother told me I need to learn to cook and suggested I ask you and our friends for help." Derek was a little confused. Olivia began to undo the knot on her bathrobe. When the knot was free, both sides of her robe hung open.

"She doesn't want me to go hungry." Olivia reached over to Derek's robe and undid the knot, allowing his robe to fall open too. "She told me she and my father will be spending the rest of the summer in Portola Valley."

"Does that mean you might get scared being here all alone at night?" he asked. "Should I come over and tuck you in and scare off the monsters?"

"I'm often afraid of strange noises," she said, inching closer to him. "I have a particular fear of things that live in dark closets. Can you help?"

"I have been known to clear out monsters from time to time. There are plenty of strange beasts living in our old house, and I get called in to help clear them out now and again."

He reached under Olivia's robe and ran his hand along the smooth skin on her hips, and then higher to her ribs, and then her breasts.

Olivia thought about his offer. "At eighteen years old, I'm an adult, but I'm still afraid of the kinds of beasts that make strange sounds in the night. Now that you have proven yourself adept at clearing out scary creatures, maybe you can help me get rid of any that remain," she said, letting go of his robe and wrapping her arms around his neck, pulling their bodies closer until their bellies touched. Derek reached around her and held her hips against his. "That is, if you aren't afraid of monsters yourself."

"I'm afraid of monsters and I'm an adult too," Derek said as he lifted her up, holding her higher and then placing her back onto the bed. He held Olivia's body even tighter against him and brushed his lips across hers. "Once the monsters are vanquished, I think we can find other things to do."

He smiled and said, "I may need your help."

"I'm glad to hear that," she said." Her smile turned into a grin. I can probably teach you a few things, to a point, but, after that," she replied, "I'm afraid I don't have any experience either."

Derek looked her in the eyes and kissed her again. "This will be the first time for me."

Olivia held his gaze. "It is the first time for me too."

With that admission she pulled Derek's robe off his shoulders and dropped it to the floor. Then he pulled her robe from under her and let it slip to the floor. Derek pushed back a step and politely took in a full view of her naked figure, allowing his eyes to gaze lightly across her exposed body, but not wanting to embarrass her.

Far from being embarrassed, she rolled back, allowing him to view her, to draw in her naked and toned figure. Next, she began slowly running her hands along his body, finding new places to hold and explore.

"We are missing something," he said as he slipped his hands from her breasts and placed them firmly on each hip.

She leaned over, reached into the drawer of her night table, and pulled out a box of condoms. "I bought these at the beginning of the summer. I was beginning to fear we wouldn't get a chance to use them."

Derek laughed. "I prepared the small bedroom in the garage for us but didn't have the nerve to ask you to join me there. So, once again, I'm the slow one."

"From what I've heard, slow is good." They moved their robes to a chair in the room and pulled the covers back on the bed.

"Olivia?"

"Yes?"

"Do you think you could help me with this?" he said, holding out a condom. I am not quite sure I'll do this right." He gave a shy glance down to the small packet in his hands and she smiled as well.

"Sure, Derek. We have a lot to learn, but we also have lots of time." They caressed each other, first with their hands then with their whole bodies, each enjoying the responses they got as they gently and lovingly ran their hands over each other. They moved slow at first and then picked up urgency, both breathing in short gasps, finding and sharing their love for one another, over and over until they tired and dozed off.

Several hours later, Olivia and Derek slept in her bed. Olivia was partially asleep but still hyper-aware of Derek and where his body touched hers. It was amazing, and confusing, she thought to herself, and silly, and sometimes embarrassing. They tried different things and drew hard lines at others. By the time they dozed off, they had put a big dent in the box of condoms.

They fumbled and accepted instructions, finding things that worked well and then laughed until each of them climaxed, unsure exactly how they caused the other such pleasure. It was their light heartedness and good humor that let her enjoy the fun and excitement she experienced today.

Olivia's phone had been chirping and buzzing, but Derek was fast asleep and Olivia chose to ignore the messages, allowing Derek to sleep for as long as possible. Finally, Oliva looked at the clock and saw it was after 6 P.M. She had nowhere to go, but unless he had informed his family of other dinner plans, Derek was expected at his house for dinner at seven o'clock each night.

·   ·   ·

"It's time to join the real world," Olivia said, and she gave Derek a nudge. "First, I might have an interesting idea. My mom told me that she and my dad will be gone for the rest of the summer. I'm here alone in a four-bedroom house." Olivia sat up and leaned back against the headboard, her sheet slipping down exposing her breasts to Derek's eyes, and then to his hands. "I'd like you to join me here for the rest of the summer. Is that something you could do? It's actually okay with my parents."

She jabbed him to see if he was awake. He responded by pulling her on top of him. "Yes. If it is your plan, I support it," he said while still half asleep.

After a moment of processing her statement, he replied, "My mom was fine with Annie and Frank, and we're heading off to college soon, so I think she'll give us some latitude on where we sleep."

"Do you know what else that means?" Olivia asked Derek. He was dozing again, so she ran her hand down his chest, across his belly, and then further down. Derek quickly grabbed her wrist and came awake. "What does it mean?"

"We have room in the house for Annie and Frank. Do you

think they would like to move into the guest bedroom?" she asked between kisses and the distraction of his roving hands. "They'd be two floors below us. It could offer them the privacy they need," she said, as she pulled her hand free and continued to explore various areas of Derek's anatomy. He started to respond, but not in a way that would help them get to dinner at Derek's house on time. To move his mind away from Olivia's teasing, he brought up one of the problems.

"I don't know if that will work. You should have heard them this past year," said Derek. "I had to drown them out with rock videos on MTV. It was embarrassing."

"I don't know whether putting them in the guest room means no more 'sounds' but it could mean we won't be near enough to hear them," she replied. "Who knows? We might make a few embarrassing sounds ourselves." Olivia was having fun arousing Derek. This was uncharted territory for them both.

She had yet to put on a robe, so Derek could barely keep his mind on their conversation. He roamed his hands freely as they spoke. They forgot about the phone ringing in the background.

Derek was thinking about the new plan. "What about your mom?" he asked. "What would she do if she came by and accidentally walked in on us all shacking up in their beach house?"

Olivia remembered her conversation with her mom before she left. "My mom suggested it! She wanted me to start having you all over for dinner, which I presumed meant that she was concerned about me becoming hungry and lonely. And, she openly said she promised not to visit unexpectedly. Then she came out and said that I am welcome to have you, Annie, and Frank stay here the rest of the summer."

Derek thought about it and agreed. "It's a good idea. If the new accommodations work out, we call your house the 'Shack,' since we're shacking up!" he laughed.

She stared with wide open eyes in shock. "Oh my God, if any of our moms hear that name, we're doomed. Do you think Frank could last a week, let alone a whole summer, without letting that slip out?" Suddenly she was concerned about the whole plan.

Derek pulled her into a hug and told her it would be fine. "The Beach Shack is catchy and cute, given how your house is quite the opposite. It shouldn't upset anyone when they hear its name. And I'll talk with Frank. He's grown up a bit and doesn't make those mistakes anymore."

Olivia held his hands and sat up. "Stop. We'll deal with names later. Right now, I think your mom's expecting us to stop by for dinner tonight. We should go now before you start stirring up too much heat. Otherwise, when we get there, everyone will know exactly what we've been up to."

"Oh, they'll know," said Derek. "It's a mom thing. My friends had it happen to them. Their mothers looked at them and said, 'You two are having sex.' All they could do was plead the fifth. I mean, we are going to ask her if we can sleep together for the rest of the summer. No sense in trying to deny it. The horse has already left the barn."

Olivia just shook her head and started pulling on her clothes from the pile on the floor. Derek started to dress and then stopped to kiss her and would never have gotten dressed if Olivia hadn't glared at him.

After dressing, they checked Olivia's answering machine. It contained a few missed calls for Derek from Frank who was at Annie's house. Derek returned the call, and Annie answered on the first ring and put it on the speaker phone in her room.

"So where are you, bud?" Frank asked. "No, strike that. I know where you are. What are you doing?" Again, he stopped. "Nope, I know what you are doing," Frank teased. "It's almost dinner time. Your mom's expecting you here, so why don't you two get dressed and come on over? "

Olivia's face flushed a deep red, and Derek just grinned.

There was a smacking sound as Annie whacked Frank across the side of his head. "You behave yourself," she said. "Remember, the Little Ones are near and can hear what you say."

"But honey," Frank said, trying to get himself out of trouble. "I meant it in only the kindest way."

Derek said, "See you in a few minutes," and hung up.

As they walked over to Derek's house, he suggested there wouldn't be much of a change with the new plan. They were already moving from house to house, having lunch with one family and dinner with the next. Now, they would simply return to the Shack every evening.

"Oh, you are a bear with such a little brain," said Olivia. "In our parents' eyes, this changes everything."

Derek's mind was back on their afternoon together. He had no desire to think about anything else.

●　●　●

The rest of the summer moved far too fast. The four friends had tense conversations with their parents, but overall, things went quite well. Their parents had already talked with one another and accurately guessed their children were already sleeping together. With the first blessing given by Olivia's mom, then Annie's mom, the rest of the parents fell in line. The only request was they be smart with birth control.

They all knew college was just around the corner, and they planned to move soon to their respective universities for orientation and to move into their living accommodations.

The restoration process on Frank's car was slow, but since the shop had given him the surf wagon for his use, he was fine with their slow pace.

There were days Olivia and Derek did not get out of bed until noon. They could not get enough of each other, and knew saying goodbye would only be that much harder.

One afternoon at Derek's house, his mother came into the kitchen and sat at the counter next to him with a mug of coffee and a determined look on her face. He knew he was in for a lecture. It was past due, given the amount of time he was now spending at Olivia's house. Annie was still in bed with Frank and was not at their parents' house yet.

"I was speaking with Frank's mom, and we thought it was time to have a conversation with all four of you. We'll bring dinner over to the Shack." She waited until Derek realized what she had said, then continued. "Yes, we listen to everything you say whether you intend for us to hear it or not. 'Shacking up at the Beach Shack,' sounds catchy." Derek's eyes were boring into the plate in front of him.

"In any event, let's meet at 6:30 P.M. at Olivia's house. Pick up a cheesecake or something to have with coffee. I'll bring lasagna. You're an adult now. It's time you started eating like one. Adults don't eat pizza five days a week."

Annie showed up a few minutes later and Derek pulled her into a rare empty room in their house. "Mom and Frank's mom are coming to Olivia's house at 6:30 tonight and bringing dinner. They want to talk."

Annie laughed. "You're so weak. What can she do? Maybe she could stop cooking for us, which would be bad. Otherwise, let's listen."

The moms arrived at Olivia's house on time, to the minute. Frank and Derek arrived earlier to set the table, prepare the coffee, and tidy up the house. Olivia and Annie gave the kitchen another go-over before the women showed up. Annie brought flowers as a centerpiece for the dining room table. Derek and Frank moved the table over by the window so they could watch the shifting colors of the sunset.

"Girls, boys, it is great to see you for a change," said Frank's mother as she took a seat at the table.

The first card was played, noted Olivia. The " kids" remained silent, wondering how this would play out. Finally, the food was served, Frank said grace, and they dug in. A light conversation began. Both moms went down the list of people in their families and what they were up to at their houses. Frank talked about his job, where he worked with Uncle Robert a few hours a week. Annie described helping with the kids, practicing her culinary skills, and trying out new recipes on her family. Derek was successful as a house sitter and had expanded to a few home restoration projects, which paid very well. Olivia spent the summer jumping from house to house, helping her friends wherever she could. A formal summer job never materialized for her, and she was fine with that.

Finally, when the food was gone, the table cleared, the coffee put on, and the dessert put in the middle of the table, the "kids" were ready for their parents' conversation.

Derek and Annie's mom spoke first. "I'm glad to see that you had a great summer. Quite eventful, with Derek's successful fight and Frank's grand discovery of a valuable car." She looked around, and everyone was listening. "And what can make the summer any better? How about two young couples in love, fresh out of school, with no adult supervision, and free use of a multi-million-dollar house overlooking the water? Each couple has a bedroom with a balcony and ocean view. How great is that?" The kids were starting to feel something was coming.

"Olivia," Frank's mom asked, "Does your mother know you're all sleeping over here every night?"

Olivia thought that was a bit forward, but when it came to asking tough questions about the lives of their children, moms were privileged in ways others were not. Still, this house belonged to Olivia's family, so her mom set the rules, and in her absence, Olivia was head of the house. "My mom knows my friends and I like to get together for dinner. So, she suggested that I invite them over so we could enjoy ourselves and the house wouldn't remain empty. I think she is afraid I will starve unless I have everyone come over to cook dinner." It was quiet. Nobody moved, waiting to see how this would turn out.

Olivia continued, "More directly to the point, she said that she liked Derek, trusted him, and that she would be fine if Derek stayed with me at my house. She expanded the invitation to include Frank and Annie, provided their parents were supportive."

Olivia looked directly at Frank's mom and then at Derek and Annie's mom. "I think she knows us well and gave me the key to a house that would be empty all summer. I don't see her having a problem with me sharing the house with my closest friends, especially since it was her idea."

Frank's mom didn't shy away. "I'm not quite sure what she expected. But I do know this, Beverly and I feel like the summer is almost gone, and we don't see enough of you. I'm okay with how you spend your evenings, and I assume you are all being safe and the girls use the pill or whatever else is available, and don't just rely on the thin little wrappers that often break and cause young couples like you to start their families earlier than expected." She looked around the table and saw that everyone except Olivia was staring at their plates. Olivia was sitting a little taller with her chin defiantly jutted forward, but she remained quiet.

Frank's mom continued, "Assuming you all are being responsible in that area, my only issue is not seeing more of you. If you are sitting around and are dressed—Frank, I'm talking to you—" They all laughed. "We'd like to get a visit from you, any of you, when you can. Feel free to come by either of our houses for coffee and a chat. Also, you don't always have to show up as a pack. It's nice to have conversations with you, one-on-one, or with two of you, not only with each couple, but two girls or two guys." She looked around. "Your thoughts?"

Derek was the first to speak. "That wasn't as painful as it started. I'm relieved. I speak only for myself, but I usually wear clothes in the late morning. Visiting shouldn't be difficult."

Everyone had a good laugh as the tension broke a little.

"Don't look at me," Frank said. "Only when I'm at home am I a clothing-optional kind of guy." More laughter, along with a look of daggers from Annie.

"I'll ensure everyone finishes this summer by spending more time with our families and using appropriate social graces," Annie said, staring at Frank the entire time.

Frank's mom cut wedges of the dessert with the large knife next to the cheesecake. Annie returned to the kitchen with a tray containing the coffee pot, cups, sugar, and creamer. Olivia filled the cups and passed them around. Derek served the cheesecake to all and then returned to his seat.

After most were finished with their desserts, Derek's mom opened another conversation with the two couples at the table. "There's only a month or so before you all head off to college. Would you care to share your plans?"

Olivia spoke first. "I'm heading off to Cambridge to attend Harvard. My parents were pleased because it's their alma mater. Although I'm a legacy kid, I like to think I was accepted on my own, but it's hard to say. Still, I'm looking forward to it."

"Derek, what about your plans?"

"I received a scholarship to UC Santa Cruz, and I plan to live here on the Point while I attend school full time." He looked awkward as Olivia looked away.

"That sounds like it will be tough on you and Olivia," said Derek's mom. "How're you going to handle it?"

Derek looked like he wanted to be anywhere but there, answering questions from his mom that he could barely discuss with Olivia. Olivia was the first to speak. "I know long-distance relationships are difficult to maintain, but we've been successful for four years, and I think we can succeed going forward. We'll have our lives in college, and when summer comes, I plan to return here from Cambridge and I expect we'll pick up where we left off."

Derek added, "We'll do what we can with summers and

school breaks. I don't have enough money to fly back and forth, and I want Olivia to have a normal life at school without me dropping in on her and making it awkward."

It was quiet around the table as each person weighed out their thoughts on the feasibility of this plan.

Olivia spoke up. "I know it isn't a great plan, but aside from one of us transferring or dropping out of school, it's our best. I love Derek, and he loves me. I think our relationship is strong enough to go the distance. I have faith in us and faith in our love. It isn't the plan that will make us successful. It is our certainty that we can overcome any obstacles that come our way."

Olivia continued. "It's the feeling I get just after waking up next to him and knowing this is right. Knowing that we're meant to be together." She looked at the startled people around the table, realizing that she had given the first proof that they were sleeping together. She continued, "There isn't a road map for us as a couple, just like there isn't a road map for us in life. But being together with the support I get from Derek is one thing I can count on.

"For example, my mom gave us the summer house; she wouldn't have done that if she thought our relationship was wrong or my friends were inappropriate. Having her support is important to me. My dad, too, even though he is quieter and still has trouble thinking that someone is sleeping with his daughter."

They all smiled but cringed a bit too, in acknowledgment of her father's concerns. It felt like too much information, but it was an open and honest conversation.

"We also have the support of Grandmother and Aunt Nora. Derek and I occasionally visit them for lunch." Olivia looked at Frank. "You two also visit them as a couple, right?"

Frank nodded, as did Annie.

"They serve us food and talk, and we listen," Olivia continued. "It is amazing how they know what is troubling us, even before we tell them. They can read between the lines." She stopped to take a sip of coffee. There was a long pause as nobody dared interrupt her.

Finally, Derek joined in. "Nora was a critical part of my support system when I was dealing with Ricky. She also told me how to deal with the other two boys, to give them an 'out' as well as a show of force so they would doubt their ability to succeed against me. I never would have expected that kind of advice from Aunt Nora. As for the rest of our visits, they helped us work through disagreements and concerns."

"They support us, which is important as we face an uncertain future. All the support we get from our families combines to help us avoid problems with our relationship. If we are meant to be together, we will make it and not get tripped up by mistakes."

Annie stepped in. "Which brings us back to your proposal, Mom or Moms. I agree we need to spend more time with each of you. Only through spending more time with you can we hear what you have to say and learn from you. Dads too. Again, there are no promises that our romances will stand the test of time. All we can do is be kind and forgive one another quickly with love. We need to be grateful for the people in our lives and treat them with respect.

"Aunt Nora also said that what we need to do the most is forgive each other when we make mistakes or hurt each other by saying careless or cruel things. If we don't forgive one another, our problems will stay with us and poison all our relationships," Annie said.

Frank's mom said, "It sounds like you're learning a few things from Grandmother and Aunt Nora."

It was quiet at the table. A great deal was shared, and it wasn't clear where to go next.

Frank's mom spoke up. "There're some people we should acknowledge who aren't at the table. I believe Derek likes to call them the Little Ones, although they haven't been little for quite some time. For example, a pair of twin girls at my house would love to get to know Annie and Olivia. Nothing is more enchanting to young girls than getting attention from beautiful young women. They don't take much time, but they'd love to have dinner with you or have you help them dress up or style their hair."

"We have three younger kids at my home who would also like to be included in the rest of the summer's festivities," Annie and Derek's mom added.

Olivia joined in, "I could invite all the kids here and let them sit on the balcony overlooking the boardwalk. We could bring food from our house and set up a lunch and make them feel like we are one big family."

Everyone thought about that for a while. It felt as if the love of the four of them stretched out to include all the families.

Frank's mom made a little ringing sound with her coffee cup and spoon. "We haven't heard from Annie and Frank about their college plans. So far, they've been very circumspect about their future."

Frank leaned over to Derek, saying, "It means cautious and careful. You know, like me." Derek shook his head in wonder at his dopy friend, but he was glad to know what the word meant.

Annie answered, "We've both been accepted to Cal Poly, San Louis Obispo. We picked out a dorm. We have separate rooms and roommates, but we can work with that. I've saved money for college my whole life and although the money will be tight, it's doable. It's a good state school not too far from here. I don't know how often I'll return to Santa Cruz during the school year, but I certainly will for family events."

Frank reached over to hold Annie's hand. "We're excited to share the same school. It's a little pricey for both of us, but I'm feeling much better knowing the car is coming along.

"I've been working with Olivia's father to set up a purchase and sales contract with one of Monterey's prominent restoration firms. The car is worth more than we originally thought. By the way, Derek, Olivia's father is a pretty good guy. He comes across as gruff, but I like him. Then again, I'm not sleeping with his daughter." Once again, everyone cringed. Derek reached across the table and punched him in the shoulder.

"They expect the car to be finished later this year," Frank continued, "and the sale is scheduled for early next year. I know that might be too much information, but I'm leading up to my point: Olivia's dad helped me set up trusts for Annie and me and loaned us enough to cover school costs until the car is sold. At this time, each trust will cover four years of tuition. The money is only for school-related costs, including room and board. One for Annie and one for me. Her trust is hers alone, no matter what happens between us. If we make it the whole way and get married, she'll have the rest of my money anyway, and in return I'll get her love forever."

Frank looked around, somewhat embarrassed to share so much with everyone at the table. "I think it is a good deal," he said to Annie. Looking at her, he asked, "What do you think, Annie?"

She burst into tears, stood up, and knocked over her chair. "How? What? Mom? What is he talking about?"

"I think he was pretty clear about the trust, but I want to hear it again: What if she breaks up with you?"

"If we break up for any reason, she keeps the money for her four years of school expenses, and I become a miserable shell of a man. Nothing is tied to us getting married."

"I think you have a keeper," Annie's mom said.

Annie leaped up and threw her arms around Frank. She felt like she would never let go.

"All of this from a pile of fenders in your garage," Derek said.

Afterward, the conversation grew lighter until the moms needed to return home to attend to the Little Ones.

●　●　●

Fall semester started in August or September, depending on the school. During the final days of August, Olivia and Derek spent an entire week at her parents' house, sharing meals from Annie. It was a week they'd never forget. The summer allowed their love to turn up the heat, and she would remember this love for the rest of her life.

Knowing they would be parting ways soon, Derek and Olivia had trouble remaining upbeat. Sometimes, Derek held Olivia while she cried, fearing being apart for the coming year would break their relationship apart.

As the end of their last week loomed, Olivia started talking about marriage, even if only in secret with Derek. He would repeatedly shake his head and tell her this was love for the ages. Their marriage deserved to be celebrated publicly, with her in a white dress, he in a black tuxedo, and a large church filled with all their families and friends.

"We're going to make it," he told her. "There are still some bumps ahead, I'm sure, but don't be afraid. We have our love for each other and the love of our parents, Aunt Nora, and Grandmother."

"On top of all that," Derek told her, as he wiped the tears from her eyes, one at a time, "We are no longer kids. Our love is real, and many family members and friends support it. We are not alone."

Olivia took comfort in his words. She knew this was a man to hold on to and never let go.

Olivia was the first to leave Santa Cruz for college. She was flying from San Jose to Boston, arriving a week before classes started for orientation. Derek offered to drive, but her father had already ordered a black car service to take her to the airport. Both Olivia and Derek knew it was a generous gesture, mainly because Derek was never confident his car would make it over the coastal mountain summit.

When the limousine pulled up in front of her house, the driver stepped out and expertly packed her bags into the spacious trunk. After loading the car, Derek asked the driver to pull the car around to his house so his family could say goodbye. Both Olivia and Derek climbed into the back of the luxurious limousine. They were inspecting the limo's creature comforts when they arrived in front of Derek's house.

He stepped out first and held his hand out for Olivia. Standing on the sidewalk, they looked around to see who joined them. Olivia couldn't believe what she was seeing. Derek's family was in front of their house, with Annie and the Little Ones leaning out of the windows. Frank's family was there, along with Aunt Nora and Grandmother. Olivia made a beeline for the two older women and hugged them together. "Thank you so much for your love and guidance. I'll never forget you both for as long as I live."

"Try to come by to see us whenever you are home," said Aunt Nora.

Olivia gave up on holding back her tears. There were so many people she loved there seeing her off. Finally, she turned back to Derek's mother. "You," she said, "I will miss the most. I promise to be right back!" She had become very close with Derek's mother over the past four years in Santa Cruz. Their hug would never have ended if Derek had not tapped her shoulder.

Derek took her hand. "There's someone else you need to say goodbye to." He pointed to the front door of his house, and there stood a short, teary-eyed woman. There she was, Olivia's biggest supporter, starting from the day she was born. She couldn't believe her mom had come to Santa Cruz to see her off. "Mom, what are you doing here?"

"I wanted to help you unpack and maybe walk around the campus with you. This is an experience we can remember for the rest of our lives."

Olivia fell into her arms. "I love you so much, Mom. I'm going to miss you."

Her mother replied. "It is only a short flight to Boston from San Francisco or San Jose—sort of." A small ripple of laughter rolled through the crowd. They all understood Boston was about as far from Santa Cruz as anywhere in the U.S. "I thought you could use some help setting up your dorm room, so if you don't mind, I'd like to accompany you to Boston and help you settle in?" Olivia gave her another big hug and stepped back to allow her access to the limo's door. Olivia was bursting with love from her friends and family. Frank, Annie, Aunt Nora, Grandmother, Derek's parents, and even Frank's parents were all there wishing her a safe journey. There was only one more person to hug.

She turned around and there was Derek. The man who knew from the beginning that she was the one for him. The one who she had picked to share the rest of her life. They only needed to stay the course, and everything would be fine. Olivia was still scared that the long distance would break their love, but her fears were receding, replaced by a new confidence that she and Derek were meant to be, that love would triumph, and that there was no need for fear.

She turned back to Derek and took each of his hands. "Just like old times," she said.

"Who knew holding hands could be so personal and so romantic." He said and smiled. Although they had moved far beyond holding hands, there was an innocent truth in his assertion. They laughed as he kissed each of her hands.

"I love you, Olivia."

"I love you too, Derek."

After one last survey of her friends and family, Olivia followed her mother into the town car, and they were off.

Over the next few days, Frank and Annie loaded their belongings into the Surf Wagon to drive to San Louis Obispo. They were setting up their dorm room suite they selected with another couple. It was built for four students, like the dorm Olivia had at Harvard. The difference was that this one had California comforts like an outdoor swimming pool, recreation rooms, and bike trails, and, as Frank pointed out many times, great surfing.

From San Louis Obispo, it was just under a four-hour drive to visit Annie's family in Livermore and two and a half hours to visit Frank's family in Aptos. Either way, they expected to spend most of their time on campus. Cal Poly was known for its rigorous academic program, but Frank and Olivia were good students and did some advanced homework, just to be prepared.

Derek did not need much preparation to start his freshman year at the University of California, Santa Cruz, or UCSC for short. What was supposed to be a side business quickly turned into a full-time job. He had a considerable workload juggling his existing clients for his vacation property management company. Each new client he landed not only required property management functions but an increasing list of special services, such as maintaining hot tubs, managing irrigation systems, and caulking and sealing windows when needed. With Olivia at school, he spent long evenings formalizing his responsibilities, including creating an inspection schedule and a list of necessary items to monitor each property.

The biggest challenge was setting up his bookkeeping for his business. Luckily, Aunt Kate was a business major in college and up to speed with the latest bookkeeping methods. Sensing a need for a more sophisticated way to manage the portfolio's finances, she was learning a popular property management software program.

At first, she gave Derek lessons and advice on basic accounting, accounts receivables, and bookkeeping. But increasingly, they realized that he was better off with her as a partner. Their skills complemented each other, and the time Derek would have needed to figure out a bookkeeping system could now be spent visiting real estate brokers and property owners to expand the business. In addition, Derek was busy with classes, homework, and managing the existing portfolio.

Unfortunately, he still wasn't busy enough to ease the ache in his heart whenever he thought of Olivia.

Eleven

After an agonizing month anticipating Olivia's return from her first year at Harvard, Derek counted the hours until their annual Castle Beach meeting on Father's Day. Unable to wait until the agreed-upon one o'clock time, he arrived over an hour early and stretched out his towel under two aluminum-framed chairs. The day was warming up, and the clouds were giving up coverage without much of a fight. The air was chilly, but it was still possible they might go in the water if the sun was hot enough to warm their skin after a frigid dunk in the waves.

Derek waited alone on the beach. Frank and Annie said they would join him after running a few errands in the afternoon. Derek was buzzing with anticipation. Meeting Olivia was exciting and terrifying at the same time. It was certainly his most anticipated day of the year.

Making it even harder for Derek to wait was his knowledge that Olivia had returned to Portola Valley over a week ago. She wanted to head straight to Santa Cruz, but her father had scheduled the cleaning service to prepare their house on the Saturday before Father's Day. Olivia chose not to argue with her father. She would still arrive in Santa Cruz on Father's Day. and spent her days in Portola Valley with her friends, sitting by their country club's pool. She enjoyed catching up with her friends and loved hearing about their horses.

Annie talked with Olivia almost daily on the phone. Derek never understood why Olivia spoke so much with Annie while he and Olivia spoke only once a week. Last year, they agreed that infrequent calls were fine, but they continued writing as well. One thing he liked about this strange, old-fashioned arrangement was that his box of cards and letters filled up over the years. He understood that it served a purpose when they were all in high school, to learn to express themselves and allowed him to see how their relationship grew. It gave him a sense of timeliness, as their relationship matured through the year.

This summer, when Olivia showed up he hoped to grab her by the hand and race up to her parents' house which they now kept for Olivia's use in summer. He saw her stepping onto the beach while holding both shoes in her hand. She carried nothing else. Was she only planning for a short visit? She approached Derek slowly. Each step was hesitant. They shared dozens of calls and many letters, but their calls were a bit stilted since their college experiences were so different—an Ivy versus a surf school, he thought. He quickly corrected his thoughts, UCSC was a great university, no doubt, but it was not Ivy League caliber.

It was reasonable to think that things remained good between them, he speculated. Nevertheless, watching her slow approach gave him a bad feeling in the pit of his stomach. If she were to break up with him, now was the time.

Derek could sense she was apprehensive about meeting him because her eyes only looked down at the sand as she approached. He put down his soda and ran toward her. She was startled by his sudden movement, but before she could turn away, he reached her and pulled her into a hug, spinning them both around. "Olivia," he implored. "Don't be afraid. We're both here." He stroked her hair back from her face.

Derek waited for her reply. Her face still reflected her startled response to his eager hug, but it quickly changed to a broad smile. "We've met at Castle Beach another year. I am so happy you're here," he said, pulling her close and initiating a long kiss. He continued, "I just need to hear it from you, too, as I'm scared you may not feel the same way." He looked at her and waited for her response.

It was her turn to talk. She hesitated, and then, looking straight into his eyes, she gave him a big smile as tears filled her eyes. "Derek, I'm here, and I'm so happy! I love you too and look forward to another summer with you. I was so scared you would have moved on."

She stepped back, and Derek took the zipper on her sweatshirt and inched it downward. As he progressed, he could see an off-yellow and pink one-piece swimsuit underneath her sweatshirt, with a Hawaiian motif of a sunset and palm trees. It was skintight fabric and hugged every curve. The top of her suit was scoop necked exposing a generous area of her breasts. He would need to make sure no other guys ever got the same vantage point.

Derek was spellbound. She was breathtaking.

"You're killing me with these new swimsuits each year." Derek was trying hard not to stare but failing miserably. "Babe, you are so beautiful that it scares me."

Derek was frozen as he began remembering their love life from the previous year. He could see the arch of her breasts seemingly fuller than last year. As he reached out with both hands, Olivia grabbed his wrists and held them. "There are laws about what we can do on a State Beach. I'd hate to have an unsuspecting mom and her young children see us if we were to lose our inhibitions."

Derek smiled. His willpower to behave was running at an all-time low. Her face was framed with wisps of dark hair while the rest was pinned into place on top of her head. He could see the subtle changes that occurred over the past year. The rounded curves of her jawline were replaced with a sharper edge, her eyes were shaded with dark makeup, but her cheekbones remained unchanged over time. She was stunning from every angle. He had to look away. He could barely believe that he deserved love from such a beautiful woman. Derek reached out to her and touched her cheek with his hand. She leaned into him.

"We can stay here and enjoy the cold air. I hope it'll warm up enough to swim," she said, slipping one of his hands under her sweatshirt, moving it in a slow circle across her breasts, and then removing it. "Or we can continue exploring the changes that occurred during the past year. But if we do that, we'll be better off moving indoors," she teased.

Derek raised his eyebrow, indicating that she should continue.

"My parents are in Europe this summer and I have the beach house, or Shack, all to myself—and you," she said casually.

Derek could not gather up his towel quickly enough. He shoved it into his beach bag. He would leave the chairs for Frank and Annie to pick up. Olivia zipped up her sweatshirt and started running back to her house. When they got to her bedroom, he quickly removed her sweats and then her swimsuit, continuing to explore her new figure. Throughout the afternoon, they cried and laughed as they realized they had passed another year and were still together as strong as ever. Olivia kept pulling back from his embrace to look at him to ensure he was really there. She could not keep her eyes off him. In return, he couldn't keep his hands off her.

Derek was awakened from an afternoon slumber by the ringing of Olivia's phone. Disoriented, he picked it up while trying to establish where he was. "Hello?"

"Dude, get dressed and come open the front door. Annie and I are here. We have lasagna and beer." Somehow Frank always knew precisely where they were.

Derek surveyed the room and then saw Olivia lying next to him under the sheets. Their clothes were scattered around the bed, and she started to stir.

A few minutes later, Annie joined Frank. "Derek! Derek! I know you're in Olivia's house. Come and open the door. The food is getting cold," Annie yelled as she pounded on the front door.

Derek tapped Olivia on the shoulder. "Frank and Annie are here. Shall I let them in, or do we have better things to do?"

"Let them in," Olivia answered through the haze of sleep. "I need food before we can pick up where we left off."

Derek kissed her lightly and then ran his hand under the sheets to confirm that she was indeed naked, just as he was. Frank guessed correctly again.

"We'll be down in a minute. Let yourselves in. The front door's unlocked, and nobody else is in the house," Derek called out.

After quickly dressing, Olivia and Derek met Frank and Annie in the dining room. It was great to see everyone. They all had grown taller and filled out. They were high school kids who went off to college and returned as adult college students.

Frank carried the food into the kitchen while Derek and Olivia set the table.

All at once, each started stories from their freshman year in college. Annie kept a running commentary on her experiences with Frank in San Louis Obispo while re setting the table to meet some artistic standard only she knew. In the end, the table was a work of art, both in content and presentation.

There was so much love and happiness in the house, that at any given time, at least two people had silent tears streaming down their faces. Frank was constantly picking up Annie and spinning her around. Olivia easily substituted for Annie if Annie wasn't close enough to keep his theatrics in motion. Once food was on the table and the participants seated, Derek gave thanks for the blessings they had received this past year and then offered a toast. "To the five summers we have shared. May there be many more."

One by one, they continued to share stories of their year as well as plans for the current summer. Olivia found a technology company in Scotts Valley that needed her help. "It's less than ten miles away, and they promise not to work the interns through twelve -hour days. So, I plan to work hard but be home for dinner."

Annie had started working in a bakery, hoping to open her own store one day. "I'll bring home samples from the bakery, so I expect you to keep up your exercise regimens. Otherwise, I'll give the goodies to the Steamer's Lane crowd."

Frank was next to comment on his future. "The auto shop finally finished all the prep work on the Mustang and removed the rust. However, they held off doing the welding and engine repairs until I arrived. They said they will take me on as an assistant mechanic. I've been in touch with Uncle Robert and with their head mechanic and I like this kind of work. Restoring cars is much more challenging than working in a gas station, replacing mufflers, and doing brake jobs. I could see doing this long-term, as long as Annie's bakery keeps me fed."

Derek was last. "I have been adding property owners to my list of clients. These houses operate as vacation homes for the families that own them and vacation rentals during the off-season. I brought on Aunt Kate to do the books, but she has a knack for this and wants to expand the business. She's starting a marketing program with the local realtors. I want to keep it small and manageable until we have all the systems in place so the business will run smoothly.

"Together, we plan to assemble crews to clean and maintain the rentals instead of hiring that out. We're also planning to buy houses for use as vacation rentals. This is an excellent little niche market overlooked by the more prominent real estate firms. I aim to balance work between spending time with Olivia, surfing, and spending time with Olivia." He laughed.

Derek looked around at blank faces. "Yes, just like that," he answered the unspoken question. "I'm going to start my day with Olivia and end it with her." He winked at the group.

There were so many things each couple wanted to do that it would take all summer to list them. Frank reported that Grandmother and Aunt Nora were in good health and were expecting them as visitors. Annie reminded everyone that the Little Ones expected to be included in the big-kid activities, since they actually were big kids now.

As they discussed their plans, Annie tapped her water glass with her spoon and called for attention.

"I want to invite a new pair of guests to our private, couples club. These people are only a few years older than we are and have been an integral part of our lives this past year. Let's include them in all our future events. Most importantly, she's just arrived at the door and brought a strawberry cheesecake. If there are no objections, I'd like to invite Aunt Kate and her boyfriend Douglas to join our group."

Everyone clapped and cheered. After the past two years together, she was well known and was well-liked by the gang. Annie opened the door and ushered them in.

Aunt Kate was startled when the door opened. The cheesecake teetered but did not fall. "Hello!" Aunt Kate tried to shake hands but instead nodded to avoid a major disaster with the dessert. "Thanks for inviting us. I know it was an easy decision once you heard about the cheesecake. I have only one request: Would it be okay if you just called me Kate? I'm not that much older than you. I just happen to have a lot of nieces and nephews."

They all laughed and invited Kate and Doug into the house. Frank looked at Derek and they smiled. The name " Aunt Kate" was here to stay. Nicknames were very hard to change, and she played the role of their aunt very well. The celebration continued. They discussed visiting parents and the not-so Little Ones at Derek's and Frank's houses, plus the extended family all around Santa Cruz.

It was a summer they would never forget. Frank grabbed a couple of beers and motioned for Derek to join him on the porch overlooking the Boardwalk. Each couple enjoyed the calm, settled feeling that comes with a long history of spending time with a loved one. In addition, they expanded their commitment to their families, making sure to stick to their promises to visit their parents and siblings.

With a dramatic flourish, Annie produced three large wall calendars. "We're hanging our official calendar on the kitchen wall in each of the three houses. The master calendar will be kept in Derek's and my house. Olivia and Frank need to keep an exact duplicate at Frank's parents' house, and Olivia needs to keep one at her house, along with all our phone numbers. We're all so busy this summer that I want us to coordinate events so we're sure to hang out as a group, not just as separate couples. This also assures that we schedule quality time with our families."

*   *   *

One of the first scheduled visits was to the grand dames of Seabright: Grandmother and Aunt Nora. The senior women finally relented to allow the young couples to host dinner in their honor at Olivia's house. After years of feeding Frank and his bottomless stomach, it was their turn to be taken care of. Annie and Olivia prepared the meal with help from their parents.

The happiest hostesses were Frank's little sisters, Sophia and Julia, who were delighted to be included in the big girls' activities. Frank reported his sisters were bouncing off the walls with excitement.

The not-so-Little Ones at Derek's house were anticipating leading age-appropriate activities with Frank's younger siblings. Frank's older sisters were frequent dinner guests at Olivia's while most full family dinners were held at Annie and Derek's house, utilizing their massive kitchen and multiple appliances.

Olivia liked to have some structure to her vacations, so she and Derek decided to become Santa Cruz tourists. She planned the local itinerary and invited everyone on their list, including Grandmother and Aunt Nora, both sets of parents, and Frank's family. They planned a group excursion.

Frank and Annie loaded up the Woody which Robert had lent to him during the Mustang restoration. Joining them were Frank's two little sisters, and Derek and Annie's three Little Ones—now teenagers—and Derek and Olivia. The older women were thankful to be invited, but politely declined when they heard there may be long walks involved. Their parents also politely declined, eager to enjoy a quiet afternoon without their kids' typical chaos.

Squeezing everyone into the car was a little tricky, but there was a seat for every adult and a lap for every child.

Olivia pre-ordered tickets to save time. Everyone born in or driving through Santa Cruz saw billboards for the Mystery Spot. It was a tourist legend, but it was not a place locals frequented so no one in the group was quite sure what to expect. The kids provided considerable speculation about what they were going to see. Derek, Olivia, Annie, and Frank spent the drive deflecting crazy notions raised by Derek's three younger siblings, such as: "You all better hold hands, otherwise you could get sucked into the cosmos! Monsters sometimes crawl out of the building and hide in your lunch boxes. Aliens might live there. We'll need to check everything before we get back in the car!"

The directions consisted of a series of billboards that showed a large black spot on a bright yellow background pointing up the hill at every intersection. They left the main highway and joined a semi-paved road that continued to climb up and into a thick redwood forest. The higher they went, the tighter the redwood groves became, until it became rare to see the blue sky. Along the roadside, dense brush and poison oak obscured any visibility into the forest around them.

Finally, they reached a widening of the road and saw cars already parked, filling the lot. Derek was concerned that with the lot so full, he wouldn't be able to park the car; however, at a space close to the Mystery Spot's main office was a reserved parking sign that read: "Only Derek and Olivia's guests may park here." The spot was long enough for the Woody, so Derek pulled right in. When the car stopped, the kids poured out into the parking lot while Olivia went to the front gate, picked up their tickets, and waited for their group to be ushered to a small shack like building which tilted at several unusual angles. Because nobody in their group had ever visited before, it was all a new experience, and everyone, regardless of their age, had fun marveling at the tour guide's claims and the optical illusions.

"Derek and Olivia?" called a woman in a brown park ranger outfit with "Mystery Spot" embroidered on her front pocket and a large black spot printed on her back. "Follow me." They counted the kids and walked up a narrow path to a board full of historical photos.

"The Mystery Spot goes back over a hundred years, to the day a group of loggers tried to build a shed to live in. Whenever they got a wall erected, it would lean to the side. They tried and tried to build the shed, but everything kept leaning or falling over."

Their guide took them down a series of walkways, each with old photos of loggers or visitors demonstrating how the strange gravitational pull of the land caused each building to lean one way or another. Finally, they reached the main building of the logging camp where the kids were included in demonstrations and optical illusions. With each display of "the unexplainable," as their guide was fond of saying, the younger kids ooh-ed and ahh-ed, and the older kids tried to remain cool, shouting out their explanations of the weird demonstrations. Derek solved the mystery after staring at the building for ten minutes, but he did not want to be the one to break the Mystery Spot's charm in front of the children.

When the tour was complete, Olivia commented to the

adults, "the adventure was half unexplainable illusions, and half tourist trap tacky adventures." She sounded confident in her explanations but had grabbed Derek's arm a little tighter at each 'unexplainable phenomenon.'

They finished the tour and headed back to the car. "I'm not afraid," said Frank to the kids who were listening with rapt attention. "I know how they did it. It is totally explainable." He looked around inside his Woody and saw it was stuffed with kids, listening to every word he said. After leaning forward for a slight suspenseful build up, he shouted, "Aliens!" The kids screamed and jumped up, shouting "Aliens in Santa Cruz!"

Some of the younger kids were frightened and started to sniffle. They were too old to cry, yet too scared not to cry.

Olivia unclicked her seatbelt and worked her way to the back of the Woody to reach the frightened children. Taking two to her lap and hugging another, she tried to lighten the mood, while scowling at Frank for his thoughtlessness. Once she got the kids' full attention, Olivia took command. "Listen up, everyone. These are not bad aliens! They've been living here for hundreds of years and never hurt anyone." All of the kids gave her their full attention. "Use your mind to imagine what they look like."

She struggled for a moment, knowing what to do but not how to do it. A memory came to her of her father making up bedtime stories for her, a long time ago. He had many tricks to keep her from becoming afraid when he told bedtime stories. She decided to use a few of his favorite tricks. "Now, think of them, aliens hiding in lunch boxes, peeking out from under the lids, and wandering around the Mystery Spot. But whenever they left their house, all of them were wearing..." she paused to ensure she had everyone's attention. "They were wearing bright-red party hats!" The children started giggling. "Now think of them at home with their puppy dogs," she whispered. "Did you know aliens love puppy dogs? Can you see the puppies licking their alien faces? Such silly aliens!" The kids all laughed at this one, and the tension was broken. Annie clapped her hand on Frank's leg and squeezed hard. "You owe Olivia for saving the day."

For once, Frank had nothing to say.

Frank started the car and Derek exclaimed, "Wasn't that a great adventure? Now check your lunch boxes for aliens and let's go. Next stop is Marianne's Ice Cream and ice cream for all."

By the time they got the kids full of ice cream and on their way to their respective homes, it was midafternoon. They were all sleepy, and all appetites for dinner were ruined, but the kids had a ball, and the couples had a fun time leading the group, while the parents at home enjoyed a quiet afternoon with the kids gone. Everyone enjoyed the day.

Twelve

Derek started the school year with the optimism of a sophomore. All problems could be worked out, reasoned Derek. No issue was too big to tackle, nothing but blue skies ahead. The only small difficulty was selecting times to schedule their calls since Olivia's schedule was packed with events.

There seemed to always be one function or another that demanded her time. Derek tried setting a schedule for weekend calls, but that somehow had a way of demonstrating—at least in his view—that he had a pathetic social life compared to Olivia. She repeatedly pointed out that very few of the girls that stopped by were close friends. Mostly they were acquaintances who were trying to drum up support for a night on the town; success was measured by the size of their crowd.

Derek had a group of four to five friends that he could count on to call him on Thursdays to make plans for the weekend. He never socialized in large groups.

Eventually, Derek was successful picking a midweek evening for their conversations when there were no interruptions from evening activities. Olivia studied alone, but even these solo study times were rescheduled for group study sessions when exams approached. Exams came and went with their second year of college. Derek and Olivia survived the school year, both earning good grades.

When Father's Day came, Derek eagerly awaited Olivia's return. He stood on their spot at Castle Beach, reminiscing about past summers since they first met. Father's Day was their agreed upon first day of summer, the day they met each year—so far. Would today be any different?

He hoped she would continue to come as he always expected she would. Santa Cruz was still their home, their grounding point. This location at the Cove on Castle Beach became their home base and the start of each summer. Meeting each other on Father's Day was just another annual challenge they met and overcame. Like the obstacles of time and distance, their love triumphed in all previous years.

Assuming she returned today, this would start their sixth summer together. Six years was a long time, he noted, especially since they were now just in their early twenties. But Derek thought it felt like a blink of an eye in the broader scheme of a lifetime. Each year came and went, disappearing in the past, leaving behind scrapbooks and boxes full of dog-eared letters and postcards, preparing them for another annual test. Each year, he asked himself the same questions: Would she show up or did she find someone new? Would this be the year one of them lost interest and walked away? In spite of Derek's sense of foreboding every Father's Day, each summer had gone well—so far. They survived each new challenge to their relationship and grew stronger through them.

Derek cleared his thoughts as he watched someone in a gray sweatsuit approach him on the beach. As the figure got closer, she pulled down her hood, displaying a young woman with shoulder length blonde hair. It was Annie.

When she reached him, she called out, "Derek? I tried to catch you before you made it to the Cove. Olivia called. She wants you to call her back." Derek looked at her dumbfounded.

He needed to return to the house to call her. Derek left everything on the beach while he and Annie walked up to their house.

When he reached the house, he phoned Oliva "It's nice to hear from you," Derek said. He was confused by the call. Shouldn't she be here on the beach?

"It's summer up here. But there are still a lot of flowers left over from spring." Olivia's voice sounded tight and strained.

"Down here, we have four seasons: cold, colder, hot, and hotter." Derek laughed at the old joke, adding, "But that's not quite true. It's summer right now and the weather is perfect."

He waited; however, it was evident she needed help, judging by the long period of awkward silence after he spoke.

"Olivia, why are you calling me? Are you still in Boston? The last time we spoke, you had a flight scheduled to bring you back to Santa Cruz today."

She turned the phone away for a moment, blew her nose, then returned to the call.

"That's what I wanted to talk with you about. My plans have changed."

Derek had a sinking feeling in his gut.

"I took a job in Boston for the summer. It starts next week and ends the week before school starts."

"What happened?"

"I couldn't find any decent jobs in Santa Cruz or San Jose that would bring me home. Some were okay but..." she trailed off.

"You are a top student from Harvard, looking for a job in one of the largest technology markets in the country. You had a couple of interesting offers. What was wrong with those?"

"My father has a friend who owns a tech company in Boston, and he got me a better job at their headquarters. I couldn't turn it down."

"Better for whom? I thought you were happy with one of them and I was happy that I would see you this summer." He waited. "What are we doing now? Nothing until next year?" Derek was crushed.

"This is why I called. I was thinking." She was fumbling with the phone, but she continued, "Given this new development, I wanted to get back to you about travel this year. I'm planning to come out at Christmas. Thanksgiving vacation is too short, and the traffic at the airport will be madness. If I come at Christmas, I could come out for at least three weeks. Does that work for you?"

"Any time works for me." Derek was numb.

"Okay. In the next week or so, I'll send you my itinerary. We can do this. It'll be great to see you then." Their conversation on the phone was awkward and disjointed but at least they had a plan.

"Will your parents allow you to spend time down here in Santa Cruz at the Shack?" Derek asked.

There was a pause. "That would be best. I'm sure I can get a week or two alone with you at my parents' beach house. But there is one thing I need to tell you. We'll need to limit any visit to Portola Valley for dinner at a restaurant instead of my home. Ricky is staying at my parents' house. He can't travel until he fully recovers. I don't think you should see him."

"Our fight was over a year ago, I'm sure he's healed up by now!"

There was another, longer pause. "Just so you know, they're not sure if he will ever fully recover. After his fight with you, he went back to the Bay Area and got in another fight. He took another blow to his head—this one was severe. Now, he's confused about where he is and who he is talking to."

The phone slipped again and fell onto the desk, and Olivia picked it up and held it. "Ricky doesn't even remember you."

Derek paused, trying to formulate what to say. "Does your dad blame me for Ricky's problems?" It was the most important question that Derek needed her to answer. He held his breath.

"Honestly, I don't know. He's buried himself so deep in his work that we rarely talk." Olivia added, "My mom doesn't blame you. Her opinion of you is very high. I'm able to talk with her, and she is very honest with herself about what happened to Ricky. She accepts that you acted in self-defense. My dad won't talk to me about it."

"And you," he asked. "Do you blame me?"

There was no hesitation in Olivia's response. "No. If you hadn't won the fight, he would have killed you. I thank God every day that you survived."

"So, instead of this summer, you're offering two or three weeks in Santa Cruz at Christmas," Derek commented, with no emotion in his voice. "It sounds like a plan." He was completely discouraged. He lost this summer with Olivia and only gained a few weeks with her at Christmas, hopefully alone with her at the Shack. But now, with plans becoming so fluid, he was not sure what plans he could actually count on.

"Should I come up to see you before then?" Derek was having trouble understanding the plans for this summer. Olivia didn't have a reply.

Finally, they moved on to other topics. After a couple of false starts on picking a travel plan for the summer, they talked a bit longer and then hung up. Derek felt like it was a total failure. He assumed she would come to Santa Cruz over Christmas, but he hadn't expected to lose her for the full summer.

He said goodbye to Olivia and went out to the garage to digest what had just happened. It was the best he could do. There were so many forces pulling at them that it was unrealistic to expect either of them to put their lives on hold to spend all their time together.

• • •

When her sophomore year was completed, Olivia spent a wonderful summer in Boston. The president of her company introduced her to all the top staff and put her on a rotational internship program to learn the roles available for new interns. Her evenings were full of staff dinners in some of Boston's finest restaurants followed by walking tours of the downtown bars. Most nights she didn't get home until midnight, or later.

Every night she talked with her new friends about the lifestyle in Boston compared with the one in Santa Cruz. "Between Boston and Santa Cruz, Boston always comes out ahead," they told her. More than one young woman advised it was not a good strategy to limit your future to accommodate a high school boyfriend who was studying at a public school in Santa Cruz, "wherever that might be," they usually added.

She said she would consider the wisdom of their words, while inwardly cringing at their disparaging remarks about UCSC. She tried not to judge their advice as elitist or narrow-minded, but she did notice that most of the girls were single and no longer involved with long-term boyfriends.

Thirteen

When summer ended, her boss took her to lunch along with the human resource director and told her how much they enjoyed having her on their team. "I know you're only a rising junior, but we'll hold an opening for you when you graduate. I assume you'll still be around next year, and if so, you are welcome to come back and work for me after graduation," he said. "I also assume we will still be around then too," he said, and his laughter filled the restaurant. He was a Harvard alum and prominent player in the mergers and acquisition market. He could laugh as loudly as he wanted. They toasted to the future. It was a better job than she had ever imagined she would get. They even offered a downtown parking space for her, should she wish to live in the suburbs and commute.

The only downside was that she felt she could not share her enthusiasm for this company with Derek. If she took the job, her romance with him would be over. He wouldn't move to Boston. It wasn't his style. He would miss his family too much. These thoughts gnawed at her stomach.

In the end, she did not have to make any hard decisions or explain anything to Derek. During her junior year she received a phone call from her dad. "Honey," he said in the voice he saved for talking with his family. "I'm afraid I have some bad news."

Olivia's mind raced through all the possible bad news she could imagine. "That's a terrible lead, Dad. I'm freaking out. What happened?"

"The company you worked for last year was just acquired by a giant company from Austin, Texas. Your boss said you are still welcome to work with him if you can survive the summers there."

It was an easy decision for Olivia. She thanked her dad for the heads-up and sent her boss a letter, thanked him for the opportunity, and wished him the best of luck as head of this new venture.

She had never been to Texas but from what she knew—which is what everyone knew—Texas has very long, hot summers. Austin would not be a good fit for her.

"Thank you for the opportunity to work for your firm. After careful consideration and in-depth research, I am afraid I must decline your offer as it would not be a good fit for me or the company."

She told her roommate about the change in her job offer. Her response was more direct than Olivia's. Her roommate took a moment to compose her thoughts. "Longhorn cattle would rise up from the dust of extinct civilizations and rule the world before I ever consider moving to Texas." She was an English lit major.

After dodging that bullet to her relationship with Derek, Olivia was glad she had not shared with him the details of the job offer, just that it would require moving to Austin, Texas. His response was similar, she discovered during one of their phone conversations. They discussed places to live, should job opportunities arise. Living in Texas, Derek mentioned in no uncertain terms, was a non-starter and she agreed.

She continued her weekly talks with Derek. They were comfortable having both long and short conversations. Most of the time the phone just helped them keep in contact, avoiding fears that one of them was falling out of love.

• • •

Derek bought a round-trip ticket to Boston to visit Olivia over Columbus Day, a holiday famous for high school relationships to reach their breaking point and crumble. For Derek and Olivia, it was the opposite. Her roommate was invited to stay at a friend's estate in Kennebunkport, Maine and would not return to their dorm room until Monday evening, leaving a place for him to stay. It was a grueling flight for Derek with lingering jet lag that lasted as long as the trip, but his time alone with her made any inconvenience well worth it; the trip was a total success.

They reached Christmas in good spirits. Derek met Olivia's parents for dinner, an evening that was surprisingly low key. Olivia's dad seemed to have exorcised the demons haunting him about Ricky, or he did a good job hiding them. Everything that could be said about Ricky had already been discussed before they got together. Olivia's parents invited Derek to have dinner with them when he dropped Olivia off at the end of the Christmas vacation. He accepted their invitation.

Christmas was a three-week affair. Frank and Annie bounced from house to house visiting Frank's parents and siblings and then off to Annie's parents' house in Livermore, sometimes for a family dinner, with all family members, and other times with only her parents. Most evenings they returned to the Shack to spend the final hours of the evening with Derek and Olivia, and weather permitting, with the windows open and the cool air flowing through their cliffside home. They spent many hours around the kitchen table with Derek and Olivia, sharing bottles of wine and talking about their colleges and their respective campus experiences.

"I'm having the time of my life," Frank declared. "A toast," he said, holding his glass high, "to sometimes having no steak, but always having a good glass of wine. To having nowhere to live but good friends willing to share their home. To having no money but having a woman who appreciates my humor, and finally, to reach that point in life when my parents ask for my advice and give up telling me what to do and how to live. That one I attribute to their faith in Annie's ability to keep me on the straight and narrow path. Cheers!"

Annie gave him a wine flavored kiss. Olivia gave him a kiss too, but without the wine flavor and just on the cheek.

For the first time in his life, Frank had a little money, enough to allow him to breathe. The car restoration shop gave him an advance on the sale of his car—not enough to jeopardize funding his education, but enough to allow him to eat out every now and then. Robert also allowed him to use the Woody until his car was sold. This summer he worked full time for the restoration shop to earn some money and learn some marketable mechanic skills.

Fortunately, most students they knew in San Louis Obispo also had little money, so being tight with the dollar was acceptable among his friends.

Fourteen

Spring semester ended, closing out their third year of college. After her spring semester, Olivia caught the first available flight home to visit Santa Cruz to work things out with Derek. The couple only had two weeks together before she would travel to Paris to start her summer semester abroad. After a surprisingly easy reconciliation, she spent her days cooking and shopping with Derek or wrapped in blankets in front of a warm fire when the windows were shrouded in fog and occasional light showers. It made them feel like they were floating in clouds.

When summer arrived, Derek, Olivia, Frank, and Annie shared the cooking and cleaning, and afterward each couple retreated to their own rooms in the Shack. After dinner, they sat around the polished granite island in the kitchen and told stories of school and new friends, or split off to walk on the beach as a couple. The first two weeks of early summer vacation were quickly over, and Olivia flew off for an eight-week semester abroad program.

Olivia arrived in Paris and checked in with her semester abroad professor to receive her formal work and study package. The semester started in early June and ended in late July, which allowed her time to study during the week and take excursions in western Europe on weekends. With the itinerary she planned, there would be plenty of time remaining in August to spend time in Santa Cruz before she returned to Boston for her senior year at Harvard.

Unfortunately, her father had different plans. Instead of returning to Santa Cruz after the program's completion, her parents surprised her with a five-star extension of her European trip including a rare chance to dine at the finest restaurants and share meals with leaders of Europe's elite international companies.

She met her parents in Paris where they started their adventures which included touring and staying in exclusive private castles and villas owned by Mr. Sutton's clients, which few other tourists had a chance to see. Olivia went to her suite at the George V, where the attendants had already unpacked for her. The room was much larger than her dorm back in Cambridge. She was living the life of the rich and famous.

Her father worked as an attorney at a successful hedge fund on Sand Hill Road in Menlo Park, California, the epicenter of an exclusive group of technology investors who parlayed their initial fortune into extensive wealth for those fortunate enough to participate. It was often said they minted money for their clients.

At Harvard, her most ambitious friends spent all their time trying to gain this type of high-power investor. Her father's personal introduction to the leaders of these firms allowed Olivia the privilege to bypass being just another name in their stack of unsolicited resumes. She enjoyed a European grand tour, stayed in first class hotels, ate at exquisite and often private restaurants. Even though she enjoyed these trappings of success, she was not convinced she wanted this career path.

Her Harvard friends, who successfully obtained jobs in high finance, spent their days and nights grinding through endless piles of merger and acquisition documents with very tight deadlines. Olivia thought it was a high price to pay for fortune and fame, which she was not even sure she wanted. It was the people she met that made her understand the allure of working at the high end of venture capital markets.

For the first time, Olivia was able to see her dad as not just her father but also as Jack Sutton, the successful attorney at the center of nearly all major corporate merger transactions. He had friends all over France, England, and Italy who were dying to show their appreciation for his help which had allowed the success of one or more of their deals. Jack became fluent in French and Italian so he could assist his clients. His clients enjoyed hearing Olivia's opinions. Being a Harvard student was a distinction that allowed her to participate in the business conversations—when they were in English—and, when the day was done, to join in other topics such as art and history while viewing their private collections of original paintings and sculptures.

Time differences and equipment failure conspired against Olivia, resulting in unreliable communication with Derek. Success came through her father's connections, and a couple of nerdy French students who were tech wizards willing to do anything to spend more time with the beautiful American student. They set her up with communication connections in several of the hotels in Paris that had business centers. Her new best friends then worked with Olivia's itinerary to link phone networks at each of the hotels she would be visiting on her trip. She was so thankful, that at the end of the summer she took the tech gang out to a very expensive restaurant and let them pretend, for an evening, that they too were high powered venture capitalists. Olivia enjoyed touring through Europe with her father's tech team and gave them rave reviews to any and every senior officer she met.

Even though she enjoyed the extended trip to Europe, her energy reserves began to run down and finally, all she really wanted was to go back to Santa Cruz to see Derek. It was mid-August before she was able to return to the U.S., which did not leave enough time for a trip to the West Coast.

Fifteen

As fall semester began and life fell back into its own routine, Derek and Olivia resumed their weekly phone calls, but often they spent more time trying to explain what they wanted to say than they did just saying it. "I'm not angry," Derek exclaimed, struggling to contain his frustration. "I'm just trying to understand what you want. I hate to say it so bluntly, but you sound like a Harvard education is too good for Santa Cruz, that you'd be wasting your time and degree if you don't work in a major city."

Olivia objected, "There are plenty of good jobs within commuting distance from Santa Cruz. Not every success story was started by Ivy League founders, nor were they all formed in Boston." She just needed to avoid asking her father for recommendations so she could look at jobs near their Santa Cruz home. She didn't share her father's belief that Boston was the center of the world.

Olivia was not done yet. "My relationship with you is more important than landing a high paying job." She held the phone away from her so Derek wouldn't hear her crying. "I want us to succeed."

After a few more minutes, they stopped arguing. It was agreed that they would both be in Santa Cruz for Christmas. It was not worth risking the promise of time together due to one of them carelessly making insensitive accusations. Olivia planned to be in California for three weeks during Christmas break. Annie and Frank planned to be home for part of the time but would take a week afterward for a surfing vacation in Hawaii.

Derek picked up Olivia at the airport in San Jose. It was a convenient, small airport, and easy to navigate. He got out of the car and loaded her bags into the trunk. He used her car for the trip because of its reliability. They kissed and he pulled away from the terminal. The trip was made in silence until they got back on the freeway. As he started to relax, Derek began making small talk, asking Olivia how her trip from Boston went and how her parents were doing.

Olivia started relaxing as well and contributed to their conversation. "Mom and Dad are planning another trip next year, if you can believe it." She shook her head. "My mom wants to go to New Zealand. The flight alone takes 14 hours—and that's nonstop—if you can get it! Can you imagine that much time on a plane?" asked Olivia.

Derek thought it over. "My parents will never go to New Zealand. They chose to have a million kids instead of travel."

"Oh, come on! The kids are worth it. You wouldn't send any back." Olivia liked joking with Derek. She enjoyed his good sense of humor even if he kept it hidden most of the time.

"Some days there are a couple that drive me to the edge. Many times I could see sending the Little Ones to New Zealand."

Olivia shifted topics. "Have you heard from Annie and Frank? Are they here yet?"

"I hope not."

Olivia looked at him and frowned.

"That is," he clarified. "I have some plans for the two of us tonight, so I told Frank and Annie to come by tomorrow night."

Olivia was quiet for the last stage of their journey. When they rolled up into their neighborhood, Derek asked, "Your house or mine?"

Olivia smiled to herself. "My house would be easiest for me. I have a few bags of clothes to unpack." Olivia hoped Derek would not complain that she packed such heavy bags. He said the same thing every time and it was such a stupid and tiresome joke, she thought.

"What do you have in these bags? Rocks?" Derek said almost the minute he pulled her luggage from the back of her car. He carried it to the back door.

Olivia bristled and grimaced as he fell back into old habits, almost daring her to start a fight.

After a beat, he continued. "Whatever they are, I'm sure they'll look beautiful on you." He gave her a quick kiss. He pulled Olivia's car into the garage and closed the door. Derek gathered Olivia's bags as if they weighed nothing and added a small travel bag he had brought for his own toiletries.

"You got me there. I'll make myself beautiful for you every day if you carry my bags!" They both laughed at the first joke of the night.

Olivia unlocked the door and stepped into the entryway and then into the living room. When she flipped on the rest of the lights, she discovered a sea of flowers everywhere she looked. "Oh, Derek! You didn't have to do this!" Olivia was overwhelmed by the gesture.

He took her hands. "I want tonight to be something we remember for our whole lives." She looked at him, a slight frown marring her otherwise happy face. Was he talking about sex? Is that all he thinks about when he is with her?

Derek continued, as if reading her mind. "It's true, I'm looking forward to having you drag me into your bedroom and leaving our clothes on the floor, but that's not what I'm referring to now. I want the flowers to show you how much I love you. If I bought you some flowers, that would mean some love. More flowers, more love. A crazy amount of flowers, and I'm talking about a crazy amount of love."

"I'm guessing this is a crazy amount of love!" gasped Olivia. Her eyes swept across the entry and dining room, with flowers of every kind, on every surface, and petals on the ground. There was also a large display of roses on a pedestal table in the middle of the room.

"No," said Derek. "What you see is not 'a crazy amount of love.' It's still a more love amount of flowers."

She tilted her head. "What does that even mean?"

"It means you haven't seen the rest of the house." He winked.

She stepped back from Derek, placed her hands on Derek's shoulders, and kissed him with glee. She took his hand and led him through the house, room by room. Before she finished the tour, she threw her arms around Derek's neck. "Oh, baby, I'm so impressed. I love you a crazy amount too. This is the most romantic thing you've ever done."

They spent the next hour wandering from room to room, as she sought out the location of all the flowers Derek had spread around the house. They played the old warm/ cold game to locate a few more bouquets that he hid. They also took time to stop looking and get involved in an increasingly heated make out session. Derek teased her as he held her hand and then pretended they reached their destination at her bedroom, but then he quickly moved them both along. By the third pass, Olivia had suffered long enough. She pulled Derek into her bedroom, flipped the comforter back, and threw him on the bed.

"The first time will be to punish you for making me wait," she said as she climbed on top of him and held his face an inch from hers. "The second time will be to reward you for buying all these flowers."

"And the third time? What will that be for?" Derek asked.

"I'm not going to tell you if there will be a third time, or a fourth time. You'll need to see for yourself." She sat up and pulled her sweatshirt off over her head, signaling the end of talking and the beginning of action. They both laughed. Olivia could be very funny when she tried to be bold. "It'll be your turn to suffer."

The next morning, insistent knocking at the door woke Derek up, only the knocking was on the door to Olivia's bedroom. Frank and Annie were past the formality of waiting on the front step to be invited into her house. Luckily, both Derek and Olivia had the comforter pulled up to their chins, covering their naked bodies.

"Dude, wake up." Frank was now tapping on the door. Derek opened an eye. Olivia kept him awake late into the night. He closed his eyes again.

Olivia was asleep on the other side of the bed and showed no sign of waking up.

"Look, you go ahead and sleep," Frank said through the door. "We'll cook some breakfast and come back for you later this morning."

After one more round in bed, Derek and Olivia finally emerged from their room. They were greeted by a Norman

Rockwell–inspired setting of a couple sitting around the dining room table, drinking coffee and reading the paper. Derek and Olivia looked warm and satisfied in their matching white bathrobes, as they reached the table and its assortment of cut fruit and pastries.

The coffee did its magic and both couples began planning activities. They wisely postponed any family obligations until the following day. Olivia spent the morning directing Derek and Frank in the re arrangement of all the flowers to allow space for a Christmas tree and decorations.

• • •

By the time Christmas arrived, the house looked like a Hallmark card, with flowers, bows, and ribbons pushed into every corner of the house, while room was left for the Christmas morning visitors. Derek even brought in fake snow he sprinkled about, knowing how Olivia loved the winter season in Boston.

Christmas Day was celebrated with an explosion of guests from every family who arrived throughout the day. Olivia, Annie, Frank, and Derek, along with their mothers, kept the food coming with a buffet style brunch to meet the demand. And of course, there were boxes of cookies and other goodies some visitors brought. A bowl of glass ornaments was placed on the table with small white tags that were labeled with the name of each child to hang the decoration.

Frank's sister Vanessa brought her Christmas puppy named Rudolph, who was immediately swarmed by the excited children. They set up a play and sleep area in the laundry room.

It was the type of celebration each large family was accustomed to. Even Olivia's parents made it down from Portola Valley for the afternoon festivities.

The next two weeks slid by with ease. There were conversations about colleges, majors, classes, parties, the friends they had met, and issues they faced.

The day after Christmas, Annie and Frank packed up their surfboards and a pair of travel bags along with several Hawaii travel guides. They headed off for their one-week surf vacation. Once Frank and Annie were dropped off at the airport, Derek commented that they could not leave soon enough. Frank was talking nonstop about how great their waves would be, and it was getting a bit tiresome. Olivia agreed with Derek but enjoyed the enthusiastic show Frank and Annie put on.

Derek exhaled. "He was like a kid dying for Christmas to come. He was packed midway through the semester. Annie was tripping over the surfboards until she made him pack them on top of the Woody. We'll certainly hear the blow-by-blow when we pick them up next week," Derek said as he navigated his way out of the airport.

Olivia had to admit that Frank was a rare one. "That guy will be a kid for the rest of his life."

"That's true, but he'll probably raise a pack of professional surfers and disappear into the South Pacific somewhere."

They rode home after successfully delivering the travelers to the airport. The return trip would be even more taxing, Derek thought. A week later, his predictions were proven correct.

When Frank and Annie returned from vacation, Derek picked them up in the Woody. Although Frank was never pale in the winter, the tan he sported was even darker than it was during the summer. Frank came off the plane wearing an expensive and tasteful Hawaiian shirt, shorts, sandals, and necklaces of black and white polished stones. Annie wore a light cotton dress, wide hat, and a multicolored jeweled necklace. Her skin showed the remains of a deep burn and peel. The smile on her face was evidence that the trip was well worth the pain of the burn.

In spite of Derek's misgivings about the ride home, Annie and Frank were somewhat subdued, holding hands and staring at each other like newlyweds.

"Did you guys get married over there?" Derek finally asked.

"No, but we thought about it." Annie giggled at some personal memory from their trip.

Derek had to admit he was jealous of the couple for making the trip happen and enjoying a beach somewhere else besides Santa Cruz. Derek enjoyed Frank's storytelling, and jealous or not, he was happy anywhere, as long as he was with Olivia.

"We can tell you about our trip but nothing we say will do it justice until we get the pictures developed and we can really show you our adventures." The next day, Frank put a rush order on the film developer and set up a slide show of the pictures that night.

After dinner they opened a bottle of wine and told stories from their surf trip. Annie had to admit that Frank was a very good surfer. Her only complaint was his ignorance about the danger he faced in the large, north shore waves.

Frank did not kid about those. "Some were very large, and some were just terrifying. I was lucky to catch a couple mid-size waves around the edges of the pipeline. I can say I surfed there, but I don't think I'll do it again."

From Frank's serious tone, Derek knew that he had been

spooked, but Frank quickly shook it off and continued sharing their pictures. Derek promised himself he and Olivia would also take a trip to Hawaii. He wanted to make some memories of their own.

• • •

The next morning, Olivia was awakened by insistent knocking on the front door. Since she rarely, if ever, received morning visitors at the Shack, Olivia awakened Derek. They quickly dressed and went downstairs together to greet the unknown visitor.

Before the door was even opened, she was greeted by a man shouting with a foreign accent, "Surprise!" As she opened the door all the way, Olivia recognized the voice belonged to a junior in her apartment complex back in Cambridge. Olivia shared coffee with him once to be polite, but he was no one she expected to see again—and certainly not in Santa Cruz.

"Darling, don't you have a kiss for me? I've been flying for days to come see you!" He was short, and younger than expected from one so self-assured.

Olivia was mortified. "What are you doing here?" she asked him.

Derek was starting to wake up and did not like what he was hearing from the stranger. Before he could say anything, Frank and Annie came running to the door while tying their robes.

"What do we have here," Frank asked Derek, ignoring the stranger at the door.

"I have no idea," said Derek. "I'm not sure what he's selling but I'm close to closing the door on him."

Olivia held the door partly open. "His name is Fritz Wilmer. He is a student with me at Harvard."

She turned to face Derek directly. "I have no idea why he is here. He's certainly not my boyfriend and has never been. He is barely an acquaintance."

"I'm standing right here." Fritz looked back and forth between Derek and Olivia, unsure how to proceed. "I thought you still loved me, Olivia, and it stings to hear you say you are not my girlfriend! I envisioned surprising you with a long weekend in Carmel. We will have a trip we will always remember." He looked at Derek and took a step back. "I even bought you a return ticket to Boston, first class."

Derek continued to hold the door, but he opened it a bit more. "You are not coming in until we know why you're here."

"Livie, I do not understand who this man is, blocking my entrance to our house. I assumed you would be pleased to see me. I thought we were a couple." Fritz was as confused as everyone else.

Derek turned to Olivia and asked, "Can you clarify this for me? How long have you had a boyfriend?"

Olivia was near tears.

Frank took charge and decided to solve the problem piece by piece before Fritz caused any real damage. "Olivia, would you go with Annie and explain to her what you think is going on? Clearly, you and Fritz have different ideas about what constitutes a girlfriend. I'll talk with Fritz, to find out what he expected from his cross-country trip to spend a weekend with her."

Frank then asked Derek to take a long walk on the beach.

After a half hour grilling Fritz, Frank was confident he understood the whole story. Leaving out Fritz's hopes and dreams, it was the story of a Harvard student who was socially challenged—maybe more than that—who had a black American Express card and decided on a whim to surprise Olivia with a visit. Fritz assumed she was single, and that this trip could give them plenty of time to get to know one another.

Frank also determined that after a great deal of bluster, Fritz finally admitted that contrary to his claims he was not currently her boyfriend and, in fact, had never been her boyfriend. He knew nothing about Olivia beyond what one learns by sharing a class together. He incorrectly answered every question about Olivia that a boyfriend would know, such as when they met and where her parents lived, where she attended high school. The one fact of his story that was also consistent with Olivia's story was that he admitted they had not slept together, she simply shared a coffee break with him—once. According to Frank's interview with Fritz, Fritz had not slept with anyone yet, and he had never even kissed Olivia.

Frank recommended that they take him back to the airport and escort him to the gate so he could fly home.

Derek was not as convinced by Frank's conclusion. "Guys don't just get on planes on a whim to visit a girl that isn't their girlfriend." He thought Olivia acted more like a girl who got caught with a second boyfriend than one who had a stalker that she knew little about. This guy clearly knew her. He just did not know her very well, like it was still a young relationship.

Annie and Olivia spoke for almost an hour, with promises to talk further once they got rid of Fritz. The story Annie heard from Olivia was consistent with the story Frank coaxed out of the student. Olivia barely knew Fritz existed. She waved when they crossed paths but didn't want to encourage him in any way. He was too weird for her. For Olivia, the worst part of this whole episode was that she was afraid Fritz's bizarre visit might jeopardize her relationship with Derek. The past two weeks with Derek were everything she wanted: romance, friendship, joking around, quiet sharing. She could never duplicate or replace Derek. She allowed herself to have friends who were guys and cut back on time with the ones who started getting more friendly. Instead of dating, she spent most of her time studying or socializing with groups of friends.

The more Derek thought about Fritz, the more convinced he was that Fritz was her secret Boston boyfriend. It set up a terrible cycle in his thoughts. He tried to believe what happened was innocent, but it was just too unbelievable. Why would a guy show up at Christmas and travel across the country for a girl he barely knew? It did not make any sense to Derek.

After Frank finally got rid of Fritz, Derek went back to his parents' house. He spoke for a bit with Frank and explained his position. When Frank told Olivia what happened, she locked herself in her room for the rest of the day.

The next day, Olivia told Frank and Annie that she was returning to Boston early—not to see Fritz—but because her relationship with Derek was so badly broken, she had no hope it could be fixed. The trust and love they built over the years was obviously not enough, since Derek did not believe in her innocence.

Sixteen

Eventually, everyone returned to their respective universities for their final semester. Olivia's graduation commencement took place on the Harvard campus in Cambridge. Her parents attended but Derek did not. Her mom could not get a straight answer from Olivia about what happened and why Derek missed her graduation.

Derek had his graduation ceremony on the campus of UC Santa Cruz. It was an informal affair. Derek and his family celebrated with a catered lunch, inviting his friends and classmates. Olivia did not attend.

The next weekend, Derek and his parents drove down to San Louis Obispo to witness Frank and Annie's graduation ceremonies. Both families sent an entourage to celebrate the occasion.

When college ended, the real challenge began. Olivia had yet to decide which job offer to take and where to establish her professional life. She had several offers from biotech and life science companies, the latest hot industries and the current darlings of Wall Street. There were still some offers from the firms in Silicon Valley that she kept open while she thought about her future and where she would like to live. She needed to decide quickly; her offers would not be open much longer.

There were many reasons for her to stay in Boston, and a few more were created by guys who surrounded her in school, trying to convince her to stay. After a careful cost-benefit analysis to weigh staying in Boston versus moving back to northern California, and with long discussions with her closest friends, she decided to give the east coast life a chance. She would live the high life in Boston and its surrounding technology areas, with their intellectually stimulating atmosphere and jobs paying more money than she could spend.

She flirted with the guys but kept them at arm's length for now. One by one, she looked at them and saw no reason for starting something with no future, something that would only lead to pain and guilt. Until Derek proclaimed that their relationship was officially over, she would not make the effort required for another serious relationship. Although she hadn't heard from him since their blow up over the uninvited guest, six months ago at Christmas, she had too much respect for Derek to start something—if there was a chance he still loved her.

Olivia thought about their relationship. In the beginning, they both made it to Castle Beach on Father's Day. However, once she moved across the country, it was harder to keep the promise. One year, she had a summer job in Boston, and the next, a study abroad program cut her time in Santa Cruz down to two mere weeks. Annie told her later that Derek went to their meeting place on time that summer but left after sitting by himself for several hours each day around Father's Day. He hated appearing foolish, sitting in a beach chair alone when he became certain she would not be there. Later that year, she paid a short visit to Santa Cruz, but the trip ended early; he was too upset about her plans to stay in Cambridge. She knew his disappointment.

The last time they spoke, they were both still unattached. She remained tight with her circle of girlfriends but refused to attend parties when invited. Her closest friends stopped trying to help her out of her personal "Santa Cruz gloom," as they called it. They knew things were left unfinished with Derek over Christmas break, but they couldn't understand why she held on to his memory so tightly.

They also knew about the death of her brother Ricky in a bar fight and what it did to her family. Her brother had been a slow train wreck. Olivia had been unable to help him. Their relationship remained distant and full of anger and hurt to the end. Many times, Olivia extended her hand in support, only to have it rejected, and her kindness thrown back at her. Her parents refused to acknowledge that Ricky had problems and needed help, professional help, that neither Olivia nor her parents could give.

Olivia recovered from her brother's death more quickly than she anticipated. There had always been the fear that he would return to Santa Cruz and attack Derek again. Personally, she had been very angry at Ricky ever since his first confrontation with Derek. His pathological need to fight people almost destroyed their family.

She could admit to herself that she was glad that Ricky was gone. Nobody should have the right to threaten someone like he threatened Derek. Her parents were broken by Ricky's death. Her dad retired and they stopped traveling. They both had aged under the constant pressure of bad news and legal problems. Her parents gave their Santa Cruz house to Olivia as they could no longer visit, the memory of Ricky's fights with Derek a constant reminder of the troubles that weighed on them.

Olivia did not recover as well from her estrangement with Derek. He had cut her off since the fiasco with her uninvited visitor during the past Christmas break. The whole final semester at Harvard had collapsed, and instead of enjoying all the activities going on during the spring, she holed up in the library and studied, even when she knew the remaining courses were worthless since they would never help fix her broken heart.

Olivia's friends couldn't understand why she held on so tightly to her relationship with Derek even when it was clear to everyone that her high school romance hadn't survived the time and distance of college. Socially, she acted like she was in a committed relationship, turning down overtures from guys who expressed interest in her. On weekends and Friday evenings, she spent most of her time with girlfriends, seeing the sights in Boston, going out in groups of friends but avoiding potential romantic entanglements.

Derek rolled up his sleeves and began putting in the time necessary to grow his business. Outside of work, he surfed with old buddies in the early morning and hung out with new friends in the evenings, enjoying live music at local venues and drinking beer. Sometimes the whole music scene seemed a bit intense so instead he headed down to a local bar to catch a Giants or A's ballgame. Derek could feel himself pulling back and spending more time by himself, not realizing it was because he was lonely and missed Olivia.

On weekends, it was not uncommon for him to see Frank and Annie. They would visit one of their parents midday on Saturdays and descend upon his family for lunch. They would stay around talking with anyone who happened to be around; they were sociable.

Frank's younger sisters, Julia and Sophia, stuck to Annie like Velcro. She played the latest cool music and had wild dance parties where they all jumped around madly, often dragging Frank onto the dance floor. Derek would usually take a rain check.

At night when the girls wound down, Frank and Annie would drop them off at their house and go with Derek to local bars and dance clubs. It was often fun, and for a few moments, Derek enjoyed himself, but mostly, by the time he made it home, he just felt lonely without Olivia, especially now that their communication had completely broken down.

Seventeen

Seasons in Boston marched along steadily from summer with its burst of heat and tourists, to fall with its vivid colors and crisp air. Olivia stayed this year in Boston, working through Christmas. Winter arrived with regular dumps of snow, and now it was spring with its cheerful flowers and blossoms everywhere. Olivia admired the charm of Boston in spring, even if she had to admit every region across the country had beautiful springs as well.

The weather, cold enough to require a light coat or sweater, did not bother her. It just gave her a reason to buy clothes for another season. The only problem with the seasonal change was that it emphasized how much she missed the California coast. She missed the most minute details of living that defined her life at home along the cliffs of Santa Cruz, and the people who resided there—like Frank's grandmother and great aunt. She missed the cold fog that blanketed them for the better half of the year. All of it was important, including the bench looking out to sea. Their old bench on Castle Beach. Individually, each memory could be found almost anywhere. But together, they all gave her a sense of belonging, like she was home.

One cool Saturday morning, Olivia sat in a small Cambridge café across the square from her apartment building. The sidewalk bustled with students and neighbors eager to get out of their homes to catch some sunlight, regardless of the cold. Because they were all on the street at the same time, seats were hard to find at the tables in front of cafés. She sat at an inside table sharing coffee with a young man, a student at Harvard who was approaching his senior year. It was the first time she recognized how different student life was from that of an alumna, and how different these roles were in life. She and the young man were seeing each other for a few weeks but she never encouraged him to believe it would be more serious than discussing careers around a cup of coffee or eating an occasional dinner in the neighborhood.

Olivia had gone down this road before with a few guys who promised they were only looking for friendship but eventually would confess that they were falling for her and were hoping to take their relationship to the next level. Like the ice cube lying near her foot, slowly melting on the warm café floor, she could see that her time in Cambridge was drawing to an end. The man she was sitting with was funny and respectful, and by all accounts had a successful career in front of him. He was just the wrong guy for her.

The café was toasty warm. Olivia continued sipping coffee and avoiding an untouched scone on the table in front of her. As he chatted about classes and on campus interviews, her mind wandered. She sat here, fondly recalling all her reasons for staying in Cambridge and determined few—if any—remained. It was a town made up of faculty holding on to faded glories of youth and students preparing for the working world. With a degree of certainty that eluded her the past year, but now had a rock-solid grip on her, she knew this door in her life was closed.

Once that thought settled into her mind, she anxiously realized she could not leave fast enough. Cambridge and the surrounding Boston area was not her home. Picking up a newspaper from the table next to her, she checked the date. Counting on her fingers, as she liked to do, Olivia calculated that Father's Day was only a week away. Getting home to California on time would be a challenge. And even then, she would be walking away from her apartment deposit, new career, and who knows what else. It didn't matter. She squared her shoulders, and with hands on her hips, leaned forward and mentally pushed past any obstacles of her life in Cambridge. She would quit her job, ship her possessions home, catch a cab, march through an airport, get onto a plane, and not stop until she was home.

Trying to understand what just happened, she began thinking to herself, waiting to hear the narrative to determine if it made any sense. She thought, "There is a boy waiting for me on the other coast. No," she corrected. "There is this particular man on the other coast, sitting in a folding chair, his feet in the cool sand at a foggy beach, waiting for me. This makes it imperative I make it to the beach in time, even if that means leaving everything behind to race across the country to prove to him this love will survive."

•   •   •

She knew as clearly as if she was viewing a movie clip that he would be there, and it was time for her to end their stalemate and make things right with him. Her mind was spinning while the student across the table was talking about how to get the best paying job possible. She had to keep herself under control as she carefully placed a twenty-dollar bill on the table, said a short goodbye, and told him she had a plane to catch.

Olivia knew the process of clearing her life out of Cambridge was a necessary step to start her new life with a clean slate. She was willing to risk that Derek had already given up on her. During Fritz's disastrous Christmas visit and the silent months that followed, they only spoke once when he called to congratulate her on her Harvard graduation. Afterward he refused her calls. She was running completely blind. Annie was a comfort and supported her, but she too was blind to Derek's feelings.

Even without any certainty that Derek would welcome her back, she had to come home. It was a true leap of faith. She gave herself no other choice. The thought of losing him and walking away from all the years of their love was too tragic for her to think about. Once Olivia decided to return to Santa Cruz, she canceled her lease and immediately started to pack. She moved as quickly as possible, keeping her focus on the task at hand, hoping Derek remembered who they were and the life they had shared. If he focused on their love, he would be at Castle Beach waiting for her. She now had to reassure him of her commitment to him.

Unwinding her four years in Boston to arrive home by Father's Day would be difficult, but as she and her friends often quoted, laughing, "Nothing is too difficult if you have money." So she hired a moving service to pack her furniture, one large wardrobe box, a box of all the small mementos collected during college, plus a few heavy boxes of books, kitchen gear, and other items.

She held a clothes-swap party with her closest friends that night, who helped her sort out what she should keep from what to give away—and what to share among those present. In the end, she eliminated most of her formal suits, leaving a more reasonable pile of her favorites. Her friends each took a healthy pile they would keep and enjoy, to remind them of their friendship with

Olivia. She saw no need for five long wool coats or twenty pairs of heels in Santa Cruz or even Silicon Valley. She thinned out her coat collection but, in the end, couldn't bear to part with any of her shoes. There were tears all around as she hugged her best friends and said goodbye; promises were made to visit if anyone's travels brought them near each other.

Olivia left one cryptic message for Annie, her lifeline to Santa Cruz. " Meet me at Castle Beach." Annie would take care of the rest. As she hung up the phone, the weight of her decision settled in her chest and made her lightheaded and giddy with anticipation. She reached out to a nearby bench for support. Then, like stepping into a warm bath, happiness swept over her. She was going home.

The mover arrived the next afternoon, boxed everything remaining, and left. Next, another mover came to ship her VW bug convertible. It was an impractical car, but it was too fun; she could not let it go—besides it would be perfect in Santa Cruz.

Later that night, she called her father's travel agent and purchased a first-class, one-way ticket from Boston to San Jose, via Chicago. It was a crack-of-dawn departure, but it was the only way she could get to Santa Cruz by 1 P.M. With no communication between her and Derek, she was afraid that being even an hour late would ruin her plan and their future for good. She could not afford to have Derek think she would not be coming at all.

Eighteen

O nce in San Jose, Olivia rented a car to drive over the coastal mountains to Santa Cruz. Her VW would arrive later that week. The plan was working. She would arrive in Santa Cruz around noon and make it to Castle Beach within the hour. She had feared her flight would be canceled or delayed. She did not have time to catch the next one, but luckily the flight was on schedule.

The question she was afraid to ask herself was whether she could survive the permanent end of a relationship with Derek. Olivia hoped she would not have to answer that question.

When she was on the highway, Olivia pushed the rental car as fast as it would go, picking up a few minutes, and then slowed when she hit the local traffic into Santa Cruz, winding her way through interminable lights, past cars that seemingly blocked her path with the sole purpose of delaying her arrival. Up the hill and over the train tracks, and then back down. She rolled ever so slowly, lowering her window while she took in the sights and smells during the last three blocks of her journey.

As she approached the shore, the bright sunshine quickly turned into gray fog which sat heavily on the cliff houses in her neighborhood. She wore a sweatshirt in the car out of habit. It was early June, very warm in San Jose when she put on her sweatshirt and turned on the air-conditioner, and very cold and damp when she arrived at her house in Santa Cruz. She expected the fog and embraced it. If she were honest with herself, she wore the sweatshirt with the faded Boardwalk logo for good luck. So far, so good. She was home.

Olivia pulled into her driveway in her nondescript rental car at 12:15 P.M. and brought the lightest pieces of luggage into the living room. The movers were expected to arrive later in the week with furniture and her remaining belongings. She wondered if Derek was already at Castle Beach. At the thought of Derek, Olivia's little inner voice went into high gear. It took all her mental strength to avoid dwelling on the problems she experienced in Santa Cruz over recent years. Instead, she took a deep breath and opened the front door. "Keep moving and unpack the car," she told herself. "One foot in front of the other. If things work out, it will be great; if not, I will survive," she repeated. It had become her mantra.

Olivia reminded herself that today was Father's Day, a ridiculous time to leave the warmth of the San Jose Bay Area and willingly enter into cold fog. She thought back to her childhood. It was a day to barbeque with her family in their back yard. Her father was the one who established Father's Day as the day they arrived in Santa Cruz to start each summer. The days before Father's Day were filled with packing and completing lists at home. The day itself became Olivia's favorite day of the year. It heralded the beginning of summer with her boyfriend and her best friends. Derek, Annie, and Frank adopted it as the first day of summer for the two couples.

Truth be told, she now had a fondness for the cold mist, almost as much as she had for the sun. She certainly enjoyed it better than Boston's snow and ice. That was all behind her now. Here, she could choose how much damp fog she wanted. If the fog became too much for her, she could rent an apartment near the tech centers in Scott's Valley, ten miles inland from Santa Cruz and where she expected to find work and warm, sunny weekends. She would continue to use the beach house under all scenarios. It had good and bad memories, but for her, the good ones were enough to keep her on the coast.

As she sat on the front stoop of her house, resting from moving her heavy luggage, she realized this was the same scene that played out when she first moved to Santa Cruz from Portola Valley when she was in high school. If Derek didn't make it... She could not go down that road now.

Olivia glanced at her watch. It was 12:45 P.M. She was still on time. She could not wait any longer. Standing in her entryway, she surveyed the house. Everything was quiet; everything was put away. Derek maintained their house and kept it clean and well-tended in case she or her family chose to visit. Olivia pulled a Red Sox ball cap off the hat rack in the entryway and set out toward the beach. The roads in her neighborhood were narrow, and although nobody was driving, cars lined the streets, leaving very little room for pedestrians. Summer visitors were in town but stayed inside, keeping warm, having lunch, and waiting until the sun came out.

She walked slowly down the hill, staying on the sidewalk to avoid getting hit by an errant driver whose vision might be limited in the thick, low fog. When the sidewalk ended, she stepped off the curb at the landing where the old castle was built so many years ago. Castle Beach was empty of visitors, with only a few seagulls standing guard.

It took great courage for Olivia to hope that he would be here. She could not think of anything else these past days, afraid of the pain she would endure if he were not there. "If he isn't there, I'll survive," she told herself and breathed in deeply. It was a long shot. She knew that. Derek had not communicated with her for a long time. She was not going to calculate the number of days.

●　●　●

After the last time he saw Olivia in person, he had not fared well. When asked why he did not return to Livermore now that college was over, he told his friends he wanted to keep his property management business running. He told his parents that Santa Cruz felt more like home. He told Annie that he thought his relationship with Olivia could be strong and wanted to be in Santa Cruz when she returned. Annie did not believe him, and neither did he. He only shared with Annie and Frank that he and Olivia had not talked since he stormed off at Christmas, refused her calls, and did not answer the door when she stopped by to tell him she was returning early to Cambridge for her final semester.

He did a poor job of handling the fiasco of Olivia's fake boyfriend. He should have known that Fritz was currently not Olivia's boyfriend and probably never was; embarrassment and damaged pride kept him from shaking off the anger he felt for the strange guy entering Olivia's house, declaring his love for her. He had channeled his anger toward Olivia at the time, but now it was squarely aimed at himself for actually believing such a wild story and suspecting her of cheating when she was always so truthful with him. At the time, Derek and Olivia had just finished two fantastic weeks of Christmas vacation together with their families, showing they were still going strong; and they were, until that stupid kid showed up uninvited and wrecked everything.

But that wasn't true, he told himself. Looking back, he realized if his anger had not blinded him from Olivia's truth, he would have sent Fritz on his way based on the advice of his friends Frank and Annie; and he should have simply accepted the truth from Olivia. It was up to him to restore their relationship and accept the peace offering of love Olivia offered him, but he froze and eventually missed the chance to reconcile with her before she left.

Derek thought about their past and their love, which only made it more painful. He remembered holding her while she cried, and how agonizing it was, but he was powerless to change anything. There were promises to forgive past misunderstandings. One self-proclaimed boyfriend unexpectedly followed Olivia to her house in Santa Cruz and it broke him—broke them. He grimaced. To be fair, some girlfriends wanted more from Derek than he was willing to give. Derek broke it off with them too. No other relationship mattered. All he could think about was the fear that this one might end.

●　●　●

Olivia continued down the sidewalk to the Cove at Castle Beach, wearing shoes instead of sandals to conserve her warmth. When the sidewalk ended, she stepped into the sand and began her trudge across the beach, carefully placing one step in front of the other. When she finally glanced up, there was a man sitting on a folding chair, his feet on the blanket and a large floppy hat on his head. Next to him was an empty chair. From this distance in the heavy fog, she could not see who he was or why there was a second chair. Scanning the empty beach, she saw no one else claiming the chair.

Olivia could barely breathe as her heart rate climbed higher and higher. How great would it be if he were here to meet her? How badly would it hurt if the stranger on the beach was not Derek? she thought. Like a ping pong ball, her mind bounced back and forth between the two possible outcomes. She continued her slow walk toward the lone figure on the beach.

Within fifty yards, she saw the stranger's profile and was relatively sure it was Derek. At twenty-five yards, she recognized his jacket and the ghastly fishing hat he refused to throw out. When she finally reached him, Derek remained seated as he glanced over and saw her standing next to him. Unsure what to do next, she sat in the empty chair which faced the shoreline, but she turned slightly toward him.

She saw a slight smile flicker across his face, registering a sign of hope, but the smile fell. Unknown to her, his smile faded from pure relief and tension release once he saw she actually made it there. He looked like he was in pain, with sadness showing as his eyes narrowed. They were red rimmed and more sunken than she remembered.

Olivia's world stood still as she settled into her beach chair. "I was afraid you wouldn't be here," she said to Derek as he continued his focus toward the shore. He didn't move, and she feared he would get up and leave.

Finally, he gave her a quick glance and then turned his focus back to the shore. "I'm here because I live here," he said almost too quietly for her to hear. "I've lived here all my life. Other people come and go."

"I live here too." She kept her eyes on him, hoping to get a clearer idea of his thoughts. "I kept the beach house. It's just for me."

He picked up a stick and poked it into the sand. "I know the guy who showed up at your house at Christmas was not your boyfriend. I'm sorry I didn't believe you. Not believing you was unforgivable."

"I don't have a boyfriend. The only boyfriend I had then was you."

"Are you just here this weekend? Will you be flying back to Boston soon?" Derek asked.

"I'm never going back to Boston."

"So, what is it that you want?" Derek needed to know because from here on out, there would be no turning back. His heart could not take it.

"It doesn't matter what I want," said Olivia, returning quick, sharp answers to his questions like short volleys made at the net on a tennis court. "What matters is what I need, and I need you."

She got out of her chair and kneeled next to him. Derek felt a stirring throughout his body as he remembered their past Father's Day reunions. It took all his willpower to keep his arms from wrapping around her and pulling her into an embrace, but he was too afraid of being hurt. Instead, he also knelt across from her and waited.

Olivia slipped her fingers under the edge of her sweatshirt, and lifted it up, above her head, until it was free. She folded the garment and placed it on his towel. With the heavy gray sweatshirt off, the T-shirt she wore was exposed, revealing a picture of a meadow showing a vast array of wildflowers. Thousands of flowers, tens of thousands, or maybe millions of flowers of all colors. The detail was incredible. Derek read the caption printed across her chest: "A Crazy Amount of Flowers," with a second line printed below: "A Crazy Amount of Love."

Derek's heart burst as he stared, first at her, and then at her T-shirt. Her shirt was so thin it clung to all her curves, revealing that she was wearing nothing beneath. "I had it printed and made a little snug," she told him. "I wanted you to like it."

Derek still hadn't responded. On her shirt was the phrase he had chosen to express his love for her when it was beyond words. Olivia waited for him to say something, afraid to look at him, but when she finally looked to see where his eyes were focused, she was surprised. Every other time she made it to the Cove on Father's Day, Derek's focus was on her swimsuit.

Today, his eyes were focused on her face. Finally, he looked at her T-shirt, as if noticing it for the first time. When he reached out to touch the shirt, she pulled his hands back. "We better not touch it while on a public beach. It's stretched pretty tight and could probably tear." That was like throwing gasoline on the fire that burned within him. Derek freed his wrists from her grasp and then sat back on his heels and held her hands loosely in his, a pair equal in control, equal in love.

Olivia realized it was easy to say it out loud now that she was sitting close to him. "There is nothing else I need," she said. Derek waited. "All I need is you, just you." She paused, then continued. "There are things I want. I want us to live in the same house. I want to raise a family on Castle Beach. That's it. You, me, our family, Castle Beach, and we're complete. I know what I need to be happy, and it isn't a high-powered, long-hour job in Boston. It isn't a high society boyfriend with a black American Express card. It isn't any of those things."

"There was never anyone else," she said, squeezing his hands. "Fritz was a weirdo with an overactive imagination. Frank and Annie told you the same thing: I was true to you. I only wanted us in my future." She tugged sharply on both of his hands to get his attention. "You should apologize to me for believing him instead of me," she said. "From now on, we'll only be on each other's side and let nobody come between us. Do you agree?" He nodded.

Olivia looked Derek in the eyes. "I just need you," she said as she continued to look at him, and he returned his gaze to the ocean. She started to despair; was there anything she could say to break his malaise?

●　●　●

Once Derek saw Olivia in person, and not just as a memory, all his hopes for how this would play out solidified. He had thought of this moment, thought of it a thousand times, each ending with her return to Santa Cruz permanently. So much time had passed without her that he was terrified to get his hopes up.

Now, seeing her in the sand next to him, he began to believe it was not a dream, that she was really with him. "You know I love you, Olivia. I'm not talking about the past. I'm only interested in the present. I need to know if you love me and are here to stay. If so, I'll never risk losing you again." He gave her a melancholy smile and reached out to her, pushing a strand of hair behind her ear, if for no other reason than to prove to himself she was there.

Finally, Derek looked at her directly, "I'm sorry. I let my fear take over my judgment. I ignored you and even ignored what my best friends were telling me: there was only you and me. I'll never cut you off again. I promise. This year's been awful without you."

Derek continued. "I need more than a summer romance. I need to be secure in knowing that every day, there will be you and me. We need to be able to count on one another to be committed to each other, our family, you by my side and me by yours."

Olivia responded, "We'll settle down, and raise our children, visit our families, and hold hands as we walk along the shore together for the rest of our lives. I need to know you are committed to this relationship the way we always hoped it would be. You and me: friends, equal partners, and lovers." She paused. "Eventually parents and, with God's grace, grandparents."

Derek reached out and took her hand, tears springing to his eyes. "From the day we first held hands, I felt we were meant to be together. I certainly had no idea what was coming down the road for us. It's been a bumpy ride, but I wouldn't change a thing if this is the road we needed to travel to be together for the rest of our lives."

Olivia was crying now too, the tears running silently down her cheeks. "I spent the past week disengaging my life from Boston. I quit my job, said goodbye to my friends, cleared out my apartment, and shipped my remaining possessions home—here to Santa Cruz."

"I went to see a guy that I occasionally shared coffee with on weekends. I made sure he understood that I was not his girlfriend and that we would never be more than friends."

"How did that go?" asked Derek, only slightly concerned.

"Surprisingly well. I think all along he had been looking for something or someone more permanent than I ever offered. He was tired of being kept at a distance by me."

"And Fritz?" Derek asked, clearing up concerns that had been clouding his judgement.

"Fritz graduated and moved to Finland. I never saw him after that humiliating Christmas."

"I'm here for you," Olivia said. "I gave up everything in Boston. I want to be with you. There's nowhere else I want to be." They each leaned in, splitting the distance between them until their lips met, softly at first and then with passion, showing they were equally ready to begin pulling their lives back together, rebuilding what they had, and creating anew the future they each dreamed about.

• • •

The early June chill kept the beach free from other visitors, most of whom were likely at home celebrating Father's Day in more traditional forms, with barbeques and gifts of bad ties or terrible cologne.

Derek pulled a small box out of his pocket. He was already on his knees while still holding Olivia's hand. He leaned back on one knee. "Olivia, I feared you wouldn't come today. I was afraid to ask if you still felt the same about me. I couldn't ask our friends about us because it would have been too painful to hear from them that we were through. I could only set up two chairs here in the Cove and pray you would show up."

Derek looked up at Olivia with an expression of hope, bright eyes and a wide, relaxed smile that told her he knew they would make it.

"Olivia, I love you. All I want is to spend my life with you. I want to make you happy and continue to share the love we built between us over the years. Will you marry me?"

He opened the box in his hand to reveal a gold engagement ring holding a bright, sparkling, solitaire diamond. "We are meant for each other. If you marry me, I know we'll continue to be as happy as we have been in the past—even happier. I know this because I have been in love with you for years. And when the problems of the world stepped aside and gave us a chance to share that love without interference, I knew that was all we needed."

Olivia pulled her hands to her face and then extended her left hand while nodding her head in acceptance of his offer. Finally, it had happened. All the waiting and all the tears were behind them. "Yes, Derek, I will marry you. I love you, and all I need to be happy is to live with you for the rest of our lives."

Derek took the ring from the box and slid it onto Olivia's outstretched finger. She stretched out her arm, eyes never leaving the ring on her hand. She tipped her hand back slightly, fully extended. It was a common pose used by a woman when she was given a diamond ring from the one she loved. It showed she was newly engaged. Olivia couldn't take her eyes off it. It was the ring's power, blending the culmination of her dreams with the awe of its beauty. She jumped up and threw her arms around him. They lost their balance, and both fell into the sand, unwilling to relinquish their embrace.

Nineteen

On a chilly Father's Day, when most people were inside, sitting around a fire, the only two people in the Cove at Castle Beach were enjoying a different kind of warmth: the beginning of the rest of their lives together.

The original castle of Castle Beach was built in stages starting at the turn of the twentieth century, but was gone by the mid-1960s, victim of a fire and powerful storms that destroyed it, followed by waves that crushed its broken pieces and washed them into Monterey Bay. Yet, Derek and Olivia had found love in the small cove where the castle once stood. The love between Olivia and Derek proved stronger than any problems time or distance could throw at them. They had persevered and prevailed over the trials and tribulations life threw their way.

They sat facing the waves, Derek on Olivia's left side, which allowed him to peek at her ring every few minutes. He purchased the ring several years ago and despaired about ever placing it on her finger. It sat in his pocket for the entire month of June, each of the past two years. The box was worn from carrying it around with the sand in his pocket, but he handled it carefully and the box remained unbroken. Now, it was finally hers.

From a distance came the sound of whooping and hollering, down West Cliff Drive and approaching the Cove. The shouting continued until they could distinguish Frank and Annie's voices. They were falling all over each other, with Frank holding onto Annie to slow her down, to no avail.

When they got to the beach, Annie stopped, saw Olivia and Derek, and ran full speed at them. Annie grabbed both by the arm and pulled them from their chairs. Annie was crying and exclaiming, "I knew you would make it. I just knew it."

Frank caught up to them. "Dude, I told her you would come." Derek looked at him. They both remembered how difficult it had been during the past years when she did not come home. That was behind them now.

Frank saw all the commotion between the girls and stepped over to see what they were discussing. A few seconds later, he watched Olivia show her ring to Annie. They laughed and cried, and both were hopping and clapping.

"She said, 'Yes!'" Derek exclaimed to Frank and Annie.

Derek looked at the ring, proud that it was still as spectacular as the day he purchased it. He looked at Frank until he drew his attention, and then tipped his head toward the ring, his eyes silently asking him when their ring would come.

It came sooner than Derek expected, as Annie suddenly raised her left hand and held it out so everyone could see. On her hand was a diamond so big that it boggled Derek's mind. He could only say, "I guess the car was worth more than you thought."

"You could say that. It was worth a beach house, two bachelor's degrees, a fleet of collector cars, more surfboards than I have room for, and a ring that makes my girl happy every day."

"I don't know why he felt he needed to buy such a large diamond." Annie pointed at him and shook her hand. "Fastest car, largest diamond. What's next?"

Everyone except Annie knew the answer. Together, they slowly said, "Largest family!"

They laughed as Annie put her hand over her mouth in shock. Finally, she said, "I want a smaller ring."

"We're engaged!" they all yelled at once.

After sharing her story about leaving Boston, Olivia announced that she was getting chilled and invited everyone to come over to "visit at my house."

They gathered Derek's beach gear and walked up the sidewalk to Olivia's house. The inflection of her tone and emphasis on "my house" made it clear to Annie and Frank that she was here to stay.

They all remembered her house where they had spent two magical summers, living a life that was beyond their means but right down the middle of their dreams, in a house overlooking the ocean and in beds they shared with their sweethearts who were now their fiancés.

"I'd like to gather all our families here at the house later this week to celebrate our engagements. Does anyone want to help?" Olivia didn't hear any response from the others, so she looked around to gauge their reaction.

"We could do that," said Annie, with a lack of enthusiasm that surprised Olivia.

Frank joined in, "That would be great. I could bring some beer."

Olivia thought they were distracted and moved along to a new topic of conversation. "Derek, where do you want us to live once we get married?" she asked. They were now within a block of her house, and everyone stopped, presumably to hear him answer her question. Olivia turned to face him as Annie and Frank fell behind.

Derek stepped forward and took her hands. "I am going to live with you. If work takes us away from our home, we'll keep the Beach Shack but buy another home and live together near work." He kissed her lightly on the lips and continued, "But if work wants us to make a long-term move away from our families, we'll find different work."

"When we first met," Derek reminisced, "I had my family, and you had your family. Now, we have only one family. I want to show it to you." With that, he slowly turned her to face her house up on the Point. There, she saw a street full of people starting to clap, with several running toward her. The first to reach her were Derek and Annie's parents, followed by the Guys.

Derek's mom ran up to Olivia and gave her a big hug. "Welcome to our family," she said.

Next were her parents, congratulating her. "Mom! Dad! How'd you know I'd be here?" Olivia was amazed at how fast the family network turned.

Olivia's parents looked at each other and smiled. They both hugged her. "We have our ways." Her mom smiled at her and quietly said, "Annie." They laughed. Annie, her best friend, was the epicenter of all the group's important news and events for too many years to count. She was the only person Olivia called when she decided to move home.

After Olivia's parents, they were followed by Frank's parents, Aunt Kate, and her husband Doug. Other guests included friends, neighbors, and Frank's older sisters, one of whom was engaged, with her fiancé pulling her through the crowd to congratulate Olivia. There were so many people, and Olivia knew them all.

•　•　•

Everyone stopped talking when a car approached them with a low rumble. People in the street moved to the sidewalk while a classic white Mustang with two dark-blue stripes idled up the road and stopped in front of Olivia and her friends. Uncle Robert turned off the engine and helped Grandmother out of the passenger seat. "Why are these cars so low to the ground?" she complained. "Don't they know about my knees?"

Derek leaned in and helped Aunt Nora out from the rear seat, which was propped up with several pillows to allow the small woman to see out of the car. "Thank you so much, Derek." She was younger than Frank's grandmother and had an easier time maneuvering in and out of the car. She put her hand on Robert's shoulder. "Go ahead and leave the keys in the ignition. I'll be taking it for a spin before I go." Everyone laughed, but Robert pocketed the keys.

"Do be a dear and bring Olivia by. I want to welcome her into the family personally," she asked Derek.

Olivia walked slowly up to Aunt Nora, shaking the hands of well-wishers along the way. It appeared everyone Olivia knew in Santa Cruz was there to greet her and celebrate her engagement. She reached Aunt Nora and gave her a gentle hug. Aunt Nora had a big personality but was small and slightly frail. Olivia never wanted the hug to end.

She let go of Olivia and clutched a bag near her side. "It seems only recently that you first visited a few old ladies at their Seabright home. We were touched that you kids had enough time for lunch with us. Of course, Frank would be at my house every day as long as the food held out, but young women willing to spend time with older folks demonstrates their good character. The men came for the food, the young women came for the advice, and the older women were there to extend their family's love to the next generation. Sometimes our advice was helpful for you—we hope. But sometimes, the purpose of the visits was to give a few old ladies the strength to live a little longer and share a peek into the future of the next generation. You and Annie are joining the next line of matriarchs in our extended family. We are so happy to have you."

Annie and Olivia surrounded them with a big hug. Frank's mom and Annie's mom also joined them. "Aunt Nora has one more item to address before we adjourn to Olivia's house for lunch," said Frank's mom.

Aunt Nora pulled two 4x6-inch framed pictures from her purse. "I will put these pictures on the mantle in our living room. The first picture shows all of us in the courtyard at our house. I included your men because, well, sometimes we must include them." Everyone laughed.

"The second is a picture of Annie and Olivia, with Grandmother and me standing by. I imagine that when Grandmother and I are long gone, this picture will spur many conversations with some young girls, asking their elders how they managed to get through some of the difficult places in life. So, I am comfortable passing the torch to Frank and Annie's mothers, Olivia's mother, and to you two women to advise the next generations." She squeezed both girls' hands as they started off to Olivia's house.

During lunch, the women talked. Annie asked Olivia if it was all right if they got a house here on the Point. Nothing too big or showy, but one near Olivia and Derek and their parents.

They agreed it was a good plan.

The guys' conversation went straight to car-talk. "Is this the million-dollar Mustang?" asked Derek.

"Are you kidding?" replied Frank. "This one isn't the restoration car, which was worth a ton. This is a more common model I bought. The other one wasn't quite worth a million dollars, but it was worth a lot more than we expected. When they completed the restoration, I sold it and invested the money in my future with Annie." He smiled and looked around to make sure they were alone before he continued. "I also got a few other things, like the Woody, which I kept, and this Mustang. As for the original Mustang, they barely let me look at it. Once it was completed, that car was put on a trailer and sold immediately. This one is almost as fast but not that type of collector's car." He rubbed his hand lightly along the fender. "I tried to get visitation rights for the original car, but that was a no-go."

"Can I at least drive this one?" asked Derek.

"No," said Frank, looking down and shaking his head with a smile. "This is still a high-performance car. Uncle Robert and I are the only ones who can drive it. I had to sign papers promising I wouldn't race it or let inexperienced drivers get behind the wheel." He patted the car fender. "That means you, unless we don't tell anyone."

Frank furtively looked up and down the street. "At the right time, you'll enjoy driving this machine. It's almost too fast to be street legal." They both nodded their heads at Frank's disregard for rules and laughed.

"Maybe we could make it the company car." Derek watched for a reaction from Frank. "I could use a partner, and I'm sure there would be opportunities for the partners to take the Mustang to business meetings."

"I'd like that," Frank said. "I mean, I'd like to join you in the business part." He put his hand on the car fender. "The Mustang will always be mine."

Looking at Frank, Derek said, "Cars aren't my thing anyway," fooling nobody, but getting a laugh from Frank.

Frank waited to get the nod from Derek, ensuring that they both understood who owned the Mustang. Frank moved the conversation along. "I could get involved by drumming up business. I know most of the families who live here."

People were walking by, congratulating them both. Their friends joked that Derek and Frank had "each out kicked their coverage," and others said, "Don't blow it, you aren't going to do any better."

"Typical guys," said Derek to Frank. "Afraid to give us credit for our accomplishments. I mean, we are good catches, aren't we?"

"No," said Frank, trying to be honest. "We are just dopey guys, still a little rough around the edges, who got extremely lucky with our gals."

"That works," said Derek. "There is only one thing I need to warn you about."

Frank looked up, giving Derek his full attention.

"Our partnership won't work if you want to do the accounting. Kate has that function sewn up tight."

"I think I can live without that part of the job." Frank exhaled in relief. "I'm not an accounting sort of guy."

There was a thunderous roar as the Mustang fired up. Everyone jumped back and looked at the source of all the noise, trying to see who was behind the wheel. All they could see was the top of a head with silver hair. Aunt Nora pulled herself up by the steering wheel, pushed her head to the level of the dash, and looked at the crowd gathered around her. "Well, come on, boys.

I don't have all day," she shouted above the rumble of the idling engine.

Uncle Robert reached into the car and turned off the ignition, pulling out the keys Aunt Nora must have lifted from his jacket pocket. "Thank goodness the car was in Park!" He opened the driver's door, escorted Aunt Nora out of the Mustang, and handed her and the keys off to Frank. Quietly, Frank slipped the keys into his pocket. "I guess you have another high-performance driver in the family," Robert said to Frank.

As she walked up to the house, Aunt Nora waved to the crowd like she was in a parade. She vowed, "Wait until I get my set of keys!" to anyone who would listen. Aunt Nora continued to wave as the group disappeared into Olivia's house for lunch.

The next generation of family was firmly established. Aunt Nora and Grandmother, along with Frank's, Olivia's, and Annie's mothers, gave their best advice to the girls who now seemed ready to chart their own way.

The fog broke, and the sunshine pushed through. Olivia reached out and held onto Derek's arm as tears filled her eyes. Derek moved to wipe them away, but Olivia stopped him. "I'm so happy; there's nothing more I could want. The tears tell me it all turned out as we hoped."

"I think you're right," Derek agreed. "But I believe the best is yet to come."

A single tear rolled down his face as he leaned over and kissed Olivia. Their prayers were answered. Now their dreams for the future were just beginning to come true.

Epilogue

Annie and Olivia sat in their favorite rocking chairs, looking out from the living room to the Boardwalk. Each had a favorite granddaughter in her lap. (Olivia explained to the girls every visit that whoever occupied her lap was her favorite grandchild—at that time.) Annie held her five-year-old granddaughter Tracy, and Olivia held her four-year-old granddaughter Ema. The sun was out, the sky was clear, and their men were off doing whatever retired men do in garages.

Today was a day for reminiscing. The girls brought over a photo album they found on Olivia's bookshelf. For what seemed the hundredth time, they wanted to see what their grandparents looked like when they were in high school, wearing silly clothes and looking funny.

"Well, boys back then sometimes wore silly clothes and always looked funny," Annie said as she ran her fingers lightly over the pictures. "They looked very cute, in their white painters bib overalls, Hawaiian print shirts, multicolored sandals, and slightly long, shaggy hair."

The pictures included one of Derek wearing a white puka shell necklace while Frank wore two necklaces, one white and one with small black seedpods. Like clockwork, when the grandchildren saw the necklaces, they squealed, "Boys don't wear jewelry!"

"There was a time when your grandmothers could get Grandpa Frank and Grandpa Derek to wear very stylish clothing and jewelry. They looked good then."

The next pictures showed the boys riding skateboards and bicycles, standing in front of their little convertible sports cars, and one the little girls called the race car. There were many pictures of Frank and Derek standing in front of the white Mustang. "Ooh, we call that the race car because it's got racing stripes," Ema explained. The girls had memorized the albums. Coming up next was one of Ema's favorites. It was of her Granddaddy Derek kissing her Grandma, Olivia, when they thought nobody was watching. "Granddaddy was so mad!" squealed Ema.

"He wasn't mad," Olivia said, more to herself than to her granddaughter, who already knew the story. "He was surprised, and afraid people would laugh at him. What he didn't know was he was already in love with me, and all the other girls wished they were me because I scooped up the handsomest man!"

"Is that a real word, 'handsomest?'" asked Tracy, who at the age of five, was already reading and wanted to know about new words.

"It was then." Olivia smiled. "And do you want to know a secret?" Olivia leaned in and took one hand from each little girl. With exaggerated movements, she looked first to the right and then to the left to make sure nobody else could hear their secret. The girls leaned in too, waiting to hear this precious information.

Olivia loved these little munchkins. She could make any story into an adventure for them; the girls were at just the right age to make story telling so satisfying. "Granddaddy was falling in love with me, and Grandpa Frank was learning that he was falling in love with your Grandma Annie too!" The girls shrieked with glee at the falling in love part. They grew up hearing princess stories which always had someone falling in love. It was the magic of love that kept the girls glued to the story.

Olivia looked at the last picture of Frank and Derek pretending to surf on one of the tables.

"This one is both of our granddaddies being silly," said Ema, stifling a yawn with the back of her hand.

"They sure were silly, but it was good fun for Grandma Annie and me. I think that was when we fell in love with them," Olivia said.

"Aww," the girls cried out together.

Annie and Olivia shared glances and were each hit with the sting of tears, which always happened when they brought out these pictures.

Olivia looked away and, in an instant, saw her life stretching back to the day she met Derek. When she looked at Castle Beach, she saw it in the past, with their towels, picnic baskets, and aluminum chairs, and then over time with their extended families, and now with the grandkids.

"It was wonderful. And now we have you two little chipmunks who we can tickle all day long." They squirmed and squealed, closing their eyes and belly laughing as loud as they could.

The girls returned to look at the pictures. In a few minutes they would want to do something else, and that would be fine. Ema was probably ready for her nap, judging by the number of times she rubbed her eyes. But for now, it was nice having the warm, squirming little bugs in their laps, reminding Olivia that life was a constant series of surprises with good little treasures like these times in her life. In spite of her happiness, she would not allow herself to cry since it would upset the girls, so she dabbed her eyes and reached over to squeeze Annie's hand. Watching the grandchildren was now one of their favorite pastimes. And unlike her old family visits to their grandparents, nothing seemed to get broken. This generation of Little Ones was being hugged and held so much their feet never touched the ground.

"Look, here's a picture of the four of us sitting in front of the whale at the park," said Olivia.

Tracy and Ema jumped up and down in excitement. "That's our whale! He's just down the street from here! And that's our picnic bench," they cried.

"That was where the four of us met, at Castle Beach," Olivia said to Annie, with a satisfied smile.

Acknowledgements

I want to thank my team of friends and family who supported me while writing this novel, including my first readers, Patty Smith and Shirley Stalder, for helping me persevere when facing go-no-go decisions about this endeavor. Writing is a solitary occupation, and their feedback was crucial to keeping me moving forward when I was uncertain that there was an audience for my work.

Thanks to my mom, who read through numerous draft manuscripts and offered kind but honest criticism and overall support for this novel.

And, of course, a big thanks to my wife, Tamara, who read this manuscript more times than I can count. Without her assistance, I would still be trying to pull together a story from piles of paper surrounding my desk.

I would never have made it through the publishing process without the professional staff at Reedsy, including my fantastic editors Ema Barnes and Kimberly Broderick, and designer Alan Barnett.

And of course, a great thanks to my guild, the Connecticut chapter of the Romance Writers of America, who offered guidance and critiques of my writing over the past few years. When I disappear into the basement for lengthy Zoom calls, I explain to my wife that I'm on the phone with a patient group of successful writers willing to share secrets of the trade.

About the Author

R.S. Ledwith grew up in Northern California, spending summers at the beach with his family. He married his college sweetheart and raised his family with elaborate bedtime stories that became legendary with his children and their friends. After retiring from a finance career in New York City, he began writing full-time. He and his wife reside in Connecticut in a small home by the sea, with a tortoise, and numerous additional animals in their menagerie.

This is his debut novel.